Merry Christmas
Paul + D
Enjoy

SHEPHERD'S INN,

the Gift

MIKE + CHRISTINA
WOULD LIKE TO BLESS YOU
WITH THIS BOOK FROM
THEIR FRIEND DAVE
ROMANS 8:18

God Bless You
Dave Stokley

DAVE STOKLEY

Trilogy Christian Publishers
A Wholly Owned Subsidiary of Trinity Broadcasting Network
2442 Michelle Drive
Tustin, CA 92780

For information, address Trilogy Christian Publishing
Rights Department, 2442 Michelle Drive, Tustin, Ca 92780.
Trilogy Christian Publishing/ TBN and colophon are trademarks of Trinity Broadcasting Network.

For information about special discounts for bulk purchases, please contact Trilogy Christian Publishing.

Manufactured in the United States of America

Trilogy Disclaimer: The views and content expressed in this book are those of the author and may not necessarily reflect the views and doctrine of Trilogy Christian Publishing or the Trinity Broadcasting Network.

10 9 8 7 6 5 4 3 2 1

Library of Congress Cataloging-in-Publication Data is available.

ISBN 978-1-64773-610-1 (Print Book)
ISBN 978-1-64773-611-8 (ebook)

Foreword

Shepherd's Inn started out as a thought that came to me as I was walking my usual daily exercise route in my Las Vegas neighborhood. Each day, as I walked, I thought about the characters, setting, and story line. Finally, I put my thought to words on a page, and the short Christmas play titled *Shepherd's Inn* was born. I assembled an excellent cast and director, and we performed the play in our local church at Christmastime. It was a qualified success.

My friend Mike suggested I write a book about it, and I thought, *Yeah, right!* But that comment stuck in my head, and a couple of years later, I wrote my first chapter. It took two agonizing years, but I finally finished. And here it is.

I want to thank all my friends and family who gave me words of encouragement as I struggled with my first book. To my friend Mike, who suggested it. To the professionals who gave me information to make the story more real. And most of all, I want to give a special thank you to my wife, Beverly, who never gave up on me and urged me to keep going. She gave me the strength to finish the work.

Chapter 1

Joe and Maria
October 29

Maria turned over and looked at the clock on the night-stand: 2:09 a.m. She had been wide awake since a little after eleven and had been to the bathroom three times to throw up. She kept trying to pray, but it seemed like every time she tried, other thoughts were keeping her from it. Meanwhile, Joe was lying there next to her, snoring so loud she was sure the neighbors next door could hear him.

How can he be so insensitive? she thought. But that was Joe. He was that way when they first met, a year ago, and he hadn't changed a bit. Oh, how she wished she had listened to her mom when she told her not to marry him. "He's no good for you," her mother had said. "Just look at the family he comes from. His dad can't hold a job, and that poor family lives in a dump." Sure, she knew his family didn't have lots of money, but he was so cute, and he did treat her nice most of the time. *It's just that sometimes he just doesn't understand me,* she thought again.

Maria had such grand plans just a couple of years ago. Having graduated from Bend High School just two short years ago, she worked for a while in a little dry cleaner's not far from her parents' house in Bend. She then decided she wanted to go to school, but not in Bend. She moved to Klamath Falls, Oregon, and enrolled in Oregon Institute of Technology (OIT). She planned to major in dental hygiene and heard that the school had a great dental program. Shortly after school started, she met Joe. He was one of those friend-of-a-friend guys. They met at a party, and when she saw him across the room, she knew she had to get to know him.

Their romance had been a whirlwind, and they were married four months after they met. Her parents were paying for her tuition, and when they couldn't talk her out of getting married, they cut off her funding. She had no choice but to drop out of school.

Now, they had been married for eight months, and she was six months pregnant. They lived in a tiny little one-bedroom house they were renting from a friend of his in Klamath Falls. Joe worked for a furniture store in the delivery section, and he came home every night complaining about his job. He had to work too hard to cover for the guy he worked with because he was the boss's son and he didn't carry his load. And the pay was minimum wage. Joe said he would quit, but there weren't any decent jobs out there for him. "Why did I drop out of high school and not get my GED?" he had said to her on more than one occasion.

But now here they were, stuck in this town, very few friends, no money, not much of a future, no hope. And her mom and dad living in Bend, Oregon, two and a half hours by car, if their junker of a car could even make it that far. Only two more months until Christmas, and Maria had no idea what was going to happen next.

Tears started to trickle down her cheeks, and her quiet sob was drowned out by Joe's snoring. "O God," she began, "what am I supposed to do? I know I haven't always been the person I should be. And I know I haven't always been the wife You want me to be to my husband. But sometimes, God, I get so mad at Joe I wish he would just go away and leave me and my baby alone." Sometimes she thought her pleas fell on deaf ears. "Why don't You answer my prayers, God? Why is my life so bad? What have I done to deserve all this?" She didn't even realize the last plea, she cried out loud.

Joe woke up and turned over to her and said, "What's up? Are you crying?" He was still half-asleep, so it sounded more like a mumble than a real question. "What time is it? Are you okay? Are you having problems with the baby? Come on, talk to me, Maria. What's going on?"

Then the tears came in a flood. "Oh, Joe, just hold me, please! Just shut up and hold me!" she shouted, and then she wrapped her arms around him and cried.

She didn't know how long she cried or when she just became numb from the pain she was feeling in her heart. She just knew her pain was not being shared when she heard Joe's breathing change to his usual rolling snore. She unwrapped her arms from around him, turned over, and spoke to the wall as she said, "I hate you, Joe Alexander. I hate you!"

There was no more sleep for Maria.

Chapter 2

October 30

I walked into the lobby of Shepherd's Inn and saw Martha dusting furniture and knickknacks. By the way, my name is Gabe Sinclair. I'm the caretaker here. I so enjoy the fact that Martha works at the inn. She is a little hard to get along with sometimes, and she definitely lives up to her biblical namesake, but besides all that, she is a very good housekeeper and cook and she has a heart of gold.

Martha

Martha came to the inn about six years ago when my wife, Hannah, got sick and couldn't do the job any longer. Martha had been a widow for over five years at that time and had worked at the only job she knew how to do, cook and clean! She had married right out of high school and never worked outside the home. She had raised three kids and taken care of her husband just like her mom and her mom's mom had done before.

Martha's husband, Cal, had been a crane operator on the docks in Portland. He loved his job and had told Martha every chance he got how much he looked forward to going to work every day. He said he liked looking down on all those little guys busting their hump every day in the cold and rain while he sat up there in his heated crane, punching buttons and flipping levers. "No hard labor for me!" he used to say. Martha knew how much he liked his job, but she was concerned that he just kept putting on weight and didn't do much of anything physical. When he came home from work, all he did was sit down in front of the TV and munch on junk food. She had even begged him to go for walks with her in the evening, but he always refused. Martha also told him he was going to die of a heart attack or stroke if he didn't do something about his health. She thought that might scare him into doing something, but Cal was as stubborn as he was lazy, so nothing ever came of that.

Cal was forty-seven years old when he didn't reach over and turn off his alarm clock on that November morning eleven years ago. When Martha tried to wake him, she could tell immediately that he was gone. That icy-cold feel of death was what she experienced when she placed her hand on his shoulder. Fear and sadness combined to overtake her as she tried to control her emotions. She had never been around a dead person except for viewing at the funeral parlor.

She didn't know what to do next. The sound of the constant, annoying *buzz buzz buzz* of the alarm clock was only a sound from far away for her. She could hear it, but her mind couldn't grasp where it was coming from. It took her several seconds before she remembered the alarm clock sound was what woke her in the first place. She got out of bed and walked around to his side and turned it off.

She then stood there in the faint light of the early-morning dawn streaming through the windows, looking down at the still, silent figure that had once been her beloved husband and friend. "Oh, Cal, Cal, my dear, sweet Cal! How can I go on without you?" Martha then turned her face toward heaven and spoke a heart-pouring, sobbing prayer, asking God for the strength to go on and asking also for her Lord to take care of her husband.

The doctor said he had suffered a massive heart attack sometime during the night, and he probably didn't even wake up.

Fortunately for Martha, the union-sponsored insurance program where he worked paid for the funeral expenses, and a life insurance policy he had taken out only two years before gave Martha enough to live on for a while before she had to look for work. Her kids had helped some, but since none of them lived in Portland any longer, except twenty-year-old Nathan, and they had their families to support, the help wasn't much. Nathan lived with Martha for a couple of years after his dad died, but "true love" got ahold of him and he and his new bride moved to Kentucky, her home state.

The next three years, she felt like she was just going through the motions. She had worked at several jobs, but nothing seemed to give her the pleasure she had taking care of Cal. Every night when she came home, she would get on her knees in her bedroom and pray that God would deliver her from this spin cycle she seemed to be on. Her heart ached for a chance to be a part of a family again.

October 30

Martha looked up from her work when she heard me enter the room and said, "How is it going with getting those rooms ready for the remodel?" She thought I had been doing way too much lifting and moving furniture for a man my age. I'm a couple of years older than Martha and have been working here at the inn for more than thirty years. It's my home and my life. No amount of scolding will stop me from doing whatever it takes to keep the inn in perfect condition.

"Just about finished with the heavy stuff. I'm so glad we hired Jake Riser to help out. He is a godsend. I don't think I have ever seen a young teenage boy work as hard. 'Course, being Pastor Nate's son might have something to do with it. I know Nate and Deanne have sure done a fine job raising those kids of theirs."

Just as I finished speaking, the phone at the counter started to ring. "I'll get it," came a voice from the hall. Lydia came in on a run and grabbed the phone after the second ring. "Good afternoon, Shepherd's Inn, this is Lydia, how my I help you?" came her perky little voice. Lydia, along with her two adorable daughters, Elisabeth and Sarah, live and work at the inn along with Martha and me. "Oh, hello, Ms. Leah. I didn't know if we would hear from you this year. How are you doing?"

The voice on the other end of the line didn't sound like it deserved the polite treatment it had just received. Her first remark when Lydia answered the phone was a very sharp "This is Leah Gardiner. I want to make a reservation." Then "And why on earth would you think you wouldn't hear from me? How many years have I been staying at your inn? And since you asked, I'm doing just fine, thank you. As if it's any of your business. I would like a reservation for the week of December 20 through the twenty-seventh."

"Ms. Leah," Lydia replied, "we are in the process of remodeling many of the rooms this winter, and I'm not sure we will have anything available."

Lydia had to hold the phone away from her ear. "What do you mean you have nothing available? How many years have I been coming to your establishment? And now you tell me I am not welcome, my money is no good? Of all the nerve! I must speak to Mr. Sinclair, immediately!"

Lydia almost dropped the phone as she tried to compose herself. She tries her best to please everyone she meets, and when someone yells at her or complains, she has trouble handling it. Of course, that could come from living with her ex-boyfriend as long as she did. But that's a whole other story, and we'll probably get to it later.

"Of course, Ms. Leah. I'm so sorry. I didn't mean to upset you. Gabe is right here." She held out the phone to me, and I was giving her that look, like talking with Leah Gardiner was the last thing I wanted to do today.

"Good afternoon, Leah. We didn't expect to hear from you this year. As Lydia told you, we are doing a major remodel project at the inn this winter and most of the rooms won't have any furniture in them. When is it you want to visit?"

"As I told your most obnoxious counter person, I would like to stay from December 20 through the twenty-seventh. I trust you could accommodate one more guest for that short amount of time."

"I tell you what, Leah? Since the project will take a few months, we'll work on a room for you first and should have it ready to go by the time you get here. How does that sound?"

"Well, that will be fine, as long as the room doesn't smell like fresh paint. I have allergies, and the smell of fresh paint causes me much anxiety."

"I'm sure," I replied, "we can have the painting done in plenty of time so the smell won't be an issue. So we can look forward to seeing you on the twentieth, then. That means you will be here for Christmas this year. We'll enjoy sharing it with you."

"I don't 'celebrate' Christmas! I will expect to be left alone as usual and not bothered with all your religious traditions. I will see you on the twentieth of December. Good day, Mr. Sinclair."

When I finally hung up the phone, Lydia and Martha were looking at me, expecting a blow-by-blow presentation of Leah's end of the conversation. They both had had the misfortune of enduring Leah Gardiner every year for the last three years. They all looked forward to the day when Leah checked out after each visit. "Hey," I said, "just think. This will give us a perfect opportunity to witness to Leah again." I said it, but in my heart I wasn't sure how much I meant it. In all my years, I could not recall ever knowing anyone as full of anger and hate as Leah Gardiner.

Chapter 3

Doc
November 1

Meriweather Veterinary operates out of a small storefront in Napa, California. Luke has been the "doc" there for over ten years. His wife worked right beside him as his assistant for the first four of those years.

Luke and Brenda met in college oh so many years ago. He was an Alpha Gamma Omega, and she was a Kappa Kappa Gamma. They had both been invited to a frat party and were introduced to each other by Luke's longtime friend Leo. The party was dragging on and not overly exciting, so Luke asked Brenda if she would like to go to a midnight movie. Brenda was reluctant. She had heard too many stories of frat boys getting girls drunk and taking advantage of them. She did think Luke was kind of cute, but her instincts told her to decline the offer.

Luke felt like a ton of bricks had been dropped on his head. He had always been on the side of shy, and he had always had trouble asking a girl out. It had taken a lot of nerve just to talk to her, but to get dumped so soon was hard for him to take. As far as he was concerned, the party was over. He headed back to the frat house feeling like he didn't belong there.

He had been turned down before, but there was something about Brenda that he couldn't explain. When she spoke to him, it was like he could see inside her soul. He wanted so much to get to know her better, but after that night, he wasn't sure if that would ever be possible.

Three days later, Luke was sitting on the grass outside the commons, studying canine anatomy, when a shadow moved over his textbook. He looked up to see Brenda standing there with a book in one hand and a soda in the other.

"Hey, there, stranger, what's a girl gotta do to get your phone number?" she said.

Luke couldn't speak; he just stared at her shaded image with the bright sun in the background.

"What's the matter? Cat got your tongue?" she asked with a twinkle in her eye and a big smile on her lips.

Finally, Luke found his voice and said, "I thought I'd never see you again."

"Why would you think that? This is a small campus. We were sure to run into each other again."

Luke worked up some courage and replied, "I got the impression the other night that you didn't want to have anything to do with me."

"Oh, don't be silly. I was just being cautious. I've heard lots of stories about you Alpha Gamma Omega guys." When she said that, she had a wide grin on her face. She had never heard of that fraternity until the night they first met. Afterward, she decided to investigate and learned that Alpha Gamma Omega was a Christian fraternity that was founded way back in 1927.

"Seriously?" was all he could say.

"Are you going to ask me to sit down?" was her reply.

"Oh, I'm sorry, yes, please sit. I was just getting bored reading about dog bones. How have you been? Been to any more parties?" Luke realized he was rambling on and making no sense. Why was it so hard to talk to the most beautiful girl on campus? "What are you reading?"

"This?" she held up the book in her hand. "This is my escape from the rigors of college life. I'm into romance novels. I especially like the ones set in the nineteenth century. I like to imagine what life and romance were like back then. What do you read for pleasure?"

"I don't know. I really don't have one certain type of book that interests me that much. Guess I like mystery novels the best. I like to see if I can unravel the mystery before it's revealed. Sorta like in real life, you know, figuring out someone by their actions and words."

She looked at him, trying to decide if he was trying to figure her out. "I think I know what you mean." Changing the subject abruptly, she continued, "Can I get a belated rain check on that offer of a midnight movie from the other night? I really would like to go out with you."

Suddenly, there was no one else around. No students or faculty walking by, no buildings surrounding them, just Luke and Brenda, alone, and she had just asked him out!

That was so many years ago, and so much had happened since then. Luke and Brenda became an item very soon. They both wanted to spend as much time with each other as possible. But they both knew their priorities and boundaries, and they kept them. They both graduated in 2000 and were married that summer.

A couple of years later, Luke and Brenda opened Meriweather Veterinary in Napa, California, and six months later, they welcomed their first child, Daniel. For those four years, life seemed to be about as perfect as it could get.

That was until that Christmas Eve, when Brenda and Danny were returning from Christmas Eve service at their little church up in the hills. Luke had to stay behind to take care of a patient. A little Silky puppy had been brought in after being poisoned by an angry neighbor. He hated to miss the service, but the poor dog was in such bad shape it was touch and go whether he would make it. The dog's owner, a cute little seven-year-old girl with blond curls framing her little cherub face, was crying her poor little eyes out. Doc's heart hurt just watching the little girl and the love she had for her little friend. Brenda understood and told him she would stay and help if he wanted. He could have used the help, but Danny was in the Christmas play, and he didn't want him to miss it.

Everything was a fog for several days after Doc opened his office door that night to see the county sheriff standing there, hat in hand. It had been a drunk driver heading home after a stop at the bar after work. He walked away from the head-on crash. Brenda and Danny died instantly.

That was six years ago, and from the next Christmas on, Doc has been a guest at Shepherd's Inn every Christmas. He had heard about the inn from a friend at church. The friend had talked to the pastor, and together they had convinced Doc to go up there the next Christmas and take his mind off his work. Take time to seek God's guidance and help him recover from the emotional roller coaster he had been on for the last year. At first, he absolutely refused. He didn't want to go anywhere. But their persistence and prayer finally convinced Doc that the trip would do him good. What he didn't know at that time was what kind of bond would be created between him and the folks at Shepherd's Inn.

Doc had just finished working on the books for the night when the phone rang. Thinking it was probably an emergency and he would be there late again tonight, he said, "Hello, Doc Luke," expecting a panic-filled voice on the other end of the line.

"Hello, Doc. This is Gabe."

With a smile and a sigh, Doc said, "Gabe, it's good to hear from you. I was just thinking about you today. Wondering how the remodel project was going."

"Oh, it's going great. But I didn't forget to save out your room for Christmas. You are still coming, aren't you? I wanted to give you a heads-up this year. We won't have but a couple of rooms available this Christmas, so there won't be a lot of people around. You'll almost have the place to yourself. But do you remember me talking about a regular guest by the name of Leah?"

"Yeah, I seem to recall she can be a bit trying at times. Is that right?"

"You are so kind, Doc. *Trying* is about the mildest word you could use to describe that woman. She is one rocky path on my Christian walk. Anyway, she has always timed her visits in the fall, but this year she wants to be here over Christmas! I can't, for the life of me, figure out why she would want to come then. She knows we go all out for Christmas. And she even told me she didn't want us to include her in our, and I quote, 'religious tradition.' Can you believe that? Anyway, she will be here the same time as you, and you two will be the only guests. So I hope you're up to it, buddy!"

"Oh, come on, Gabe! She can't be that bad. I'm sure we'll get along fine. Maybe we can all go out and have a good ole snowball fight! You are going to have snow for me this year, aren't you?"

"Well, I just wanted to give you a heads-up. Don't say I didn't warn you. And about that snow, we haven't had any yet, and I know it's still early, but we usually have a little by this time. We'll just have to wait and see what the Lord has in store for us. See you on the twenty-third, right?"

"Yep. I got everything set up with Dr. Gordon, and he'll handle all my patients. See you then. Good hearing from you, Gabe."

Doc leaned back in his chair and thought about Christmas Eve six years ago. Although he had managed to resume a somewhat-normal life, his heart ached every day for Brenda and Danny. Many nights he had cried out to God, "Why?" And the answer never came. He wondered, Was there a purpose, a reason, a part of God's plan that he was not privileged to understand? Only time would tell. He reached up and turned off the lamp on his desk, picked up his keys, and headed for the door. Another night alone. They all ran together now. Would the hurting ever stop?

Chapter 4

Shepherd's Inn snuggles itself up against the eastern slopes of the Cascade Range in southern Oregon. Nothing big or fancy about the inn, just a handful of rooms and a couple of cabins off the main house. The approach to the inn is spectacular. The narrow gravel drive crosses a rickety old bridge over Little Jordan Creek. Just a short distance beyond the creek, the trees open to a small well-maintained parking area fronting the inn. Usually, first-time visitors, and even some repeat customers, stop right there and just look in awe. The main house is a single-story log structure with a high gabled roof of cedar shakes. A large natural stone fireplace rises up from one end. Log columns support a porch across the front of the house that runs from corner to corner. Handmade bentwood rockers are placed alongside small pinewood side tables. Guests find the chairs hard to resist when they are looking for a quiet place to read or just relax and enjoy the fresh mountain air. At each end of the porch hang handwoven hammocks that are so inviting at first glance that they are usually the first place guests try out upon their arrival.

The main house is surrounded by ponderosa pines and well-manicured grounds of pine needles, ground cover, and a few native shrubs such as manzanita and buckbrush. All the outbuildings are spaced out behind and are all miniatures of the main house. A couple of them are one room with a bath for guests. There is also a combination toolshed, pump house, and emergency generator building located next to the main house near the spacious kitchen. Natural stone paths connect all the buildings. Cedar shake roofs held up by lodgepole pine posts cover each path. There are patches of grass between the buildings.

The consensus of guests to the inn is that there is something about the place that makes them forget about all the trials and troubles in their lives and lets them concentrate on healing their soul.

The inn has been operating as a bed-and-breakfast for many, many years, and there are quite a few guests who make a regular pilgrimage at the same time each year. Every season has a special significance for most everyone.

Summer seems to be the busiest season, since the weather is almost always warm and sunny on the east side of the Cascade mountain range in Oregon. However, nights can be cool, and a jacket or sweater is usually the uniform of the day. Long walks along the creek and back into the meadow for bird-watching and looking at all the wildlife that make this part of the forest home is a popular activity for most of our guests.

Springtime can be very fickle, with the possibility of light snow and freezing nights as well as rainy, windy days. But the benefit of the season is watching all the new growth of plant life and the little forest critters coming out of hibernation and foraging for food.

Fall, in all its colorful splendor, is the second busiest time at the inn. The weather is turning cooler, the leaves are putting on a show, and it's a great time to come and relax before starting a busy cycle of holiday gatherings: Thanksgiving, Christmas, New Year's Day.

Wintertime is normally our slowest season. Because we are situated at the foot of the amazing Oregon Cascade Range, winters can bring lots of snow and cold weather. Although many people like to visit winter recreation areas during the ski season, none of the normal winter recreational activities are available at Shepherd's Inn. It's our time to snuggle up next to the fireplace with a warm blanket, a hot cup of cocoa, a good book, or excellent conversation. It has always been that way, and it will probably stay that way.

Chapter 5

Abel and Annabelle Sinclair, Scott and Cory Brewster

Abel Sinclair built the inn over seventy years ago as a place to get away from it all when business weighed too heavily on him. Abel was a self-made millionaire, the son of a Civil War veteran who fought for the South after his father and his brother were killed in that same war. Abel loved to give his money away to unsuspecting strangers. As for his children and grandchildren, he had told them they could get rich the same way he did—earn it! Most of them did.

In the mid-seventies, when Abel was over one hundred years old, he met Scott Brewster one night in the University of San Francisco Medical Center ER waiting room. Scott's wife, Cory, had OD'd on some bad drugs and was clinging to life. Abel's wife, Annabelle, was "going to be with the Lord," as she had told Abel on the way to the hospital.

Why she wanted to go to the hospital when she knew it was only a matter of a few hours at most for her, most people couldn't understand. "Why not stay at home around your family?" some people asked. But Abel knew there was a very purposeful reason for them to go to the hospital for her last hours. He wasn't sure what that purpose was until he met Scott in the waiting room.

As he waited and prayed in that waiting room, the Lord revealed to him that a young couple needed him now or the young lady would surely die within a few months. That was all God revealed to him, but Abel had always had a very close relationship with his Lord and was certain that Scott and Cory Brewster were the couple God was talking about.

While Abel and Scott sat in the waiting room, dreading what news they might receive, Abel began to talk to Scott about his life and the life of his wife, Cory.

Scott and Cory both had run away from home while in their teens and used their thumbs to work their way across the country to San Francisco. At the height of the Vietnam War, they had rebelled along with many of their peers, thinking they had all the answers and everyone could get along with peace and love and a "joint." They lived among hippie communes for a few years and then finally got married in the early seventies. They were always heavy into the drug culture and never had much to show for their sporadic work except for a small loft apartment and some used furniture that had either been given to them by friends or picked up from the curbside, abandoned by previous owners.

Abel was very observant and had a gift of recognizing a person's inner self while talking to them. He knew very quickly that Scott was seeking something, but he had no idea what it was. As they talked, Abel asked him if he knew where Cory would go if she did not recover. At first, Scott was defensive, refusing to accept the possibility that she might not survive. But eventually he began to accept that likelihood and allowed Abel to introduce him to Jesus.

For almost an hour, Abel told Scott about God's Son. Scott and Cory both had been raised in homes that were absent the presence of the Holy Spirit. Scott reluctantly listened for a while, then slowly began to understand some of what Abel was telling him. But part of him was more concerned with the possibility that his wife, Cory, would not survive the night.

A nurse came in a while later and told Abel that it was time. As he was leaving Scott to be by his wife's side, he gave him a big hug and told him he would continue to pray for both of them.

Early the next morning, Annabelle did go to be with the Lord. Abel was sitting by her side as they said their final goodbyes and she quietly slipped from life on earth. Abel sat quietly by her side for a couple of hours, just praying and remembering some of the great times they had experienced over all those many years together. He thought about the obvious fact that he, too, would soon be following her to sit at the right hand of their Lord. It gave him a sense of comfort and relief knowing it would be soon.

After the funeral for Annabelle, Abel had found out that Cory Brewster had indeed recovered from her drug overdose and she and Scott had returned to their life of drugs in Haight Ashbury.

Sometime later, Abel went to Haight Ashbury to visit with the Brewsters. Scott was blown away when he opened the door and saw that little old man he had met just a few weeks ago in the ER. Of course, Abel and Cory had never met, but she had heard what Scott had told her about their chance meeting while she was clinging to life.

They spent several minutes talking about the ER experience and her recovery, and then Abel got down to the real reason for his visit. He told the couple that he was going to give them a cabin in the woods of the Oregon Cascades. At first, they thought he was just some crazy old man talking trash. They had no reason to believe someone would give them anything, especially a cabin in the woods. As he continued to talk with them, there was a knock on the door, and a well-dressed man in a three-piece business suit, carrying a briefcase, was standing in the doorway.

Abel looked up and called the man by name and said, "Come on in and join us. I assume you have all the necessary paperwork?"

"Yes, sir, Mr. Sinclair, I have everything prepared for your signatures."

Scott and Cory could only stare at each other in disbelief. How could something like this be happening to them? And more importantly, what was the catch? What did they have to do to "claim their prize"?

For the next hour or so, the stranger at the door explained to the Brewsters what Abel was intending to do for them. He told them that there were no preset requirements for them to accept the gift. Once they were declared legal owners of the property, they could do with it whatever they wanted. They could move there, they could rent it out, they could sell it, they could let it sit idle. The choice was up to them. After many questions, Scott and Cory finally realized this was not a dream, Abel was not some kook, and they were really going to own their own inn.

So the paperwork was drawn up and the ownership of the inn was transferred to the Brewsters, and the stranger in the three-piece suit gathered up everything into his briefcase and vanished from their lives.

Along with giving full ownership of the inn to the Brewsters, Abel gave them $100,000 to maintain the place and enjoy a new life together, hopefully away from the drugs and culture that had brought them almost to the brink of eternal death.

When the three of them were alone again, Abel began to talk to them about their salvation. Scott had explained to Cory, after she came home from the hospital, how he and Abel had discussed that very thing in the ER waiting room. For a feeble one-hundred-plus-year-old man, Abel's witness was as strong as ever, and before he left their house, both Scott and Cory had accepted Jesus as their Savior.

When Abel finally departed, it was preceded by lots of hugs and tears and a promise by them to take good care of Shepherd's Inn.

Shortly after that visit, Scott and Cory packed up what few personal items that meant anything to them and headed into the unknown. Next stop, Shepherd's Inn, outside a little mountain town called New Bethlehem. They had no idea what they were in for.

A couple of years later, Abel Sinclair did go to be with the Lord, as his beloved Annabelle had done two years before. But the legacy of love they left behind has been felt by hundreds of families over the years.

When Scott and Cory took over the inn in 1974, the only thing there was the main house with three bedrooms and a couple of bathrooms. Over the next few years, they converted the inn to a B and B and added more bedrooms, bathrooms, and a couple of cabins behind. They loved the work they were doing there, even though the days were long and hard. They had done most of the work by themselves, with the help of a few contractors and handymen to put the plans together. So in the 1980s, they had a full-fledged mountain retreat.

By that time, their longing to do more for the Lord became stronger and stronger, and they knew they needed to get away from the inn and become traveling missionaries. But who could they trust to take care of the inn with them gone? There were a few people down in New Bethlehem, the town at the bottom of the hill, who could help, but no one capable of running the inn. They spent many hours and days in prayer for God to send someone to take over.

Chapter 6

Gabe and Hannah Sinclair

One of Abel's great-grandsons was a young man named Gabriel Sinclair. That's me.

My wife, Hannah, and I had moved to Oregon from Sacramento a couple of years earlier and had been managing a motel in southern Oregon. We both loved what we did, but a change in ownership meant the end of our job. Now, with no job and no money coming in, we needed to find something fast.

During my prayer time one day, I remembered my great-grandpa, Abel, had once owned a place not far from where we were living. I had heard it had been turned into a B and B and wondered if the owners needed any help. I talked with Hannah, and together we decided to take a drive up there and see for ourselves.

As we pulled up to the inn, we were amazed at the beauty of the area and the grandeur of the inn that we had heard so much about. When I opened the car door, a couple stepped out onto the porch of the inn. The man took one look at me and said, "You're a Sinclair! I can see it in your eyes. When can you start work?"

We just stood there with our mouths open. How could these folks know who we were and what we were here for? Finally, I said, "Well, I guess we can start today." Then looking at Hannah, I added, "If that's all right with you?"

The Brewsters invited us in, and over the next several hours, cups of coffee, and a marvelous lunch, Scott and Cory explained to Hannah and me what the Lord had in store for them. There were funny stories, tears of joy, and an instant bond between us. Cory told me she would make me the official caretaker of the inn, and Hannah would become the housekeeper and cook. There was one other employee who took care of reservations and acted as concierge. Other than that, Hannah and I would have complete control over hiring and firing and all other aspects of running the inn.

Hannah and I could hardly believe how God had blessed us in this time of need. But then again, we knew that nothing is impossible with God. So we accepted the terms of the agreement Scott had prepared, and over the next few weeks, the transition began.

Soon it was time for Scott and Cory to begin their missionary work. The church in New Bethlehem went all out for a going-away party. Just about everyone in the area came to wish them well. The night before they left, both the Brewsters and Hannah and I sat down together and prayed for one another. The friendship that had been established would never be broken, and the coming years would prove that fact. Hannah and I took over the inn and prospered for many years.

There was one thing that eluded us, and that was a family of our own. A couple of years after we started working at the inn, Hannah came home from town one day and informed me I was going to be a dad. She had been to the doctor, and he confirmed she was going to have a baby.

For the next few months, she busied herself with preparing for a new resident at Shepherd's Inn. Then, in her fifth month, she woke up one night in horrible pain. We rushed down the hill to the small clinic in New Bethlehem, and that was where we endured the agony of a miscarriage. We were both heartbroken. We had so looked forward to a child, and now only sadness. We would never have the opportunity to hold our precious little baby girl.

I took Hannah to the hospital in Bend, where her doctor wanted to run some tests before she could be released. After waiting several hours for the results to come in, we were visited by a grim-faced doctor. "Hannah, I'm sorry to have to tell you, but it looks like you have ovarian cancer. That is why you miscarried. Now, before you start asking me a lot of questions, let me tell you that you need to have a complete hysterectomy. After that, some radiation, and I am confident we can get rid of the cancer."

Hannah could feel the tears building up, ready to explode down her cheeks. No baby, no chance for any more babies, and cancer. *O Lord,* she thought, *why?* But all she could do was cry. I took her in my arms, and together we cried.

Hannah stayed in the hospital in Bend. I returned to the inn and arranged for some friends from church to hold down the fort at the inn until Hannah could get back on her feet and we could return to run the inn. The surgery and treatment were successful, and we returned to operate the inn a few months later. The folks from church stayed on and helped out for several more weeks as Hannah regained her strength. She couldn't thank them enough. Several of them took turns coming up to the inn to cook, clean, change beds, scrub bathrooms, and do anything else that needed to be done. And no one would accept one penny for their labor.

"It's our ministry to you," they would say, with a smile and a wave as they left.

Things eventually got back to normal (as normal as they could get, thought Hannah), and again the inn prospered. Scott and Cory would come back to visit every few years, and the four of us would have a great time catching up on what was happening in their lives. Other than those times, it was just Hannah and me and one hired front desk person.

"You really do need to go see the doctor about that cough, Hannah," I told her one morning.

"Oh, it's nothing. I think I'm allergic to something around here."

"What could you be allergic to? We've been living here for twenty-six years. There's nothing new here that hasn't been here all along. You're just being stubborn."

"Me, stubborn?" she said, complete with an eye roll. "You have a lot of nerve." She felt hurt by my remark, I could tell. In fact, she had been feeling hurt by a lot of what I had done lately. She wasn't sure why, because nothing much had changed in our relationship in the last twenty-six years. We still loved each other as much now as we did the day we were married. What was it, then, that was causing her to feel this way?

"Well, all I'm sayin' is, you've been looking a little tired lately, and you've had that cough for several weeks now. I think it wouldn't hurt to let the doc take a look at it."

"Okay, if it'll make you feel any better, I'll call and make an appointment."

Sitting in the exam room, Hannah was feeling a little more tired than she had before. Now she was waiting for the doctor to give her a prescription for something to perk her up. As the doctor walked into the exam room, she felt a heavy weight just push down on her. She held her breath. Not sure what was going on.

"Hannah, I'm sorry, but we have discovered a large mass in one of your lungs. I can't be absolutely sure until I do a biopsy, but it looks very much like cancer."

Oh no, she thought. *There is that horrible C-word again. Oh, Lord, why me, why now?* She couldn't speak. She just sat there and looked at the doctor and felt the tears running down her cheeks, again!

"Hannah, I know this is hard for you to accept, but we have to schedule you for that biopsy now and then consider all the options you have available. Do you understand? Do you want me to call Gabe?"

"No, no, don't call Gabe. I have to tell him. I don't want him to find out from anybody else." She could feel everything around her spiraling down. And she couldn't make it stop.

When she got home, she broke down before she could say anything. She wrapped her arms around me and just held me tight and cried. I didn't say a word. I didn't know what was wrong, but I knew she would tell me when she was ready, whatever it was.

After all the tests, x-rays, pokes, and prods, the results were in. Terminal lung cancer. Chemo would only extend her life maybe a couple of months. And they would be very painful months.

"Oh, Lord, I know Your ways are mysterious ways for us, and I know You love me with Your unconditional love, but, Lord, I still don't understand why now, why this way. You have blessed Gabe and me in so many ways over our life together, and we are so very thankful for that. But, Lord, what is Gabe going to do? My heart aches for him and what he must be going through. Please, Lord, give me the peace only You can give right now. Give me the strength to go through the next months. Give Gabe the strength he needs to go on our journey alone."

Hannah was now back at the inn, resting comfortably while the world went on outside her room. I had put up a notice in town and at the church, looking for someone to take over the duties of housekeeper and cook at the inn. I knew I would never find someone who could take Hannah's place, but hopefully someone would be able to at least keep things going for a while.

Scott and Cory had come back to visit with us, and Cory had told me that whatever it took, whatever we needed, cost was not an issue. Hire someone to take care of Hannah full-time if necessary.

Hannah was so glad they had come back to visit. She loved them both so much and was so thankful for all they had done for us. She had thought how much she was going to miss them. Then her heart took a leap when she realized and spoke aloud in her empty room. "I'm going to be with my Lord and Savior. He has just decided it's time for me to come home. I should be happy. Sorry, Lord, guess I'm still working on that part. Please forgive my delay." She smiled as she thought of what she had just said to her God. "I sure hope He likes my sense of humor."

Chapter 7

Martha and Stephanie

"Aunt Martha, this is Stephanie."

"Why, Stephanie, I haven't heard from you in ages. How are you, child? Are you still living in Seattle?"

"I'm living in a little town in Oregon called New Bethlehem. I've been here for about a year. I started going to church, Aunt Martha!" Stephanie sounded excited about this news.

"Oh, I'm so happy to hear that. How about your mom and dad? Are they there with you?"

"No, they're still up in Seattle. I don't hear much from them. I ran away from home and was heading south when I found this job as a waitress. I really like it. Most of the people who come in are locals, and they are so nice. They treat me like I'm somebody important. Like they've known me all their lives. And they invited me to a church called Eternal Hope, and well, I met this boy, and he's so nice to me, and I'm learning all about God and I'm not smokin' weed anymore and I found you a job!"

"Slow down, Stephanie. I'm so proud of you for going to church and stopping with the drugs. What's this about you finding me a job?" Martha was having trouble sorting out everything Stephanie had said.

"Well, I remembered way back when you came to visit us once when you said you would love to get away from the Portland rat race and find a little B and B or something like that where you could work around people who really cared."

"You remembered that?" Martha said. "Why, you couldn't have been more than ten or eleven when I said that."

"I remembered lots of things you said, Aunt Martha. I know my mom is your sister, but whenever you came to visit, I pretended you were my mom. I love you so much, Aunt Martha, and you were always so nice to me."

Martha was having trouble holding the phone in her hand. She knew her sister was not the "mom" type and that they had had trouble with Stephanie for several years, but she never imagined how much of an impact she, Martha, had had on her life. She wanted to reach through the phone line and give her a big hug.

"Anyway," Stephanie continued, "there's this place up in the mountains called Shepherd's Inn. The folks who run it go to my church, and the lady is the housekeeper and cook and she got cancer and she's gonna die and they need someone to take her place."

Martha couldn't believe what she was hearing. She felt horrible for the lady, whatever her name was, but the thought of having a job like that sounded too good to be true. "So how did you find out about all this?"

"Like I told you, they go to my church, and everybody knows everybody and they take care of one another and they are so nice and I can give you their phone number and you can call and find out about the job and if it's still open." Stephanie had always been high-strung and talked a blue streak without paying much attention to what she was saying. This was one of those times.

"Yes, Stephanie, give me their number. I'll be sure to call them. And even if the job is no longer available, I promise I'm going to come visit you real soon. Also, give me your phone number and address, so I'll know how to find you."

After she ended the call with Stephanie, Martha went into the kitchen and made herself a cup of hot tea. She went back into her living room and sat down in her favorite chair. It was the same chair her husband, Cal, sat in every evening for so many years. She still felt a closeness to him every time she sat down.

"Oh, Lord, thank You for my sweet niece Stephanie. Thank You for guiding her and taking care of her at her young age. Thank You for leading her to loving Christian brothers and sisters who have taken her in and cared for her. And thank You for the phone call from her today. Lord, please give me guidance now as I ponder this new information. Lord, if I am supposed to move from here and take this job, then all I ask is that You give me the tools I need to make it happen. I love You, Lord."

Martha reached over and picked up the piece of paper with the name and phone number Stephanie had given her. Her hand was trembling as she reached over and picked up the phone.

"Hello, Shepherd's Inn. This is Gabe. How may I help you?"

"Mr. Sinclair, my name is Martha Peterson, and I was told by my niece that you may have a position open for housekeeper, cook. Is that position still available?"

"Why, yes, it is. And you say your niece told you we were looking for someone?" I said. I figured someone at the church had given her the info.

"My niece is Stephanie Anderson, and she attends the same church as you, and she called me and told me about it. I now live in Portland, but I am available and willing to relocate."

"Stephanie, huh? Well, if she got her personality and charm from your side of the family, then I'm sure we could talk about you working here. What did she tell you about the job?"

"She just said your wife is ill, and I am so sorry to hear that. Please accept my deepest sympathy."

"Thank you," I said. "We're working our way through it. Anyway, you were saying?"

"Well, she said you are looking for a housekeeper/cook, and that has been my specialty all my adult life. I have plenty of references if you wish. I was just wondering if there are places to live near there so I wouldn't have to commute very far. I've never been a particularly good driver, and this Portland traffic drives me crazy."

"Oh, I guess Stephanie didn't tell you, the job includes room and board. You wouldn't have to drive at all unless you want to go to town."

"Oh my lord! That sounds too good to be true. Could I possibly come and interview for the position? I could be there in the next day or two if you need me that soon."

I started, "Mrs. Peterson—"

But she cut me off.

"Please call me Martha."

"Okay, Martha, let me tell you something. I have been a man of faith all my life. I grew up in the church, believe what the Bible, God's Word, tells me, and I turn to Him for all my needs. He guides me in the way I should go, and He advises me when I need His helping hand. I can tell you right now that you are on the phone with me right now because God sent you here. Martha, I don't need you to come here for an interview."

Oh no, Martha thought. *He's going to tell me God told him not to consider me for the job.* She felt the weight of the world on her shoulders. She was just about to start crying, and she wanted so much to beg him for at least a chance to interview.

After a short pause, I continued, "I need you to come here and go to work. It's Thursday now. Can you be here by Monday?"

Martha couldn't believe what she was hearing. Her heart was beating so fast and hard she could hear it pounding in her chest. She started hyperventilating and couldn't speak.

"Martha, are you still there?"

She said a quick thank-you prayer, then finally found her voice. "Yes, I'm here. I just can't believe what you just said. You really want to hire me without even meeting me or checking any of my references or my background?"

"I'll tell you what? If it'll make you feel any better, I'll talk with Stephanie on Sunday, and if she says you're okay, then that's good enough for me. But I still want you here Monday." I hoped she could hear the smile in my voice as I spoke. "Is it a deal?"

"Oh, yes, yes, it's a deal. I don't know how to thank you, Mr. Sinclair."

"I'm sure your thanks will be in doing a great job here at the inn. And by the way, that's the last time I want to hear you call me Mr. Sinclair. I am Gabe, always have been, always will be. Let me give you directions to the inn, and we'll see you on Monday."

When Martha placed the receiver back in the cradle, she had to try three times before she got it to stay. She was shaking so hard she thought she was going to pass out.

Lord, help me, please, to control myself and understand what has just happened, she silently prayed.

After a few minutes, she reached over to take a sip of her tea. By now it was cold, so she slowly got to her feet and took the cup into the kitchen to warm it in the microwave. As she stood there, watching the cup go 'round and 'round, she thought how her life seemed to be going 'round and 'round right then as well. One minute she was living in Portland, working at an okay job, and was satisfied, more or less, with her life. Then, suddenly, a couple of phone calls changed everything.

The chime of the microwave timer brought her back to the present. She opened the door, took out the cup of now-warm tea, and went back into the living room.

As she sat in her favorite chair, she started thinking about all the things she had to do between now and Monday. "I have to start making a list," she said out loud. If anything, Martha was always good at organizing and preparing things in advance. One thing she didn't like was surprises.

After a few minutes of writing down the first things that came to her mind, she thought she should call Stephanie back and tell her the good news. This time, when she reached for the phone, there was no tremble in her hand. Only a confidence that God was in control and she had nothing to worry about.

Chapter 8

Joe and Maria
November 3

Joe got off work at five on a normal day, but most days weren't normal. That slug of a coworker made it hard for them to finish their deliveries on time. So most days it was after six before he came walking in the door.

It was already after seven and Joe wasn't home yet, and he had not texted to tell Maria he would be late. She had tried his cell, and it went straight to message. She kept sending him texts, and he didn't reply. He had turned it off or the battery was dead, or something had happened. Fear was starting to build for Maria, and she didn't know what to do. She had called just about everyone she could think of who might know where he was, but no one had heard from him. The furniture store was closed, so she couldn't call there, but then she remembered Joe's boss's name and gave him a call.

"No, Joe didn't work late tonight. In fact, both the guys left a little early today. Sorry, I can't help you. If I hear from him, I'll let you know."

"Oh, God," Maria started to pray, "please help me. I don't know what to do. Please keep Joe safe and bring him home to me. Our baby needs him so much."

By nine that evening, she was in panic. She had even called the hospital to see if he had been admitted.

Was that a car pulling into the driveway she heard? She ran to the front window and looked out. The streetlight on the corner gave her a good view of the driveway. When she saw his car, sudden relief washed over her, knowing he was safely home. That relief was immediately replaced with rage when she watched Joe try to get out of the car and stumble and fall on the front lawn. "He's drunk!" she said. "He's stinking drunk!"

Joe managed to pick himself up and start toward the house. With lots of difficulty, he finally managed to make it up the steps to the front door. As he was fiddling with his keys, trying to find the front door key, the door flew open and he could feel Maria pounding on his chest.

"Where have you been? Why are you coming home stinking drunk? Why didn't you text me and tell me where you were? How could you do this to me?" she kept repeating as she kept pounding on his chest. Finally, she just grabbed ahold of his shirt and sank slowly to her knees in front of him. She had nothing else left. She was physically and emotionally exhausted. She wanted to run and not stop running. She didn't want to be around Joe anymore, and she hoped he would just turn around and leave. She didn't care if he was drunk and could get picked up for drunk driving. She didn't even care if he had a wreck and killed himself.

Joe reached down and held her arms and slowly picked her up. Even though he had had way too much to drink, he knew what a mess he had made. In his clouded mind, he wondered what it would take to make things right again. "I'm sorry, baby" was all that came out.

Maria turned and ran to the bedroom and slammed the door. "Get away from me! Leave me alone!" she screamed from behind the closed door. She hated this. She hated Joe. She hated what her life had become. She worried if this latest episode had harmed her baby. She knew she had made a mess of her life, and she wanted to blame it all on Joe. But in her heart, she knew that she had to take some of the responsibility for how her life had turned out. "Oh, God," she started, "I need You so bad right now. I don't know what else to do. Why would Joe go out and get drunk when we don't even have enough money to pay the bills? Why would he not text me and tell me where he was? How can I love him when he doesn't seem to love me? Lord, it seems ever since I got pregnant, he hasn't been the same man I married. He doesn't touch me the same way he used to, he doesn't love me the same way he used to. He doesn't even talk to me the same way anymore. God, am I that bad a person that he doesn't love me anymore? Please, Lord, tell me what to do!"

Maria cried herself to sleep. It wasn't a restful sleep. Her dreams were a mix of the fun times they had had together, along with nightmares of her being alone in the forest and going into labor. There was no one around as she cried out for Joe. She saw several people standing around her, but Joe was not among them. She woke up several times during the night and thought about going out to see if Joe was still there. But her feelings were so jumbled up that she wasn't sure if she wanted to see if he was all right or find out that he was gone.

Finally, at a little after 6:00 a.m., she got up and opened the bedroom door. She hadn't been to the bathroom all night, and she really had to go. She was surprised that this was the first night in months that she hadn't thrown up. She quietly walked around the corner to the bathroom, hoping Joe wouldn't hear her. So far, so good. She closed the bathroom door and turned the lock. She looked in the mirror and was shocked at what she saw. The last thing she wanted was for him to see her like this. After she had washed her face and run a brush through her hair, she thought maybe she looked a little better. Not the greatest, but he didn't deserve the greatest.

Where had the other Maria gone? Less than a year ago, she was *hot*. Small, five foot one, 110 pounds. High cheekbones and a button nose. Inset Brown eyes that prompted many people, both male and female, to comment. Dark-brown hair almost down to her tiny waist and a figure that made the guys take a second look. Now the hair was mousy and stringy. That tiny waist was nowhere in sight, and even her husband wasn't taking a second look. She was fat. She hated how she looked. *No wonder he wanted to get drunk, so he wouldn't have to look at me,* she thought.

Maria walked into the living room and saw a crumpled-up blanket on the sofa but no Joe. Then she heard a noise from the kitchen and hesitated briefly before going in. *What will I say, how will I handle his response, how is this going to end?* she thought.

As she turned toward the kitchen, there was Joe, standing in the doorway. Wearing only his jeans and a T-shirt, no shoes or socks, hair messed up with bed head, and dark bags under his eyes. She had thought she had looked bad this morning, but Joe had her beat.

Before she could say a word, Joe spoke. "Maria, I know I don't deserve to be forgiven for last night. All I can say is I'm so, so sorry. I was feeling really bummed yesterday after work, and instead of coming to talk to you about it, I went to a bar. I don't even know why I went there. You know I don't like the taste of beer, and I can't stand being around a lot of cigarette smoke. But that's where I wound up." Maria started to interrupt, but Joe stopped her. "Just let me finish, please! They told me at work yesterday that my hours are going to be cut. Bill, from the office, said they couldn't afford to pay for insurance for all the employees, so they were cutting most of us down to part-time. After the first of the year, I'll be cut to twenty hours a week and we will lose our insurance. I don't know what to do. I know I have to start looking for another job, but you know as well as I do that there isn't much out there. I guess I just lost it."

Maria rushed up to Joe, and they held each other as they both started to cry. Finally, Joe spoke. "I'm so sorry I let you down. I'm sorry I haven't been the husband you deserve. Maybe your mom is right. Maybe you should go up to Bend and stay with them until the baby is born. I could stay here and crash with friends to save on rent. I could send you money every week and maybe come up there once in a while."

Maria put a finger to his lips. "I'm not living anywhere without you. I love you, Joe. We'll work it out somehow. Just please, don't do any more stupid stuff like getting drunk. Our baby needs you. I need you."

Joe and Maria walked into the kitchen, and she put on a pot of water to make her some tea. Joe had already started a pot of coffee, and she poured him a cup. For the next several hours, they sat and talked about their future. Joe was still talking about her going to Bend, and Maria was beginning to wonder if he wanted that for her or him. She did love him, but most of the time, she had trouble understanding why he did some of the things he did. The more they talked, the more she started to believe that perhaps her going to Bend would be a good idea. But deep down inside, she wondered if that would be the beginning of the end for their marriage. Was their love strong enough to handle the separation? She didn't know the answer, but she knew what she had to do, and that was pray.

Chapter 9

November 5

Martha, Lydia and her twin daughters, and I were just leaving church to get into the van when Pastor Nate caught up with us on the front steps. "Hey, folks, not often we get the whole gang from Shepherd's Inn here on a Sunday morning. What's the big occasion?"

"Oh, nothin' special," I replied. "It's just that we normally have guests at the inn and somebody has to stay behind to babysit." Everyone gave a little chuckle at that last comment. They all could remember some of the more colorful guests from the past who really did need a babysitter. "Hey," I continued, "why don't you and Deanne and the kids come up for supper sometime this week? We haven't had you up for a while, and I'd like to show you some of the hard work Jake did helping me move furniture."

"Sounds like a plan," Nate replied. "I'll just have to run it by the family planning director to get it cleared." He smiled at his feeble attempt at humor just as Deanne walked up to join the conversation. Nate gave her a light kiss on the cheek and spoke in her direction. "Honey, Gabe just invited us all up to the inn for dinner sometime this week. How does that sound?"

"That sounds great. We haven't been up to the inn in ages. I've always loved it up there. I feel a real closeness to God when I'm there. We have Thursday open. How does that sound?"

Martha was listening to all this conversation, thinking, *Gabe never ran that by me first. He knows I'm going to be the one having to do all the cleaning and making the dinner. I adore that old man, but sometimes he just makes me so mad not thinking of all the work I'll have to do.* Her thoughts turned to words as she said to the pastor and his wife, "Oh, that'll be wonderful. I have a new recipe I've only tried once, but everyone thought it was great. I'm sure you'll like it. You'll have to pardon the look around the place, though. With all the mess of remodeling, things are a little less tidy as I would like them to be." She shot a glance at me and Lydia and continued, "But I'm sure everybody will pitch in to clean up the big messes!"

I knew I had overstepped my bounds with handing out the invitation without checking first with Martha. Nothing to do now but wait for her comments when we got home. "Okay," I said to the group, "we'll look forward to having a good time on Thursday. Come on up early so we can maybe take a walk down by the creek and look at the quaking aspens. They are late turning this year, and there are still a few colorful leaves to look at."

We all talked for a few more minutes, and then my crew and I climbed into the van and headed back up to the inn. As I drove back up the narrow gravel road, I noticed I needed to do something about the sign at the bottom of the hill. It was getting a little faded and needed some sprucing up. I also noticed a few more potholes in the road that could use some work. Seemed like there was always something to do to keep the inn in tip-top shape. And keeping it in tip-top shape was the one thing I liked to do more than anything. I treasure the inn as if it were my own. As we got closer and could see the inn through the trees, I thought about all the years, tears, and laughs that had passed through this little valley we call home. A little chill ran up my spine as I recalled Hannah and me working side by side all those years. A little prayer passed through my mind as I thanked God for all we had been given.

When we crossed the bridge over the Little Jordan Creek, one of the twins, Elisabeth, said, "Gramps, why does this bridge make so many funny noises when we go over it?" The twins, Elisabeth and Sarah, were eight years old and the apple of my eye. I thought of them more as the grandkids I never had, and their mother, Lydia, as the daughter I never had.

Chapter 10

Lydia, Elisabeth, and Sarah

Lydia and the girls had come to the inn three years ago. It was a cold, rainy September afternoon when the bus pulled into the parking lane next to Crawford's Restaurant in New Bethlehem. Lydia and her five-year-old twin daughters had just traveled over five hundred miles and a couple of bus changes as they left behind a shattered life in Olympia, Washington. She and Cade had lived together for six years. She had always known what she was doing was wrong, but she felt powerless to do anything about it. Cade often talked about them "gettin' hitched," but every time she pressed him about it, he would go off into one of his rages and accuse her of trying to run his life.

Things between them had been good at first. Cade was always bringing her little gifts, like a bracelet or earrings or perfume. And he always treated her nice—nothing special, but nice at least. It wasn't until after the twins were born that things changed. When she first found out she was pregnant, he had told her to get an abortion. "Get rid of it!" he said. "We don't need no kid around to tie us down."

She couldn't believe what he was saying. She realized later that she should have left right then. She could have moved back with her parents then. In fact, they had offered to take her in as long as Cade wasn't part of the package. They hated Cade and didn't hesitate to tell her so. Of course, at eighteen she was not going to be intimidated into something by her parents. She was a grown woman, and she could make her own decisions.

After a couple of months, Cade calmed down a little and seemed to accept the fact he was going to be a daddy. Then, when she told him she was having twins, that was the first time he actually hit her. It was a slap in the face, and Lydia couldn't believe he would do such a thing. Of course, he was quick to apologize and tell her he was sorry and wouldn't do it again. But he did do it again, and again, and again! As she kept getting bigger, he kept getting more distant. He spent most of his time at a bar or over at his friends' houses, drinking beer and watching sports on TV. In some ways she was glad when he was gone because that meant he wasn't there to mistreat her. She felt like he considered her his property that he could do with what he wanted.

When the twins were born, he didn't even come to the hospital. She had driven herself there after she had called him at work and told him she was going into labor. He told her he couldn't get away from work right then and he would catch up with her later. She couldn't believe what she was hearing. She felt so alone and so trapped.

Elisabeth and Sarah were the best thing that had ever happened to her. She had named them after Elizabeth and Sarah from the Bible. She had loved the stories of these women in Scripture and their strength and courage. She hoped the names would help to make her daughters stronger than she was.

For the next five years, they all lived in chaos. Cade would be kind and loving for a while, then something would happen, or she would say something and he would go off on a tirade again. She figured she was doing a good job of covering up the bruises. And most of the time, he hit her where it wouldn't show. But he never hit the girls. She didn't know what she would do if that ever happened. She had nowhere to go and no one she could turn to. Her relationship with her parents had deteriorated to the point where she hardly ever heard from them. They would send gifts to the twins on their birthday and Christmas, but that was about all they did. They never came to visit because, as her dad had stated once, "I will never set foot in the same house as that no-good piece of garbage!"

Shortly after the twins turned five, Cade came home drunk one day. When he came in the house, Lydia could tell he was in one of his moods. She didn't say anything, but she did give him a look that said she hated the way he was. Cade knew that look. He had seen it many times. This time he wasn't going to put up with it. "Don't give me that look," he said. "I'm sick and tired of putting up with your crap all the time!" Then he backhanded her in the face.

Elisabeth came running into the room, crying, and said, "Daddy, please don't hit Mommy! Please don't be mean to my mommy!"

Cade turned to Elisabeth and slapped her in the face. "Shut up, you little whore!" he said. "That's what you're going to be, a little whore, just like your mother!"

Lydia didn't even realize what she was doing when she grabbed the skillet from the stove. With both hands she swung the skillet and hit him right behind his left ear. He dropped like a rock to the floor, and she couldn't tell if he was dead or just knocked out. Part of her didn't even care. The girls started screaming and crying, and she just stood there holding the skillet. Finally, she told the girls to go into their room and don't come out until she told them to.

What was she going to do? She knew that if he was dead, she was a murderer and she would never see her babies again. If he was just knocked out, he would probably kill her when he came to. She had to do something, and fast. She checked his carotid artery and saw that he was still alive, but blood was trickling from his left ear. She got some extension cords from the pantry and tied his hands and feet. Then she duct-taped him to a dining chair. She then took a dish towel and wrapped it around his mouth and secured it with more duct tape. If he came to, she didn't want him yelling and alerting the neighbors.

After she figured she had done all she could to immobilize him, she took out his wallet and took all the money he had. She couldn't believe how much money he had in there. She hurriedly counted it, and there was over five hundred dollars. She checked his pockets and found a bag of white powder. *Cocaine? Was he using or selling?* she wondered. Whatever, she poured it down the drain. She checked other pockets and found another six hundred in one hundred-dollar bills.

Her mind was racing. Get the girls and get out now. She hurried into the girls' room and started grabbing clothes out of the closet. She took a duffel bag and filled it up. The girls were crying and asking her what they were going to do. She could see the girls were in a state of panic, so she tried to slow down and talk to the girls about going away.

"Elisabeth, Sarah, we are going to have to go away for a while. Daddy's not going with us. He is sick, and he is going to have to go see the doctor. One of his friends is going to come over later and take care of him. We're going into Mommy's room now and get some more clothes put in a bag, and then we are going to leave. You girls are going to have to be brave and strong and do just what Mommy tells you to do. Do you understand?"

Tears streamed down both girls' faces. They were crying so hard all they could do was nod. The girls had been through so much heartache in their young lives that they somehow knew that their mommy had to stop their daddy from hurting Elisabeth. But still they were shaking so hard with fear that all they could do was cling to each other and watch their mommy put her clothes in a bag.

Lydia hurried around the house, gathering up as much stuff as she could think of that she needed to take with them. Social Security cards, birth certificates, family photos, jewelry, medications, cell phone and charger, whatever she could think of. When she had loaded it all in duffel bags, she grabbed their coats and headed for the car. As they were leaving the house, she could hear Cade starting to move around in the kitchen. She never turned around. She and the girls went out the front door and never looked back.

Heading south from Olympia on I-5, Lydia was relieved when they passed through Tumwater, just south of the city. She pulled off at the next exit and called one of Cade's drinking buddies, Lester, and told him Cade wanted him to come over for a beer. Lester asked her why Cade didn't call, and she said he was in the shower and asked her to call. He didn't sound too convinced but said he'd be over in about an hour. Lydia figured that would give her plenty of time to get far away from Olympia before Cade would have a chance to start looking for them.

As she pulled back out onto the freeway, she thought everything would be okay. But what if he called the cops and gave them a description of her car? She hadn't thought of that. *Now, what do I do?* she wondered. As she passed a sign telling her how far it was to Centralia, she got another idea. She would drive to the bus station and leave the car in Centralia.

When they left the freeway again, she stopped at a gas station and asked where the bus station was. The young girl working behind the counter gave her a deer-in-the-headlights look and mumbled a faint "I don't know, lady."

"Perhaps I can help you, ma'am," came the voice of the gentleman standing behind her. "My office happens to be just down the street from the bus station. I'm driving the blue Jeep out there. I'm heading back to the office right now. If you want, you can follow me. We'll pass the bus station before my office, so I'll just hold my hand out the window and point to it."

Lydia was afraid at first to even think of following a complete stranger, but she didn't have a lot of options. She figured, as long as he didn't try to lead her somewhere out in the country, they would be fine. What she didn't know was that the man who offered to guide her to the bus station had had a conversation with God just a short while earlier.

Rance Malone didn't have an office downtown. In fact, he didn't even live in Centralia. He had been traveling north and had planned to pull off the freeway to get a bite to eat and fill up his tank. Rance was a semiretired pastor from northern California and was traveling to Seattle to visit family. As he drove, he often prayed and continued to listen for God's still, quiet voice to give him guidance in his daily life. On this particular day, as he drove past the freeway sign indicating "Centralia, next two exits," he also saw a young woman holding a sign that said, "Can't afford bus fare." He knew hitchhiking on the freeway was against the law, and he was also concerned for this young woman's welfare. He knew he had to do something, so he quickly pulled over to the side of the road and motioned for the young girl to get in his car. He knew it was a dangerous thing to do, but he also knew that the Lord had put that young woman there in his path for a purpose.

The uninhibited girl seemed to have no second thoughts about jumping into a car with a complete stranger. He asked her where she was headed, and she said Spokane. She then asked him how far he was going, and he immediately knew what he had to tell her. "I'm only going as far as the bus station, young lady. I'm going to buy you a bus ticket to Spokane. This is a dangerous world we live in, and I know God doesn't want you out here on the highway all alone."

"What do I gotta do in return?" she asked, thinking no matter what this guy said about God, he was probably some pervert. She was prepared to open the door and run if he made any moves on her.

"Actually, all you have to do is tell me your name and allow me to pray for you," Rance replied.

"Well, I don't believe in no prayer stuff, but if you want to, knock yourself out. My name's Cindy."

"Thank you, Cindy," said Rance, and he began to pray. As he sat there on the shoulder of I-5, on the outskirts of Centralia, Washington, he prayed for a young woman he didn't know, and as he did, he poured his soul out to God. Cindy sat there looking at him at first like he was some kook. But as she continued to listen to him, she had a peacefulness wash over her that she had never experienced.

When Rance had finished, he pulled back on the freeway and headed for the Centralia exit. He asked Cindy if she knew where the bus station was, and she told him how to get there. When they got there and parked, Rance was true to his word, and he went into the station with her and purchased Cindy a ticket from Centralia to Spokane. He wished her a safe journey and hurried out of the station as she yelled a "Thank you, mister" as he vanished from her life. A life that would never be the same.

After dropping Cindy off, Rance drove a little farther through town toward the north end freeway entrance. Just before the entrance there was a gas station, so he pulled in to fill up before continuing his journey north. That was when he overheard Lydia asking for directions to the bus station.

When Rance passed the bus station, he held his hand out and motioned to Lydia. He then gave her a friendly wave and drove away. Lydia was looking for a parking space and saying a quiet prayer to God for bringing this stranger into her life for a brief period. She wondered who he was, where his office was, what he did for a living, and if he was married. But she knew she would never find out because her primary focus right at that moment was to get herself and her daughters as far away from Olympia and Cade as she could.

She lugged her heavy duffel bags into the station and went straight to the ticket counter. As good fortune would have it, there was a bus leaving, heading south in just over two hours. That would work, she thought, and she purchased three one-way tickets to Portland. She figured she could decide once she got there which way to go next. Then she rented a couple of lockers and placed the bags inside. She had to figure out what to do with the car so it wouldn't be discovered for a while.

Lydia ushered the twins back outside and into the car again. She figured, if she parked it on a residential street, no one would get suspicious for a while. The longer, the better, she hoped. She didn't want Cade to figure out she had taken a bus. As she drove around the block, she noticed a quiet neighborhood just a couple of blocks from the bus station. *This will have to work,* she thought as she parked near a house with a "For sale" sign in front. It looked vacant, and she figured the neighbors might not get too nosy for a few days. Then she and the girls walked the short distance back to the bus station to wait.

When they arrived in Portland, she checked all the possibilities and thought a trip to The Dalles would get them off the I-5 corridor, where Cade or the police might start looking. The next bus in that direction would get them there late in the evening, but she figured they could get a motel there for the night and figure out something else in the morning.

The motel near the bus station in The Dalles wasn't much to look at from the front, but the room was clean and there were two queen beds for her and the girls. When she laid her head on the pillow, after getting the girls settled and prayers said, she thought about the consequences of her actions that day. She prayed for forgiveness for using violence against Cade and asked the Lord to be with him and heal him both physically and spiritually. As she finally drifted off to sleep, she dreamed of a place far from all the turmoil of the past several years, where the three of them were surrounded by a loving family. It was the best night's sleep she had had in years.

The next morning, she got the girls and herself ready and headed next door for a hearty breakfast. Afterward, they went back to the bus station and she purchased tickets to Klamath Falls. The ticket agent told her it was a milk run and it would stop in several towns along the way. He said she could wait till later and there was a direct bus. She thought about that and decided the milk run would be just fine. That way, she could check out all the little towns along the way.

After four stops and several hours driving in the rain, the bus pulled in to the "Bus Only" parking space in front of Crawford's Restaurant. The bus driver announced, "New

Bethlehem, folks." An older couple got up and started for the front. Lydia looked out at the town and thought of the words of the Christmas song, "O little town of Bethlehem, how still we see thee lie."

"Come on, girls, this is going to be our new home." She had no idea how she was going to support herself or her daughters, but she knew this was where the Lord wanted her to be.

They hurried to the front of the bus and got off just as the driver was finishing getting the luggage for the older couple. She said, "Excuse me, but we have decided we want to get off here. Will you please get our bags for us?"

"Suit yourself, lady, but your tickets were for Klamath Falls. I can't refund you any money for not goin' all the way there."

"That's all right," she said. "If you'll just get our bags, we would appreciate it."

For some unknown reason, the driver seemed a little put out that he had to get their bags. She couldn't understand why, but instead of worrying about it, she just said a quiet little prayer for him before she and the girls headed for the restaurant.

Under an awning near the front door, there was a large bulletin board where it appeared everyone in town posted want ads, notices, and whatnot. There was a distinguished older man in a typical plaid flannel shirt, denim vest, old worn jeans, suspenders, and well-used hiking boots. He had just a fringe of gray hair surrounding a very tan bald head. His hands looked like the hands of a hard worker. He was in the process of putting something on the bulletin board, and as she looked to see what he was doing, she noticed in bold type on the top of his notice were the words "Help Wanted."

"Afternoon, ma'am," he said as he glanced her way. "My, oh, my, those sure are pretty-lookin' little ladies you have there. Are they twins?"

Lydia had usually been cautious when strangers spoke to her, especially when they were in an unfamiliar area. But for some reason, she felt quite comfortable speaking to this kind-looking gentleman. Besides, she wanted to get out of the rain, and there was plenty of room for all four of them under the awning. "Yes, they are," she said, "and thank you. My name is Lydia, and this is Elisabeth and Sarah. I couldn't help but notice the 'Help Wanted' sign you just posted. We just arrived in town, and I'm looking for a job." She couldn't believe how bold she was acting. This was not her nature. She didn't know what had come over her to act this way, but it felt good. She felt better than she had felt in a long time.

"Well, ma'am, I'm the caretaker of a small inn up in the mountains, and we have an opening for a front desk person. It doesn't pay a lot, but the job includes room and board, 'cause we're kinda far from town. Do you suppose you might be interested?"

"Yes," she replied, "I think I'd be very interested. But would that room and board include my two girls?"

"Well, we usually have a single person fill that job, but I don't reckon a couple of little pint-size girls would be much trouble. Do you have any experience in front desk operations?"

She wanted to say yes, but it had been so long ago, and if she gave him references, he might contact them, and Cade would find out. "No, sir, I don't. But I'm a quick learner, I like people, and since the Lord guided me to this town, I'm sure he would guide me in any job I might do." *Oh no*, she thought. *What if my mention of God makes him think I'm some kind of religious kook? Too late now.*

The old man reached up and pulled the notice off the board and turned to Lydia. "My name is Gabe. And I reckon I'm your new boss. If the Lord told you to do something, then it's not up to me to second-guess Him. When can you start work?"

Lydia's jaw dropped. *Could this really be happening? Is he really offering me a job? Oh, thank You, Lord,* she prayed in her heart. Tears started rolling down her cheeks, but this time they were tears of joy. Joy for the first time in a long time. "We just got off the bus. These bags are all we have in the world. I don't have a car. I don't have a place to live. I don't—"

Gabe cut her off in midsentence. "Ma'am, like I told you, the job includes room and board. You'll be staying right there at the inn. It's called Shepherd's Inn, and it has quite a history behind it. I've got my truck right around the corner, and there's plenty of room for all of us to jump right in and head on up. That is, if it's okay with you and Elisabeth and Sarah."

Lydia was crying so hard she could hardly speak. Sarah and Elisabeth started crying, too, because they thought their mommy was sad. Sarah spoke first and said, "What's wrong, Mommy? Why are you crying?"

Lydia had almost forgotten about her girls standing there beside her. She turned and held them both in her arms and said, "Oh, no, Elisabeth and Sarah, nothing is wrong. In fact, everything is going to be just fine. We're going to our new home." She then turned to Gabe, and without even thinking, she gave him a big hug. "I accept! I accept! I accept!" she said through her tears.

Gabe thought about what he had just done and smiled a great big country smile and raised his eyes skyward. "At Your service, Lord," he said. "At Your service." Then, looking down at Elisabeth, Sarah, and Lydia, he said to them, "Okay, ladies, let's go meet Martha and get you settled in."

And that was how I first met Lydia, Elisabeth, and Sarah!

Chapter 11

November 5

"Well, Elisabeth, I reckon that ole bridge is sorta like me. We're both kinda old. Sometimes when I get up in the mornin', my bones creak, just like that ole bridge. Let's just pray it stays standing for a few more years."

When we got back to the inn, Lydia and the girls headed to their room to change out of their Sunday clothes. As soon as they were out of sight, Martha turned to me and said, "Why did you invite the pastor and his family to supper without checking with me first? You know how much I have to do around here, and now I have to get a big meal ready to boot. Gabe, sometimes I think you never even give a thought to my feelings."

"Martha, I'm sorry that I didn't run this by you first, but it was just a spur-of-the-moment thing and I didn't figure it would be that big a deal. Besides, since we don't have any guests right now, you don't have any rooms to change or other big meals this week. Guess I just didn't think it would be a problem."

Martha's cheeks flushed as she held back saying what was on her mind. This old geezer seemed to do a lot of things without thinking them through. Then she remembered the time several years ago when I gave her this job without thinking it through. That was the best thing that ever happened to her. So instead of commenting further, she just gave me a little hug and said, "That's all right. Just try to remember next time." She knew I wouldn't, though.

The next week was filled with working on the renovation projects. I made it a point to start working first on Leah Gardiner's favorite room. She was such an impossible guest, but I believed she was more at peace here at the inn than at any other time in her life for several years. She had confided in me that she was divorced, and she had given me a few specifics, but for the most part she had kept her past to herself.

I took special pains to ensure her room would be in excellent condition for her arrival. With the help of Martha and Lydia, we chose a paint color that the women thought would provide a calming atmosphere. We made a special trip to buy some new sheets and a comforter set that would, according to Martha, appeal to any woman with a lick of decency!

The curtains were starting to look a little worn and faded, so when we got the comforter, we also purchased matching curtains for the window. By the time we were finished with the room, we all agreed that if this didn't please Leah, then nothing would.

I had felt an urgent need to make the room transformation as perfect as I could. So I spent most of the week on her room.

By Thursday afternoon, I had completed most of the work and started helping pick up things around the great room in preparation for our dinner guests, Nate, Deanne, and their two children. By the time we were finished, I was exhausted, but I felt a great sense of accomplishment and knew that as soon as our guests arrived, I would be able to relax and unwind.

Chapter 12

Leah

Leah had been married to a very wealthy businessman from San Francisco. She became accustomed to the life of the superrich. They traveled extensively and threw extravagant parties for all their friends and associates. What Leah wasn't aware of, though, was that her husband had a roving eye and it had zeroed in on Leah's younger sister, Jessie. When a friend of hers accidentally let the cat out of the so-called bag, Leah confronted him about it. At first, he denied everything, but after she presented the evidence she had received, he confessed to his infidelity. But instead of asking forgiveness and telling her it was over, he announced that he was leaving Leah and taking up with Jessie.

"I will provide a stipend for you so you won't be out on the street," he said. But he said it so casually it sent rage through Leah's heart.

"A stipend!" she shouted. "How dare you throw me out like yesterday's garbage! After all I've done for you, smiling like the 'good wife' at all those horrendous parties. Fighting off advances by so many of your so-called friends who didn't miss a chance to grope me or leer at me when they thought no one was looking. And all that time you couldn't keep your hands off Jessie. We'll see about a stipend after I talk with an attorney."

"I would suggest you not bother wasting your time with an attorney," he said. "If you recall, you signed a rather-rigid agreement when we were married that if we were to end our marriage, you would receive nothing. I think a stipend is a generous offer."

Never had she thought he could be so cold and calculating. Apparently, he had been planning this all along; he was just looking for an opportunity to put it into action. "Very well," she replied. "If that is the way it's going to be, I shall make arrangements to find suitable quarters for myself immediately. I would assume you will take care of all the legal matters necessary to terminate this charade of a marriage." Before he could reply, she turned and walked out of the room.

After she had established herself in her own apartment in Oakland (she could no longer afford to live in San Francisco on the small alimony she received), she began to search for a comfortable place to get away for a while. While thumbing through a travel magazine about Oregon, she came across an article about this quaint little inn nestled in the mountains of southern Oregon. The article said it had no website and there was just one phone number available.

She knew that sometimes magazine writers liked to describe resort locales with a little more flourish than they deserved, but she decided to take a chance. She called the inn and made a reservation for a week in October. That was four years ago, and she had returned each fall since then. It might not be as grand as the accommodations she had been accustomed to, but she felt a peace there that she wasn't able to describe. All she knew was she wanted to return.

Chapter 13

November 9

Nate, Deanne, and family drove into the parking lot around four in the afternoon. The sun was already heading close to the horizon, and Nate wanted to see those aspens before it got dark.

Elisabeth and Sarah came bounding out the front door and ran up to their car. Jake and Lauren often helped in children's church and couldn't get enough of the twins. They couldn't believe how smart and polite the girls were. Some of the kids in church were a bit too much to handle, but these two were their favorites. And the twins felt the same way about Jake and Lauren. So when they got together, there was always lots of fun and giggling and playing games. So off the four went, bounding through the trees without a care in the world.

Deanne smiled as she watched them take off and thought of how much she loved this place and these people. She was glad they had been invited up for dinner. She was planning on really enjoying herself tonight. The past few weeks had been a little hectic at church. First, there was the remodel project in the nursery. Then, she had been busy getting things ready for the ladies' fall tea and social scheduled for the Saturday before Thanksgiving. It was always one of the most fun events for the ladies of the church and their daughters. A few years before, a former member of the church donated most of her collection of collector cups and saucers. She and her husband moved to Hawaii, and they had to downsize. So every table at the social was set with a beautiful cup and saucer. It was always a treat to watch the young girls as they acted so dignified as they sipped their tea from such fine china. Now here they were at the inn, and all was peaceful.

Everyone else came out and greeted their special guests. After hugs all around, Martha, Lydia, and Deanne went inside while Nate and I stood by the car and talked for a few minutes. "Gabe," Nate said, with a touch of seriousness in his voice, "I got a call last week from a church up in Bend. It was from one of the elders. He said they are searching for a new pastor and my name had come up for consideration. Seems someone from there had visited Eternal Hope a while back and they took back a CD of my sermon. The elder board had listened to it, and I guess they liked what they heard. Anyway, I was kinda caught off guard. I haven't been looking for a new church to pastor."

I was surprised at what I heard. Nate and Deanne had been pastoring Eternal Hope since before Jake and Lauren were born. It wasn't a very big congregation, but it was a strong church with a solid scriptural base. I couldn't imagine Eternal Hope without Nate in the pulpit. "Wow, that's quite a surprise. So what did you tell them? Have you talked to Deanne and the kids about it?"

Nate gave me a troubled look. "Oh, yes, we've talked about it. I talked with Deanne first, and she said she has mixed emotions about it. She likes Bend, and she could do so much more for the Lord in a bigger church. But she would miss New Bethlehem and our church family here. We sat down with the kids, and when we told them they went ballistic. You know, at their age and all their friends in high school, they didn't like the idea at all. And with Jake in his senior year, I can't really blame him for wanting to finish out high school here. We even talked about me possibly going on ahead and the rest of the family moving up in the summer. Deanne was not too thrilled with that idea."

"Sounds like you have a dilemma on your hands, son." I placed my hand on Nate's shoulder. "Of course, you probably know what I think, not that it matters. I can't imagine a Sunday morning at Eternal Hope without Nate Riser preaching the message. You are that church, you know. When you came here, we were nothing but a bunch of ragtag Christians doing our best to serve the Lord, but without a strong leader at the helm. From the day you walked in, you were a positive force who brought us all together as one voice. I know you are going to do what the Lord has for you to do. But let me tell you right now, you and your family would be greatly missed."

"Let's head down to those aspens before it gets too dark. We can continue this conversation along the way." Nate smiled as he continued, "Nothing like a walk in God's backyard to give a fella a better perspective on things."

"Amen to that," I said. "And up here, in this place, it's almost as if you could just reach out and touch His robe. That's why I don't intend to ever live anyplace else." I moved the conversation back to the matter at hand. "So are your knees all bruised yet from all that kneeling in prayer over this?"

"You can be sure of that. I don't think I've prayed so hard in my life. But so far, God hasn't given me an answer. I'm sort of at a loss, Gabe. I just don't know what to do.

They want me to come up next week and meet with them. I haven't given them an answer yet, but I told them I would let them know by the weekend."

"I reckon you have a whole lot of decision-making to do over the next couple of days. Let me pray with you while we walk." I placed my hand on Nate's shoulder again and prayed for guidance for my dear Christian brother. I prayed for wisdom and patience. I prayed that Nate would have no doubt when the time came to decide that it would be from the Lord. As I spoke my amen, we rounded a huge boulder by the trail and set our eyes on the small meadow of aspen trees lining the banks of the Little Jordan Creek. Buckbrush and manzanita mixed in with a few scrub pines covered the slopes up to a thick stand of red fir and a few ponderosas. It was a sight neither one of us ever got tired of.

Nate and I sat down on an old fallen log and spoke not a word for several minutes. We knew what each other was thinking, and there was no need for words. Instead of the silence being uncomfortable, we each shared a peace, knowing the bond we had through our love of Christ.

After tossing a couple of stones into the creek and looking up to see a bald eagle circling over the valley, looking for his own supper, we finally stood and headed back to the inn. As we approached the main house, Nate turned to me and said, "Thanks, brother. I finally got that message I have been waiting for." That was all he said, and I didn't press him for any more info. I knew Nate would tell me when the time was right.

The women were scurrying about with the final preparations for supper. The recipe Martha had prepared was a new way to make a pot roast. The smell coming from the kitchen made everyone's mouth water. "Gabe," Martha said, "will you please go ring the dinner bell for the kids? I think everything is ready."

I walked out on the front porch and rang the old cowboy-style triangle that had been hanging there since the original inn was built over seventy years ago. I could hear the screams and giggles of the kids as they came bounding out of the trees, heading for the porch.

"Don't forget to wash up," Martha said to them as they came through the front door. Even though Martha could be a little grumpy at times, she loved having children around the inn. She often spoke of her children and grandchildren and how much she missed them.

As everyone gathered around the big pine plank dining table, I asked Nate if he would ask the blessing. As he finished asking for blessing for friends, family, and food, Nate ended with, "And thank You, Lord, for answered prayer, in the name of our Savior, Jesus Christ. Amen."

Deanne looked at Nate with a question in her eyes. I looked at Nate with a smile on my face. Everyone else dug in.

The pot roast was delicious. Martha had outdone herself, and she accepted all the praise for such a great meal with her usual "Aw, it was nothing" comments. But on the inside, she swelled up with pride, knowing she was doing what God wanted her to do.

After the pie and ice cream had been served and everyone was almost finished eating, Nate addressed everyone at the table. He knew Deanne had talked to Martha and Lydia about the job offer, so it wasn't a secret, except maybe for the twins. "As you all know, I was offered the pastor position at a big church up in Bend. It would mean a big pay increase, but also more responsibility and more work. It would mean we'd have to move to Bend and the kids would have to change schools. It would also mean we would be leaving behind our church family here in New Bethlehem." He paused and took a sip of ice tea. "We've all been praying about this for a while, and I just didn't know what to do. Well, I was reminded tonight to listen for God's voice. That sometimes He speaks to us without words but with everything around us." He was having a little trouble continuing. That knot in his throat, he figured, was a good thing. It was keeping the tears out of his eyes.

"Anyway, as Gabe and I were standing down there in the aspen meadow, the Lord revealed what plans He has for us. He reminded me of when Deanne and I first came to Eternal Hope, how that small group of believers took us in like family and made sure we had enough to take care of ourselves. How when you two, Jake and Lauren, were born, everybody pitched in to watch over you on Sundays while your mom and I were busy tending to business. He blessed me with memories of all those little babies who have been born into our church and whom I had the honor of dedicating to Christ. Martha, I was reminded of your niece Stephanie, who came to the church as a down-and-out nonbeliever. How she accepted the Lord as her Savior, met her future husband, Alex, and is now raising her little babies in a Christian home.

"I saw all the love being poured out as we gathered to celebrate the life of Hannah Sinclair when she went home to be with the Lord. There wasn't a building in New Bethlehem big enough to hold the multitude that turned out to honor her."

Deanne sat watching Nate, trying to figure out what he was going to say next. He didn't keep her waiting long as he finished by saying, "I now know that the Lord wants us to continue our ministry right here in New Bethlehem. There is still work to be done, and He wants us to complete it."

Everyone around the table voiced their approval in one way or another. Jake and Lauren gave a big high five to each other and then turned and said, "Thanks, Dad!"

Deanne was sitting across the table from Nate, but instead of getting up and going over to him, she just gave him a look and a smile that told him, and everyone else at the table, that she was very pleased with his decision. No words need be spoken.

I broke that silence with a prayer, as everyone quickly bowed their heads while I continued, "Dear Lord, thank You so much for giving our brother the answer he needed. Thank You for giving us the honor of being here with him and his family as we celebrate this moment. In all things we give thanks in the name of our Lord and Savior, Jesus Christ. Amen."

Martha rose from the table first and said, "Nate and Deanne, you two go into the living room and enjoy yourselves. The rest of us will clean up this mess and come join you in a little while." At that, everyone started getting up and carrying their dirty dishes into the kitchen. To Martha's surprise, Jake and Lauren immediately started cleaning up the plates and putting them into the dishwasher. They told her they would take care of everything; she could just go sit down.

A little later, as everyone was sitting around, chatting and just enjoying the evening, I sat off to the side of the room and looked at the gathering. I was so proud of Nate for who he was and what he had done. But most of all, I was humbled by God's presence in the room. I felt His presence as I often do up here in the mountains at Shepherd's Inn. "Yes, Lord," I said to myself, "this sure is a special place you have provided for us up here. I pray for Your continued blessing."

At a little after nine, Deanne finally broke up the festivities by announcing, "I think we better head on back home now. It's getting late, and you kids have school tomorrow. Tell everybody goodbye."

After a little grumbling, all the goodbyes were said, and the Riser family piled into their car and headed back down the mountain and home. Things returned to normal, at least as normal as they ever get.

Chapter 14

Leah
November 12

Leah Gardiner sat looking at the article in the *San Francisco Chronicle* about the business conference being held in Paris for many of the movers and shakers in the Bay Area business community. Philip Gardiner, Leah's ex-husband, was mentioned as one of the organizers of the conference. What the article didn't mention was the fact that Leah's sister, Jessie, was partly responsible for the conference being held in Paris. Jessie loved to travel around Europe and was more than capable of influencing her companion, Philip, whenever she wanted something.

Leah hated her sister for what she had done. They were about six years apart in age, and Leah, being the eldest, had always had to make allowances for her little sister. Jessie had been born premature and had several health issues as a child. She learned quickly how to take advantage of those issues to get whatever she wanted. As a result, Leah had always taken a back seat to her "poor little sister."

When she met Philip, who was fresh out of Yale Law School, Leah finally felt like she was becoming her own woman. Philip wanted her and not little Jessie. But that didn't mean Jessie didn't try. On more than one occasion, Leah observed her sister making subtle little advances toward Philip. *Fortunately,* she thought, *he isn't interested in her.*

After Leah and Philip were married, things seemed perfect for many years. Philip used his business and law degrees to work his way rapidly up the corporate ladder. In only a few short years, he was making a name for himself as a tycoon in the business world. And Leah was making a name for herself as the good wife who stood behind her husband and let him take the spotlight. That part of her life was the hardest part, and it caused her to become more bitter as the years went by. By the time Leah found out her husband had been having an affair with her sister, she was so filled with hate that most of her friends no longer wanted to associate with her. And when the money was gone, they weren't interested in Leah at all.

So she read the article and looked at the bottle of sleeping pills her doctor had prescribed for her. *Is that the answer?* she thought. *Just go to sleep and never wake up?* But who would find her? She might lie dead in her apartment for days before someone found her. That thought made her sick to her stomach. *No,* she thought, *I have the perfect solution.* "I have the perfect plan," she said aloud to herself. "I shall take my pills with me when I go to that inn next month and plan my demise there. Then that self-centered, always-complaining witch of a housekeeper will have the misfortune of finding my body. That would serve her right for always being so disagreeable."

Immediately, anger and jealousy toward her sister were replaced with a mixture of resolve and revenge. Her thoughts moved toward documenting all her ideas and putting them in a letter that would implicate both Phillip and Jessie as co-conspirators in forcing her to commit such a destructive act. She would tell the world all about the lies, deceit, secrecy, and ego that prompted these two individuals to act as one to destroy the honor and integrity of one Leah Gardiner.

As she thought, she started writing down dates, locations, and occasions that she could prove how unfaithful her husband had been and how selfish and hateful her sister had been.

Hours later, after much writing, rewriting, copying, and correcting, she had what she considered the perfect suicide letter.

She now had her plan. It was only a matter of time until she would put it into action.

Chapter 15

Joe and Maria
November 12

The morning sickness was back. Maria had hoped it was gone for good after that horrible night when Joe came home drunk. But now it was four in the morning, and she had thrown up twice so far. She couldn't figure out how she could have a healthy baby when it felt like she was ripping out her insides every time.

Joe had become more understanding since that night. She knew he was really worried about finding a job where he could get medical insurance for her and the baby. Nearly every day he would bring home a job application to fill out and drop off the next day. Maria always helped him fill them out since Joe had difficulty with his reading and spelling.

Maria's parents had called and invited them to come up to Bend for Thanksgiving, but Maria was in no mood to listen to her dad talk about what a shame it was that they couldn't move there and Joe could go to work for him. She knew how horrible it would be for Joe to have her dad, Derek Belknap, belittle him every day. So she gave her the excuse that Joe was going to have to work that weekend and they wouldn't be able to get away. She knew it was a lie, but she just didn't want to face her parents right now.

"Well, how about Christmas?" her mom said. "You know we have plenty of room for you, and I'm sure Joseph could manage to get at least a few days off then. We really miss you and would love to have you here."

Maria could tell by her mom's tone that when she said, "We miss you," she was not including Joe in that statement. And there was no way she would go to Bend by herself for Christmas. This was going to be their first Christmas as husband and wife, and she wanted it to be special.

Little did she know how special it was going to be.

Chapter 16

November 13

Lydia was busy working on the books for the inn. Besides overseeing the front desk, she was also the bookkeeper and managed all reservations. She had taken some correspondence courses after she went to work at the inn and had become extremely proficient at handling all the finances. I didn't mind at all that she had taken over the finances. That was a part of the job I disliked the most.

While she was checking the reservation schedule for the next three months, she couldn't help but think about one of their guests she wished would visit more often.

She had only been working at the inn for a few months when Lucas Meriweather checked in a few days before Christmas three years ago. When he walked up to the counter and spoke, Lydia was speechless. Her heart was pounding so hard she was sure he could see it through her blouse. As she looked at him walking toward her, she knew she was looking at the most handsome man she had ever seen. Tall, dark, and handsome didn't even come close to describing what she saw. He had a rugged, outdoorsy look that he complemented with faded jeans, a denim shirt under a worn leather jacket, and a soft leather hat that he quickly removed as he walked through the door, revealing a full head of jet-black hair with just a hint of gray along the sides. His well-shined brown cowboy boots completed his wardrobe, and Lydia had taken it all in with one glance.

"Good morning, I'm Doc Meriweather. You must be Lydia."

All Lydia could do for a few seconds was stare at him. If love at first sight really worked, then this was it.

"Excuse me," Doc continued. "Are you all right?"

"Oh, I'm sorry, I guess my mind was on something else for a second." Lydia fumbled with the reservation list and dropped her pen on the floor. It rolled across the floor, and as she hurried to retrieve it, she caught her foot on the corner of the counter and took a header across the room. Doc was immediately by her side, asking if she was all right.

I'll be just fine, she thought, *if I can just crawl under the counter and never come out again!* She could feel her cheeks flush and didn't have the nerve to look him in the eye. "I'm fine, I just...I'm sorry...I'll be fine." She started to get up, and Doc reached down and took ahold of her arm to help her up. She could feel the strength in his hand as he lifted her to a standing position. "I'm really sorry," she said. "I don't know what happened. I'm usually not that klutzy. Thank you for helping me up."

"Are you sure you're okay?" he said. "No broken bones or anything?"

"No, I'm fine. Just my pride is a little bruised." She blushed again as she said that. "Now, let's see about getting you checked in."

That was three years ago, and she had had a crush on Doc ever since. But she was sure he didn't have the same feeling for her. And how could she let him know how she felt? She was certain if she said anything and he wasn't interested, he would probably say something to Gabe, and she would lose her job. She surely couldn't afford that. So for the last three years, she had just kept her feelings to herself.

Now her daughters were a different story. Elisabeth and Sarah had taken to Doc from the first day. And Doc took to them. Whenever Doc was staying at the inn, Elisabeth and Sarah were never far from his side. Since Lydia was homeschooling the girls, they always had "homework" they wanted him to help them with. They would sit on the sofa, one on each side of him, and he would read to them from the study books they brought in. Sometimes he would read from children's novels, and he was such a good storyteller that he could make the books come alive. Lydia loved to watch how gentle and caring he was around her girls. At times it made her heart ache just watching and knowing she wasn't a part of that sharing.

She brought her focus back to the job at hand. They were already busy getting the remodeling project off the ground. The rooms had been emptied of their contents, and Gabe was busy painting walls and trim. The floors were all hardwood, and the scratches and scrapes just needed a little touch-up to make things look better and still retain that rustic look that so many guests enjoyed. But there was still lots more work to do before they were back to a full schedule that was to begin in a couple of months.

Elisabeth and Sarah were busy with schoolwork at the big table in the dining room. It was just off the lobby and visible from the front counter. Lydia watched them as they worked, thinking how fortunate she was to have her girls so close to her all the time. She was so thankful they had gotten away from the horrible environment they lived in while she was with Cade.

She often wondered how he was doing after she almost killed him three years ago. She had contacted a friend of hers in Olympia a few weeks after she left and found out that by the time his friend had shown up at the house, Cade had gone ballistic. He was still tied to the chair, and he couldn't stand up. His friend knocked on the door several times and was about ready to leave when he heard a crashing sound from somewhere inside. He tried the door, and it was unlocked, so he opened it and went in. The crashing sound seemed to be coming from the kitchen. He called out for Cade, and the sound got louder. He went in to the kitchen and couldn't believe what he saw. Cade was lying on his side on the floor, still tied to the chair. The towel was still around his mouth, and his eyes were as wide as saucers.

Cade's friend hurried over and took the towel from his mouth. "I'm going to kill that…" were the first words out of his mouth. Cade was no stranger to foul language, and as his friend untied him, he spit forth a multitude of obscenities describing what he was going to do to Lydia when he caught up with her. Fortunately for Lydia, notifying the police was not part of his plans. He had had too many run-ins with the law over the years, and he didn't trust them to do anything about what she had done to him. He figured he could take care of matters all by himself.

For three years, he had been trying to find Lydia without success. He had contacted every one of her friends that he knew of, and none of them knew where she had gone. The friend Lydia had called did tell him about the call, but she didn't know where it came from, so she was of no help. Lydia just hoped and prayed that Cade would never find her and the girls. Her mind worked its way back to the business at hand.

The inn was in a narrow valley up in the mountains west of New Bethlehem. Because of the remote location, there was no cell service and their only communication with the town was a landline in the lobby. They also had internet, but the service was slow and frustrating at times. Lydia had become accustomed to working with it and didn't seem concerned about the speed. Most of the work she did on the computer was offline, so it was no problem. They did take reservations online, but that was about the limit of their activity. Gabe and Martha were not very handy with computers, so they hardly ever even went near it. Lydia knew that the girls were going to have to start doing more computer work along with their schooling, and she was a little concerned about that. But so far they were doing okay with what they had.

I walked in as she was finishing printing out a list of future reservations. I had a smile on my face, which I usually had, but this time it seemed a little more joyful. "Boy, I love this time of year," I said. "I was just out back, clearing some brush from around the pump house, and I saw the sun low on the horizon casting light through the trees. The shadows the trees were making on the side of the inn looked like something you would see on a postcard." It was just a simple statement, but I was lost in my love for my blessed Shepherd's Inn. I have devoted most of my adult life to the inn, and I know every nook and cranny of the place. I also see my beloved Hannah everywhere I look. It had taken a few years before I could get over the sorrow of losing her and remembering the joy we shared together. It was days like this, with a crisp fall air, bright sunshine, and a gentle breeze, that finally helped me to recover. And now I was at complete peace with my life in this valley.

"Gonna start working on Ms. Leah's room first thing tomorrow morning. I reckon I should have it ready to go in a couple of days, and that should give it plenty of time to air out. I swear that woman can be trying, but I know the Lord has a plan for her, and He just hasn't revealed it to me yet. I am wondering if it has anything to do with her coming this year at Christmastime. She never has been here when we have things all decked out. I have a hunch it'll be very interesting."

Lydia looked at me with a smile and just nodded. She did not like Leah Gardiner, and every time she came to visit, it took all of Lydia's strength to remain polite in her presence. She would say a little prayer every time Leah came into the room, asking for that strength from God. She had even told the girls to try to avoid Leah whenever they could because she had seen how hateful Leah could be around them. She didn't want to see her sweet daughters affected by such an evil woman. *Hopefully, this time things would be different,* she thought. *God performs miracles up here all the time. Maybe this year it would be with Leah.* She smiled again at that thought.

Chapter 17

Hank Lassiter and Belinda Claybaugh
November 15

I pulled into the parking lot at the hardware store. I had realized I needed a few items to finish the remodel project. Hank Lassiter was just walking out the door as I got out of my truck.

Hank had been the local sheriff since before I moved to the area. He had been so popular there usually weren't even any other candidates on the ballot when he ran for re-election. But Hank was getting up in years, and he didn't move as fast as he used to. Last year, he had been out in the woods, looking for a couple of young boys who had tried to steal a woman's purse. They were local boys, and he couldn't, for the life of him, figure out why they would do such a stupid thing. The woman was just passing through, so she didn't know who the boys were, but when she described them to Hank, he knew exactly whom he was looking for.

Hank drove out to the house of one of the boys. It was just outside of town and backed up to the forest. When he asked at the house where her son was, the boy's mother said, "Why do you want to know? What did he do this time?"

Hank explained to her what had happened, and he just wanted to ask him some questions. She told him her son and a friend of his had gone out to a place in the woods where they always hung out. She gave him directions, and he set out to find the boys.

After he had been walking uphill for a couple hundred yards, he was having trouble breathing. He couldn't figure out what was wrong. He had done this hundreds of times and never had a problem like this. "Boys, I know you're up here. Why don't you come down here so I can talk to you? This is Sheriff Lassiter. I'm sure we can work this out."

The boys were looking out from the lean-to they had built in a clump of trees and could see the sheriff just a few yards away. Before they could even think about coming out of their hiding place, they saw Hank start rubbing his left arm, and then he stumbled and fell.

Hank woke up and couldn't figure out where he was. Wherever it was, it smelled like antiseptic. He could hear something going *beep beep*, and he realized he was lying in a bed with wires stuck out all over his body. The last thing he remembered was being out in the woods and feeling his arm starting to throb. Did he have a heart attack? Was he dead? What the heck was going on? he thought.

"Well, it looks like our sheriff is awake finally. Hello, Hank. How are you feeling?"

Hank was still in a fog, and he had no idea who was talking to him. He mumbled, "Where am I, and who are you?"

"It's Dr. Brownwood, and you're at the New Bethlehem emergency clinic. You had a heart attack yesterday, and you've been here ever since."

"How did I get here?"

"Those two boys you were chasing yesterday, do you remember that? Well, they saw you fall, and they ran to get help. They said they knew you were chasing them because they had tried to steal a woman's purse, but they couldn't just let you die out there."

"They did that? Well, I'll be darned!"

"In fact," Dr. Brownwood continued, "if you hadn't gotten here when you did, we would all be going to your funeral. Those two boys saved your life."

"So how long do I have to stay here before I can get back to work?" Hank was hoping it was just something minor and he would be back to work in no time.

"Well, Hank, I don't think going back to work is part of the plan right now. You had a massive myocardial infarction. There was some damage to your heart, and you're going to have to take it easy from now on. No more running around out in the woods like a kid. You're seventy-one years old, Hank. It's time to step down and let someone younger take over."

Hank felt like someone just put a huge rock on his chest. He was having trouble breathing again and he felt his face getting warm. He couldn't believe what he had just heard. Step down. Is that what the doctor said? How could he step down? Being sheriff of Cabel County was all he knew. It was who he was. Now they wanted him to just step down. Go home and die?

"Hank, I'm sorry to have to tell you that, but you're fortunate you didn't die out there. This was no little episode. I'm sure in time you will be able to resume a relatively normal life. But the rigors of being sheriff just won't fit into those plans."

Hank had never been a religious man. Oh, he believed in God, but he hadn't set foot inside a church in years. And he couldn't remember the last time he prayed. He thought about that and wondered if it was time to get started. He closed his eyes and began a silent prayer for forgiveness and for healing. He wasn't even sure how to go about praying, but he just spoke in his mind to God and really felt like God was listening.

"Hank, are you all right?" Dr. Brownwood said. He wasn't sure what was happening when Hank closed his eyes like that, and the heart monitor showed a slower heart rate.

"Doc, I think I'm gonna be just fine." Hank felt a peace come over him that he couldn't explain, but he just knew it had come from God. "By the way, what happened to those boys after they called for help?"

"Now that's the interesting part. One of the boys ran down to their house and called 911. He waited for the EMTs to show up and led them right up to where you were. The other boy stayed with you and started CPR. He had been learning about how to perform it in health class at school, so he knew just what to do. Deputy Claybaugh heard the call, and she was there too. Well, after they got you stable and into the ambulance, those boys rode along with the deputy to the clinic. On their way, they told her everything that happened. They said they knew they had been stupid for trying to steal the purse and they were ready to accept their punishment. They said they felt really bad because it was their fault that you had the heart attack. Can you believe that?"

"Where are the boys now? Did Belinda lock them up?"

"I'll let her tell you the rest. She's waiting out in the hall." Dr. Brownwood opened the door and called to the deputy. Belinda Claybaugh walked into the room and over to the bed.

"Hey, Hank, you had us pretty scared for a while there. How are you feeling?"

"Not too bad, I guess, considering what I've been through. Looks like you're going to have to take over things for a while around here."

"Let's not worry about that right now. Let's just concentrate on getting you well. Can I bring you anything?" she said.

"Well, as a matter of fact," Hank replied, "there is one thing you can bring me. In my desk at the office, in the third drawer down on the right side, there's a Bible. It probably has a lot of dust on it. Don't think I've used it for quite a while. Will you bring that to me?"

"Sure thing, Hank. Is there anything else?"

"Nope," he said. "That should do it for now. By the way, what happened to those two boys? Did you lock them up?"

"As a matter of fact, after we got you here and found out you were going to be okay, they went with me down to the office. The lady they tried to rob had been waiting to identify them. When we walked into the office, before the woman could even speak, one of the boys said, 'We're really sorry, ma'am, for trying to steal your purse.' Well, the woman was taken by surprise. She figured they'd try to lie their way out of it. Anyway, I explained to her what all had happened, how you had gone looking for them and had a heart attack and the boys saved your life. When I got through telling her all that, she asked me if she could talk to the boys. I told her it would be okay, and she asked them to sit down.

"She told them how frightened she had been when they ran by and grabbed her purse. She said she had been robbed once up in Portland and the thieves stole her purse and knocked her down. She said one of the thieves had a gun and he pointed it at her and looked like he was going to shoot her. His partner in crime said, 'Hey, come on, man, let's get out of here. She ain't gonna know who we are.'

"By the time she finished her story, she had those two boys crying like little babies. They were apologizing all over the place. Anyway, she then blew me away when she told them she wasn't going to press charges if they would do one thing for her. When they asked her what that was, she said, 'Let me pray for you. Right here, right now.' Well, the boys couldn't believe their good fortune. They thought that was an easy thing to do, so the woman started to pray for them. Now, Hank, you've never heard the kind of prayer that woman spoke. She prayed for the boys, she prayed for you, she prayed for the doctor, she prayed for just about everyone involved in what had happened. She had tears running down the cheeks of those boys, and me too.

"When she was finished, she and the boys stood up, and she gave them a great big hug. Hank, it was the most remarkable scene I think I've ever witnessed. Now, I think the boys have something they want to tell you." She turned toward the door and went out. A couple of seconds later, the boys came into the room and over to the bed.

One of the boys spoke. "Hello, Sheriff, how you doin'? We're really sorry for what happened to you and for what we'd done. We sure hope you get well quick."

"Thank you, boys. I really appreciate that. I hear that lady dropped the charges against you. That was pretty nice of her, wasn't it?"

The other boy then spoke. "It sure was. And 'cause we were kinda responsible for you gettin' sick and all, we kinda thought we had to do somethin' to make it up to you. So if it's okay with you, Sheriff, we want to help you out while you get well. We'll do chores around your house and run errands or whatever else you want for us to do. We feel really bad and don't want no hard feelings. Will that be okay with you?"

Hank couldn't believe what he was hearing. What kind of prayer did that woman pray that changed the hearts of these boys so? Whatever it was, he was thankful for it. "That sounds like a deal to me. Why don't you boys come back tomorrow, when I'm feeling a little better, and we'll talk more?"

Days and weeks went by, and Hank and those boys became the best of friends. Hank sort of became the grandfather they never had.

Hank retired two months after his heart attack. It was difficult at first, but he seemed to settle into a routine of eating better, getting exercise, and reading his Bible daily. He started going to church every week, and before long, he was helping there with small chores that weren't too stressful. Hank was at peace with his life.

The county held a special election, and Belinda Claybaugh was elected sheriff by a landslide. She was the first ever female sheriff in Cabel County.

Hank spotted me and walked over to greet me. "Hey, Gabe, how are things going with the remodel? Didn't expect to see you around for a while. Figured you'd be up to your elbows in work up at the inn and not have time for us folks here in town."

I smiled. "Hank, I always have time for you. Besides, I needed a few more things to finish what I'm doing up there. I hadn't realized how run-down the place had gotten. I have to get two rooms ready real quick 'cause a couple of our regulars are coming for Christmas. You remember Doc Meriweather, don't you?"

"Yeah, he's the guy who lost his wife and kid in a drunk-driving thing several years back, right?"

"Yep, he's the one. He still struggles with that. But I think when he comes up here, he can get away from the things that remind him of his family. He's talked about selling out down there in California and starting a new practice up here, but I think he just doesn't have the motivation right now to do it. I figure the Lord is workin' on him and it will happen in due time.

"What's new with you, Hank? The old ticker still running like a fine Swiss watch?"

"Funny you should ask. I went up to Bend just last week for a checkup, and the doctor up there told me he couldn't see any evidence of heart damage. Said I should be good to go for another twenty or thirty years if I take care of myself and don't overdo it. Tell you the truth, I never realized how stressful things had gotten when I was sheriff.

"Back in the days when I first got elected, things were really quiet around here. But over the years, we just kept getting more and more outsiders comin' in and messin' things up. 'Course, now that Belinda is on the job, she's got a lot more spunk than I had. I hear tell she has all her deputies towin' the line. I had a lot of trouble accepting the fact that I had gotten soft over the years and kinda let things slide. Well, she's gettin' 'em back in shape. I'm proud of what she has done in such a short time. And she doesn't come across as a pain in the you-know-what. Strictly professional.

"You know, Gabe, as hard as it was givin' up my job, I know it was the best thing that ever happened to me. And especially now that those two boys turned out so well. It just never ceases to amaze me what the Lord can do with even crusty old codgers like me!" Hank laughed at that comment.

I smiled at my old friend Hank. "He certainly does do wonders, doesn't He? I know we have surely been blessed up at the inn. Speaking of the inn, I better get in there and get those supplies. Martha's wanting me to get one room finished really quick. Got one of our regulars coming who is very particular. Says she doesn't want fresh paint smell in her room. I kinda feel sorry for her, so I try to make things as comfortable for her as I can. I know the Lord is workin' on her, but I think it's just going to take a lot of time or something big to happen to open up that woman's heart. Just keep us all in prayer, Hank, and I'm sure everything will turn out fine.

"And congratulations on the fine report from the doctor. You're lookin' great. Are you still planning on coming up to the inn for Thanksgiving?"

"I'll be there. I do love Martha's cookin'. See you then."

As Hank walked on down the street and I went into the hardware store, I couldn't help but think about my old friend. I thought, too, about all the many friends I have in New Bethlehem. Reflecting on my life here, I feel so blessed to be a part of all that had gone on here over the last several years.

Sometimes in our busy lives, we tend to forget about the many people who come into our lives for a season or a lifetime. There have been so many fine folks who have moved to New Bethlehem and many others who have only come to visit. But each one of them has made an impact on our little community in the woods. I can remember a few as if it were yesterday.

For example, there was a middle-aged couple from eastern Oregon who came to stay at the inn several years back. The town they lived in was near the Oregon/Idaho border, and most of their ranching business was with people from Idaho.

They told me they wanted to come stay with us because they had heard that Shepherd's Inn was a good place to get away from the hustle and bustle of life. And they had come to the point in their lives where raising cattle and dealing with all the hassles that came with the job had begun to take its toll on them.

They said there were times in the summer when it got so hot over there and trying to deal with it was almost unbearable. All they wanted to do was get away for a while.

As it turned out, their week at the inn was a real turnaround for them. They told me later in a letter that after they got back home, they sat down with their children and discussed the future of their ranch. It turned out their boys were more than anxious to take over the day-to-day operations.

Later on, I received another letter from them telling me they had decided to start a B and B type of dude ranch on part of their property. They had so enjoyed their time here and wanted to do something like that so they might help others who were fed up with the rat race.

Last I heard, they were doing just fine and the rest of their ranch was doing even better with their sons in charge.

Another remembrance is of a young runaway from Silverton, Oregon, who happened to wind up in New Bethlehem by accident. He thought his girlfriend was living in town, and he had run away from home to be with her.

Her parents had forbidden her from seeing him and shipped her off to live with relatives in another town. But when he heard about it, he only got part of the story, and somehow the town of Bethlehem had come up in the conversation. The young lad, having no experience with or knowledge of the Bible, or world geography, ran to the only Bethlehem he knew. What he didn't know was his girlfriend's family was Jewish and the girl had been sent to Israel!

Chapter 18

After I left the hardware store, I got into my truck and headed south on Main Street instead of going straight back to the inn. About half a mile out of town, I came to a turnoff to the cemetery. As I looked up at the road sign, I thought about the irony of what it said. The road sign said, "Cemetery Rd." But the sign underneath stated, "Dead End." I thought of all the souls interred in this place who had most surely reached their "dead end." Those lost souls who never knew their Lord and Savior. But I also knew there were many people who had made this their final resting place and who were now with their Lord in heaven. Included in that list is my dear, sweet Hannah.

As I pulled into the drive, I thought of all the times I have been here over the last five years, spending time with my Hannah. Stopping at the same spot where I always parked, I got out and walked over to the headstone marking her final resting place.

I took off my hat and knelt down by the headstone. "I'm here, Hannah. I miss you as much today as I have every day since you went home to the Lord. I know you are at peace there, and I look forward to joining you someday.

"Thought I'd bring you up-to-date on what's been going on at the inn. I told you about Lydia, Sarah, and Elisabeth, who came to be with us about three years ago. Well, those girls have grown so much since then. And I don't mean just in size. They are the brightest, sweetest, most polite girls I've ever known. You would have loved them.

"I know you always felt like it was all your fault that we didn't have any children of our own. But, Hannah, my dear, I know the Lord had a plan for us, and that plan is still unfolding. I can only believe you are sitting there now, giving instructions to the angels who are watching over all of us. Well, let me tell you, I'm doing the best I can to take care of them like they are my own. And their mama, Lydia, now there is one woman who has been down a rough road and come out the better for it. She hasn't told me everything about what went on with her and that so-called boyfriend of hers, but she said enough that I can read between the lines and know that she would never let herself be caught up in something like that again. Of course, you probably know all that. As a matter of fact, you probably had a hand in sending her our way in the first place."

I smiled as I reflected on what I just said. *Oh, how I love the time I can spend here with Hannah.* Her spirit seemed to be all around me as I knelt at her grave. Even though the sorrow had scarcely diminished in the last five years, I had accepted the fact that Hannah would want me to move on with my life. All our years together would be for naught if I dwelled only on my sorrow and not on her glory.

"Well, my love, I reckon I best be getting back to the inn now. I still have a lot of work to do before Christmas. I'll be back to visit real soon." With that, I stood up slowly, put my hat back on my head, and turned toward my truck. As I turned, I looked up and saw a bald eagle soaring overhead. The eagle seemed to look down at me, tip his wings, and turned and soared toward the heavens. I just looked, nodded a reply, and walked to the truck.

Chapter 19

Back at the inn, Martha was scurrying around, getting things ready to prepare supper. She had walked into the dining room and had her back to the hallway when Elisabeth and Sarah came running in, the former chasing the latter. There was a squeal of delight from one of the girls, and Martha, not expecting them, jumped with a start. She had just put the plates down on the table but was still holding a handful of silverware. When she jumped, the silverware went clattering on the plates and the table. "You girls settle down now! You scared me clear into next week. You better be glad I didn't have all those plates in my hands. If I'da dropped them, you girls would be in a heap of trouble."

The girls both stood in fear. They knew Martha could get upset if things didn't go just like they were supposed to. They didn't want to get into trouble. "We're sorry, Ms. Martha, we were just playing," Elisabeth said. "We didn't mean to scare you."

"Why don't you go outside and play? It's such a nice day today, and you know it's going to get a lot colder soon, and you won't want to play out so much then. Where's your mama, anyway? Aren't you two supposed to be doing schoolwork?"

"Mommy said we could take a recess if we wanted to. She said we are getting too smart for her and she's going to have to get some bigger books for us to study from." Sarah beamed as she repeated what her mother had said.

Martha couldn't help but grin at what Sarah said. Martha had watched the girls over the last couple of years as Lydia homeschooled them, and she could hardly believe how much the girls had learned. They were both very smart for eight-year-olds. "Well, if you're so smart, tell me what we're having for supper."

Elisabeth and Sarah sniffed the air like little puppy dogs, then looked at each other, and exclaimed in unison, "Meatloaf! We love meatloaf!"

Martha bent over and gave them both a hug and said, "I'm glad you like my meatloaf, but run along now. You know how I don't like people getting in my way when I'm working. I have so much to do around here, and you girls just slow me down. Now git, before I go get a switch."

The girls gave a little scream and raced out the front door, giggling all the way. Martha smiled as the girls left the room and picked up where she had left off setting the table.

She really did love those girls, but they were a handful. Just like everything else around here. She loved her job and all the people of the inn, but she knew that everyone else didn't share her urgency in getting things done. Oh, Gabe took care of things outside, and when it came to repairs inside, he saw to it that things got repaired okay. And he was good at buying groceries and supplies. And Lydia was very good at keeping the books and reservations and greeting the guests when they arrived. But Martha knew that the place would fall apart if she weren't there to take care of housecleaning and cooking. She knew also that she worried a lot about everything getting done in a timely manner, but that was who she was, and she wasn't going to change. She didn't like surprises, she didn't like last-minute changes in plans, and she didn't like it when no one else could see the urgency in staying on a schedule.

Lydia had just sent the girls to play after a rather-long study session. She was so proud of how well they both did with homeschooling, but she worried that she would not be able to keep up with them. With only a high school education, she wasn't sure she could continue the education of her daughters much longer. Some days she felt like she was already over her head. As she sat looking at the school catalog and figuring out what she needed to order next, her mind drifted back toward Doc again. It seemed like lately all she could do was fantasize about him. He was so good with the girls, and they loved him. And he was so handsome and strong. And whatever cologne he used drove her up the wall. She knew he was a righteous man, loved the Lord, and practiced it. She had often watched him sit in the great room of the inn when he came to visit, quietly reading his Bible by the fireplace. And she had overheard bits of conversations he had with Gabe as they shared each other's lives. His voice was soft and caring, but there was also a strength that came from a man with confidence.

Reality check, girl, she thought. *This guy has a degree in veterinary medicine. He is smart, handsome, wealthy, and independent. Why on earth do you think he would be interested in a woman like you when he is probably surrounded by well-educated, wealthy women back home in California?* The thought formed a cloud over her, and she was suddenly overcome with sadness. She crossed the room to her bed and sat down as a tear started to trickle down her cheek. She turned and knelt beside the bed and began to cry. "Father God," she prayed, "what am I to do? You know, Lord, that I love living here at the inn. I love my girls with everything that's in me. I love the family I have here in Gabe and Martha, and I love my job. But, God, I feel like I am going nowhere. I ache for the gentle touch of a man by my side. My daughters need a father figure in their life who is a man of faith and who could help me raise the girls in a loving Christian home. To educate them in a way that I'm not capable. I know I sound like I want it all, God, but I really don't. I just don't know which way to turn. I am surrounded by love, and still I'm lonely. Father, please speak to me in a way that I can understand. What do You want me to do?" When Lydia finished her prayer, she cried herself to sleep.

I had returned from town and was starting to finish up some details in the room I was getting ready for Leah. Sarah came into the room as I was finishing up and said, "Hi, Gramps. Are you getting this room ready for Ms. Leah?"

"Why, yes, I am, little lady. How did you know that?"

"Ms. Martha told me. Could you put some sugar in the paint when you paint the walls?"

"Now, Sarah, why on earth would you want me to put sugar in the paint?"

"'Cause then when Ms. Leah sleeps here, maybe the sugar would make her a little sweeter."

I had to bite my tongue to keep from laughing. "Well, little darlin', I'm not sure sugar on the walls would do the trick. But I do know that God wants all of us to be kind to everybody, especially our enemies. So if you let Ms. Leah see the sweetness that God gave you, then some of it might rub off on her. What do you think of that?"

"Well," she said as she put her hands on her hips and took on an air of wisdom, "I tried to do that the last time she was here, and she told me to go away. She said, 'I don't like little children underfoot. Go away and leave me alone.' I was just trying to be nice."

"Sarah, the Lord makes all kinds of people on this earth. Some of them are nice, some aren't. But He also gives everybody something called free will. And what that means is that everybody can decide for themselves whether they want to be nice or not nice. But for those of us who decide to be nice, He gives us something else. He gives us a gift of sharing our 'nice' with people who aren't nice. And when we do that, after a while, some of those people who aren't nice, well, some of our nice rubs off on them. Does that make sense to you?"

"Sorta," she said, with a puzzled look on her face. "But does some of her not-nice rub off on us?"

"It probably would except for one thing that we have that they don't. We have God sitting right there on our shoulder, brushing the not-nice away. When God is sitting on our shoulder, He is called the Holy Spirit. You can't see Him, you can't feel Him, you can't touch Him, but He's there just as sure as I'm sitting here with you."

Sarah looked at me with a puzzled look on her face and was just about to say something else when they heard Martha calling them to supper.

I said, "We'll talk about this some other day, okay?"

"Okay, Gramps. As you always say, let's eat!" And off we went, hand in hand, to supper.

You're probably wondering right now why Sarah would call me Gramps. Now, that's an interesting story.

A couple of years ago, I had gone to town with Sarah and Elisabeth in tow. We had just finished picking up the things from the grocery list and loading them in the back of the truck. As I started to walk back to the cab, I didn't notice a young man hurriedly walking down the street and looking at his cell phone. We bumped each other slightly, and the young man looked up and said "Hey, watch it, Gramps!"

The girls were standing by the door of the truck and saw and heard all that happened. After the young man walked away, still working on something on his cell phone, Sarah asked me why the man called me Gramps.

"Well," I said, "some people call their grandfathers Gramps instead of Grandpa or Papa or Granddaddy or other pet names."

"But you're not his grandpa. Why would he call you that?"

"Guess he just thought I was old enough to be his gramps," I replied.

I'm not sure why this particular episode was so humorous to the girls, but they started laughing and making comments about how silly that was for him to call me Gramps. Then Elisabeth said, "I kinda like the name Gramps. Can we call you Gramps, Uncle Gabe? You're not really our uncle, and we still call you that. Why can't we call you Gramps even if you aren't really our grandpa?"

From that day on, I have been Gramps to those two precious girls.

Chapter 20

Doc
November 17

Doc had just finished surgery on a customer's cat that had reached her limit on litters and came to the clinic to eliminate that issue for the remainder of her life. Sophie was her name, and she was a lovable Himalayan ball of fur. She was mostly white with a hint of color around her face and in her tail. She also had an attitude that matched her stature. But with all her arrogance at ignoring commands, she was a loving cat that was content snuggling up next to her owner on the sofa.

As Doc was walking back to the front of the office, a young couple came in carrying a bundle in a worn beach towel.

"Doctor, we were just around the corner when we saw a car hit this dog and just drive off. We could see the dog was still alive, but he looked like he was hurt pretty bad." The young man was obviously distraught along with his girlfriend, but he was trying to look brave and in charge.

The girl started talking then. "We don't know where he came from, but we knew your office was right around the corner, so we thought we'd come here and see if you could help."

"Let me see what we have here." Doc took the bundle from the young man and set it on an exam table in the room next to the office. As he unwrapped the towel, he could see an adorable little Jack Russell that didn't look more than a year or two old. It looked like the dog had at least a broken front leg and possible internal injuries. Doc would know more after x-rays. A quick check also revealed a microchip in the dog, so Doc had all the info he needed to contact the owners.

As it happened, the owners of the little dog lived only a couple of blocks from the clinic, but they had just moved to town from the LA area only a few weeks before and hadn't changed their address. So when Doc called the number from the chip, he thought he was probably dealing with a family on vacation when the dog got loose. The dad answered the phone, and when Doc told him what happened, they weren't even aware that the little dog had gotten out of the yard.

Dad, mom, son (about ten), and daughter (about seven) came rushing into the office in panic. The kids were both crying, and the mom was trying to console them. Doc explained to them what had happened and introduced them to the couple who brought the dog in. Hugs and thank-yous were immediately administered, and the dad told Doc to do whatever it took to save their beloved dog Scooter.

Fortunately for the family and the dog, the injuries weren't as serious as first expected. A broken right front leg and some scrapes and bruises were the extent of the injuries. Doc was sure he would have the dog up and around in a day or two and told the family he wanted to keep Scooter at least overnight for observation. By that time, most of the tears from the kids had decreased and everyone was in a little better spirit.

Doc watched the family, however, and envied their life. Here was a husband and wife with two children, a dog, and what appeared to be a happy life together. Oh, how he missed his family. Scenes like this brought back horrible memories of that night when they were taken away from him. *I wonder if I will ever be able to have a life like that again,* he thought. How could he when he spent all his time wrapped up in his practice?

Oh, he had dated a few women in the last few years. But none of them could measure up to Brenda. He knew it was wrong to think that way, but the memory of what they had together was still strong, even after all these years.

As a matter of fact, Doc was going to have Thanksgiving dinner next week with a woman he had met at a Chamber of Commerce meeting. Her name was Carolyn Miller, and they had gone for coffee a couple of times and went to a movie a couple of weeks ago. Carolyn was office manager in a law firm in town, and she had been single for a couple of years. Her ex-husband couldn't handle the fact that she made more money than he did, and he left. *So much for richer or poorer,* Doc thought as she told him about that. Anyway, Carolyn was very attractive and friendly, and they seemed to hit it off together fairly well. But still, there was something missing, and Doc couldn't put his finger on it.

Doc's mind drifted back to the business at hand. Scooter was a tough little pup, and after his leg was put in a cast and an e-collar put around his neck so he wouldn't try to bite if off, he seemed to be recovering very well. The family finally went home and promised to be back first thing in the morning. Doc said even though it would be Saturday, he would come in and check up on Scooter. With a little good fortune perhaps, he could go home tomorrow.

After everyone left, Doc again started thinking about his family, and the longing started again. He had no family. He had no siblings, and his parents had died when he was much younger. His dad had died of lung cancer after working many years around asbestos. No one knew back then the harm it was doing to them until it was too late. His mom died a few years later of what he called a broken heart. After his dad died, Doc's mom went through a long period of depression. Her husband had been her life, and without him, she felt abandoned. She didn't have to work because of the insurance money she received when her husband died. So she did almost nothing. Physically, she didn't take care of herself, and she began to gain a lot of weight. She stayed closed up in her house most of the time and got very little exercise. Doc had tried to get her active, but nothing seemed to work. After a few years of neglecting her health, she developed a case of bronchitis. She didn't tell anyone about it until it was too late. Doc had gone over to visit her one day, and she was in bed with a horrible cough. He got her up and dressed and took her to the emergency room, and she was admitted immediately. For several days, it seemed like she might be getting better, but then she developed a fever. The actual cause of death was listed as a heart attack, but Doc knew that she had just given up.

Only about a month, he thought, and he would be at Shepherd's Inn. That brought a smile to his face. When he was there, he felt like he was around family. Maybe he needed to spend more than a week a year there. He couldn't help but think about Lydia, the first time he met her. He could tell she was extremely nervous, and at first, he figured it was because she was relatively new at the job. But as that week progressed, he could tell that she was interested in him. She was cute, and very likeable, and her girls were the sweetest things he had ever seen. But it was Christmastime. Time to reflect on that Christmas when the drunk driver took his Brenda and Danny from him. His thoughts were always tangled up at Christmas.

Maybe this year would be different. Maybe he could spend more time enjoying everyone's company and spend less time wallowing in self-pity. Only time would tell.

Chapter 21

Martha
November 20

Martha was busy with plans for Thanksgiving. She and Gabe had talked about this year's Thanksgiving and what they were going to do, since there would be no guests at the inn. Martha had mentioned inviting some of the less-fortunate children from town to come up for dinner. Gabe liked the idea immediately, and they had contacted the Children's Services office and floated the idea with them. Before long, they had a list of about ten foster children who had been bounced around from one foster home to another. Most of them had come from horrible surroundings, and they had some discipline issues. Gabe and Martha knew that might be a problem, but after a couple of days of prayer, they knew that was what God wanted them to do.

Martha and Lydia and the twins had worked hard making table decorations and little gifts for the kids. Of course, Martha worried and fussed about every little detail, but now things were coming together, and it looked like things were all set. The menu was going to be a traditional turkey and dressing, mashed potatoes and gravy, green bean casserole, cranberry sauce, pumpkin pie with whipped cream topping, the works. Martha was pleased.

Now she was busy cleaning house. Things were never as clean as they should be for Martha. So here she was on Monday, dusting every flat surface and making sure everything was perfect. She would have Gabe build a fire in the big fireplace at the end of the great room. She would have dishes of nuts and candy on the tables and hot spiced cider ready when they arrived. The kids were coming up in the big CSD van, and the driver was also going to stay for the meal. Martha was in her element. She loved putting together such an event. She just wished she could do something like this more often.

By the end of the day, Martha was exhausted, but she laid her head on her pillow that night with a smile on her face. How she loved Shepherd's Inn. How she loved Lydia and the twins. How she loved Gabe and wondered how it would be to become Mrs. Gabe Sinclair. "What are you thinking, you old fool?" she said to herself as she lay there. "You've been here five years already, and that old man hasn't given you a second look. Don't go trying to start something you can't finish." She admonished herself. But her thoughts still wandered back to thoughts of Gabe. He was the kindest, most gentle man she had ever known. And she couldn't help but have a tender place in her heart for him. Even if nothing ever came of it.

November 23

The van pulled into the parking lot at Shepherd's Inn, and ten screaming, yelling kids piled out of it and headed toward the front door. The day was crisp and cold, and there was a couple inches of new snow on the ground. Even though it was almost December, they hadn't had as much snow as they usually had by this time of year. Gabe was starting to worry that they might have an unusually dry winter, and that would increase the fire danger next summer. Anyway, he hoped that wouldn't be the case.

The kids were busy throwing snowballs at one another as they scurried around, heading for the inn. They had known for several days about this day, and they all had saved up all their energy for it. Two kids, however, weren't showing the enthusiasm as the others. A boy and girl, both younger than the rest of the kids, were hanging back a little and not engaging in the snowball fight. They stood by the van until the driver got out and then walked with him toward the front door. Gabe couldn't help but notice and wondered what kind of issues they had that caused them to be so shy.

As all the kids finally got inside, the van driver, Cecil, and I stopped on the front porch for a couple of minutes. Cecil said, "Them two young'uns have a heap of problems. They are brother and sister, and they came to us from over in Burns. Seems they watched their papa beat their mama to death a few months ago. He took off and hasn't been caught yet, and the state figured it would be better if the kids were taken out of the Burns area for their safety. None of their family over there knows where they are right now, and we want to keep it that way. You know what I mean?"

"Yep," I replied, "I sure do. One thing's for sure, they are safe here. Maybe they can have a day to just enjoy themselves and not have to think about what happened. We'll sure try to help with that. Why don't we go in now and start digging in to Martha's fixin's? I know you're gonna love it."

The day was a complete success. The kids scurried around, eating candy and nuts and drinking hot cider. They loved to stand in the warmth of the big fireplace that was probably the biggest one any of them had ever seen. They all had appetites that didn't match their small stature, and when the meal was finished, there were hardly any leftovers at all. I had to frown at that fact, since I love leftover turkey and dressing. But I was happy that the children had such a good time. I was also proud of Elisabeth and Sarah and how they helped entertain all the others. They were perfect hostesses, and they made their guests feel like they were special.

By the time they were ready to leave, a light snow had begun to fall again, and it was getting close to dark. The air was still, and the snow fell in tiny flakes that glistened in the light of the front porch. Smoke trailed straight up from the fireplace, and there was a quiet stillness that took everyone's breath away. Even the children could sense the special feel of the night. As they all gathered 'round and headed for the van, I asked everyone to hold hands and form a circle. I then led them all in prayer for God's blessings on them this day. When I finished, I noticed that several of the children were wiping a tear from their eye, and I felt the Lord's presence in this small circle of His children. I looked up and, under my breath, said, "At Your service, Lord!"

Chapter 22

Doc
November 23

Carolyn had a very nice downtown apartment on the second floor with a view of the main street. It was a cool day in northern California's Napa Valley. There was a slight haze that filtered the sun, and a gentle breeze that held a chill in the air.

Doc had assumed there would be several people in attendance at dinner, and he was looking forward to meeting some of Carolyn's friends. However, when he arrived a little after two in the afternoon, there was no one else there except Carolyn. "Am I early?" he said. "Am I the first to arrive?"

"No, you're right on time," Carolyn replied, "and you are the first and last. I was hoping we could enjoy Thanksgiving with just the two of us."

There was a tone to her voice that sounded a bit too romantic for Doc. He liked Carolyn, but this occasion had all the markings of a next step in their relationship that he wasn't ready for. But if nothing else, Doc was a gentleman, and there was no way he wanted to hurt her feelings. "That sounds great," he said, even though he didn't mean it. He was uncomfortable, and he didn't want to show it.

"Would you care for something to drink while we wait? Dinner isn't quite ready. We could have a cocktail and some hors d'oeuvres. Have a seat on the sofa. I'll get you something. What would you like?"

"Just a soda would be fine." Doc did not drink alcohol and wasn't about to start now.

"I hope you don't mind if I have something stronger," Carolyn replied. "I've been working all morning getting things prepared, and I'm ready to let my hair down a little and relax."

Doc had arrived for dinner wearing dress slacks, a V-neck sweater over a cream-colored dress shirt with an open collar, and a sports coat. Carolyn was wearing a floor-length dress with no sleeves, and it was cut very low in the back. Doc was beginning to think she had more in mind for this dinner than he had figured, and he was becoming more and more uncomfortable by the minute.

How do I convey to her that I am not interested in anything more than just friendship right now? he thought. *I don't want to hurt her feelings, but what can I do?* He quietly said a small prayer asking God for guidance, accepted the soda offered to him, and watched as Carolyn sat down next to him with drink in hand.

"So, Lucas, we have known each other for several months now, and I know hardly anything about you. What do you do for fun?"

"Now that you mention it, I guess I don't do much of anything for fun. I spend most of my time taking care of animals. My practice is really going great, and I don't seem to have much extra time on my hands."

"You told me a few weeks ago that your wife and son died in a car accident several years ago. That must have been hard. Is that something you would like to talk about?"

Doc was caught completely off guard. *Why would this woman want me to talk about my family?* If she was interested in romance, this was not the way to go about it. "Not really," he said. "It's something I've had to live with for a long time, and I'm trying hard to move on with my life. What about you? You said your ex had some inferiority issues. That must have been hard to take?"

"Not really," she said. "We met in college, and when we graduated, we both wanted to get settled in our profession before we got married. After a couple of years, he had secured a middle-management position with a manufacturer in Sacramento, and I had become a legal secretary. We got married and settled in Sacramento, but a few years later, his company downsized and he got the ax. We couldn't live on just my income, and he wasn't looking very hard for another job. I finally applied for the job I have now, and it was a big raise, but we had to move. He never did accept the fact that I could get a better job and he couldn't. After a year here, he came to me one day and said he was leaving. Said he wanted to 'find himself!' Boy, what a load of malarkey. I knew what he wanted, and it wasn't me. He wanted some little chippie he could control. He had made it clear many times how he thought I was too bossy and demanding. Can you believe that?"

"Wow," Doc replied. He didn't quite know what else to say. But he had to say something. "Sounds like he was just a little insecure. You don't seem bossy or demanding to me."

She laughed at that. "He was and is just an immature little jerk. I should have known how things would work out. We dated several years before we got married, and I could see that. But I guess I was just a foolish woman and figured he would change. He never did. Now you, on the other hand, seem to be very secure in your life and your work."

Here it comes again, he thought. *How do I move this subject to something more platonic?* "That dinner sure smells great. I hope we can eat soon. I'm starved."

That seemed to break the pattern of the conversation, and Carolyn said, "I'll go check. It should be just about ready. It'll just take a minute to put it on the table. Why don't you take off your jacket and make yourself comfortable?" And she moved into the kitchen.

While they ate, their conversation was casual small talk. They each talked about their jobs, and Carolyn talked about where she grew up in Cleveland, Ohio. She told him how much different life was back in the Midwest compared to California. She said she wouldn't go back for anything. Even though her entire family was still there, she had no desire to live there. She said she didn't like hot, muggy summers and cold, icy winters. Doc told her he was born and raised in California and had only traveled outside the state a few times in his life. He did tell her about his Christmas vacations in Oregon and then regretted saying anything about it. He didn't want to encourage her or give her the opportunity to invite herself along. He was surprised when she didn't seem to pick up on that and carry the conversation any further.

After dinner, Carolyn told Doc to go sit in the living room while she cleaned up, but he said he wanted to help and she said okay. They talked some more as they cleaned up the kitchen and then went into the living room and sat on the sofa with a cup of coffee for each of them. Doc was feeling more comfortable and thought he might have misread Carolyn's intentions when he first arrived. They sat and talked for over two hours after that, and they both got to know a lot more about each other.

Carolyn really surprised Doc when she finally said, "I don't ever plan on getting married again. I like to have flings,

I like to have fun with men, but I don't ever want to be tied down again. I could tell tonight that even though I like you very much and you are an extremely handsome man, we could never have a lasting relationship. You need a lot more than I could ever offer."

Doc was speechless. He never guessed that was who she was, and he was surprised. He thought he was a better judge of a person's character, but he really missed the mark with Carolyn.

"I hope I haven't upset you," she said. "I guess I just like to tell it like it is, and I couldn't feed you a line and pretend to be someone I'm not."

"Carolyn, I have pretty tough skin, and no, you didn't upset me. Surprise, maybe. I appreciate your honesty, and I do like you as a friend. I hope you find what you're looking for, and I want to tell you that I will pray for you."

Pray for me, Carolyn thought. *Now that's a twist I wasn't expecting. I never figured him for a Jesus fanatic.* "I'm not into prayer and stuff. I don't believe in it. I figure we're born, we die, and what's in between is all we have."

Doc couldn't believe he had known this woman for several months, had talked with her about many different topics, and he had never talked to her about God. He was so ashamed. *I'm sorry, Lord, for hiding my lamp under a bush. I pray you guide me as I try to witness to this woman, your child.* He prayed silently. "I would love to have the opportunity to talk with you more about that. I don't want to come on to you as some Bible-thumper, but I would like to introduce you to God and to His Son, Jesus."

"Maybe some other time," she said. "It's getting kinda late, and I have a lot to do tomorrow. I want to go take advantage of those Black Friday sales, if you know what I mean."

"Okay," Doc said, as she was starting to get up from the sofa. She reached for his jacket, handed it to him, and started toward the door. *Lord, I touched a nerve. I know You have plans for her, and I hope You give me the opportunity to help her see.*

"Carolyn, I had a great time. Thanks so much for the wonderful dinner and conversation. I hope we can get together again soon."

"Oh, Lucas, I had a good time too, and thanks for coming over. I hope I didn't upset you with my comments, but like I said, I tell it like it is."

With that, Doc opened the door, Carolyn gave him a light kiss on the cheek, and he was gone. All the way home he prayed for God to guide him in re-entering Carolyn's life and leading her toward a better understanding of His plans for her life. He was still praying when he got home and got ready for bed.

Chapter 23

Joe and Maria
November 23

The morning broke snowy and cold. The forecast was for snow all day and temperatures only in the low twenties. Their house was warmed by baseboard heaters, and none of them worked very well. Maria was cold, she was tired, and she was throwing up again. She wasn't looking forward to this day. Joe was still asleep, and she didn't want to wake him because she didn't want to get into an argument with him again. It seemed all they did lately was argue. Sometimes about money, sometimes about the baby, sometimes about his job, sometimes about her family. It didn't make any difference what the issue was; they always seemed to wind up arguing about it.

She went into the kitchen and took a frozen turkey breast out of the freezer. Since it would be just the two of them for Thanksgiving, she saw no need in preparing an entire turkey that would probably go to waste. Last year, Joe's boss gave him a turkey for Thanksgiving, but she guessed he was too cheap to do it again this year. Anyway, baked turkey breast, Stove Top stuffing, mashed potatoes from a package, and gravy from a jar were all they were having today.

Maria's cell phone rang, and when she saw who was calling, she almost didn't want to answer it. "Hello, Mom."

"Good morning, sweetheart. Happy Thanksgiving. Are you going to have a big dinner for you and your husband today?" Maria's mom almost always addressed Joe as "your husband." It made Maria so angry, and she had told her mom that many times, but it didn't do any good. Her mom did not like Joe, and she was not shy about making that feeling clear to her daughter.

"Yes, Mom," she lied, "we're having turkey, dressing, and all the fixings. I just got up a little while ago and haven't gotten started yet, but soon."

"I wish you and your husband could have come up here to have Thanksgiving with us. I'm sure we would have had a great dinner. You know how I love to prepare a large dinner. We are having some friends over. A couple who work for your dad, and another couple. He owns an auto parts store. Is it snowing down there? It's been snowing all morning here, and it just looks beautiful outside. I am so looking forward to Christmas.

"That reminds me, do you suppose you two could manage to come up here for Christmas? You know we would love to have you, and I have already bought lots of clothes and gifts for the baby."

Maria knew this was coming, and she had been dreading it. She did want to be with her parents for Christmas, but she was afraid if she mentioned it to Joe, it would just start another argument. "I don't know, Mom." She sighed. "I'll have to talk to Joe about it. I don't know if he can get enough time off."

If anything, Maria's mom, Wanda Belknap, was persistent. "Well, you know, sweetheart, Christmas this year is on Monday, so he should have Saturday and Sunday off as well. That would give you three days."

"Mom, you know Joe has to work on Saturdays, and he will probably be very busy that Saturday. But I will talk to him about it, and maybe we could come up on Sunday and go home on Monday. How does that sound?"

"I guess we'll take what we can get," Wanda said with a strong sigh of disappointment. "Please do talk with him and let me know as soon as possible. I will need to make preparations and do some more shopping. Guess I had better get going and get busy for our dinner. You take care, sweetheart, and happy Thanksgiving to both of you."

When she hung up from the call, Maria realized that her mom had not once asked her how she was feeling. *So much for a loving mom who cares for me,* she thought. Ever since Maria had told her parents she was pregnant, her mom had not seemed at all excited about being a grandmother. And she didn't seem to care at all that Maria was having a very rough time with the pregnancy. All Wanda had said was she hoped it was a boy and they could name him after her uncle Dexter, who had been killed in action in Vietnam. He had been a Navy pilot and was shot down while on a bombing mission. Maria didn't really like the name Dexter, but she did feel a bit of obligation toward her family. Joe was against it from the start, and that had been another subject of argument between them.

Joe came walking into the kitchen, wiping the sleep from his eyes. He had a bad case of bed head, and he looked like he hadn't shaved in a couple of days. "Is there any coffee?" he said before anything else.

"Good morning to you too," Maria shot back. "I haven't been up very long, and I just got off the phone with my mom. I haven't made any coffee yet. Guess you'll have to make it yourself." There was a distinct note of sarcasm in her voice.

"I'm sorry, baby. Good morning. How are you feeling this morning?"

Wow! she thought. *Where did that come from? He hasn't been that nice in weeks.* "I'm not feeling very good this morning. I was sick, again. As usual. I can't understand how this baby is going to be born healthy with me being so sick. It can't be good for him."

"Why don't you go sit down in the living room and I'll make coffee? Would you like me to make you some breakfast?" As he said that, Joe ran his hand along her back and leaned over and gave her a kiss on the cheek.

Joe is in way too good of a mood this morning. What is going on? That was what she thought, but her reply was, "No breakfast for me. I'm getting sick again just thinking about it. But thanks for asking, honey." *I don't know where this is coming from, Lord, but I like it,* she prayed. *Do I dare bring up the invitation to go to Bend for Christmas? Maybe let him at least have one cup of coffee first.*

"Okay, I'll get the coffee started. Are you going to feel like making a big dinner today, or do you want to go out and eat? Mason's Café is having a Thanksgiving buffet today. We could go there if you'd like."

Wow! Again. "Oh, Joe, that would be great, but it is so expensive. And I have some stuff to cook here." She also didn't feel like getting all dressed up to go out, but she wasn't going to tell him that.

"Don't worry about the cost," he said. "Do you remember Mrs. Wicker, that old lady who lives across the street from my friend Gary? Well, when I used to hang out at Gary's house before we got married, I used to talk with her a lot. She is a widow, has been for several years, and I think she was just lonely. Anyway, she kinda took a liking to me and even invited me over for lunch a couple of times. Nothing kinky or anything. She was just a nice old lady.

"Anyway, I had a delivery to her yesterday. She bought a new sofa and chairs. When she saw I was the delivery guy, she just about had a fit. She hugged me and asked me how I was doing. She knew I had gotten married, but she didn't even know we are going to have a baby. So after we got the sofa and chairs unloaded and in the house, she pulled me aside and slipped me an envelope. She whispered in my ear, 'A little something extra for you and your family.' Well, I didn't know what to think. I said thank you and went out and got into the truck, and we went back to the store.

"I kinda forgot about the envelope until after I got off work. I felt it in my pocket when I went to get my keys to the car. I got in the car and started it up to get it warmed up, and I looked in the envelope. I'm not kiddin', babe, my jaw just dropped when I looked inside. There was a hundred-dollar bill inside! You were asleep when I got home, so I figured I'd wait till this morning to tell you."

"Oh, Joe, I can't believe it. She gave us a hundred dollars?" Tears started running down Maria's cheeks. "A hundred dollars! Do you know what that means?"

Joe interrupted, "It means I can take my beautiful wife out to a really nice Thanksgiving dinner." The tears on Maria's cheeks became contagious, as Joe also started to cry.

Joe was an enormously proud man, and that was one of the things Maria liked about him. Even though sometimes his pride became a little too strong. But today, right now, she saw a humility about him that was even more pleasing. *Lord, I know You are working in him, and I thank You. Please keep him safe and humble and loving just like he is this morning,* she prayed.

Joe took Maria in his arms and kissed her lightly on the lips. Maria couldn't believe the tenderness of the kiss. This was the Joe she loved. This was the Joe she married. She thought, *I hope this lasts forever.* They walked into the living room, and Joe put a blanket across Maria's lap as she sat down on the frayed and worn sofa. *It may be worn,* she thought, *but it's comfortable and it is our home.*

"I'll get the coffee going and be right back. Can I get you anything else?"

"No, this is fine, honey. I love you, Joe!"

"I love you too, baby." And he went back into the kitchen.

Maria thought about the hundred dollars. She thought about Mrs. Wicker. She hardly knew the lady. She had spoken to her once when she and Joe were dating, but she couldn't even remember what she looked like. Such a dear, sweet lady to do such a kind thing, especially at Thanksgiving. Maria prayed a prayer of thanks to God for His kindness and love displayed in that old lady.

By some people's standards, Mason's Café would not be their definition of a wonderful Thanksgiving dinner. Mason's was not the finest restaurant in town. It was not in the best of neighborhoods, and it looked like it hadn't been remodeled anytime in this century. But for Maria, it was heavenly.

She had taken a short nap after she lay down on the sofa and woke up feeling better than she had in several days. She took a long, hot shower, shaved her legs, washed her hair, and enjoyed every minute of it. She fixed her hair just the way Joe liked it, long soft curls hanging around her shoulders. She put on makeup and lipstick for the first time in quite a while. As she looked at herself in the mirror, she said to herself, "Not too bad for a fat pregnant woman!" She didn't have a very big wardrobe of maternity clothes, but she found a skirt and sweater that looked pretty good and covered up some of the bulge that represented a seven-month-old baby in the womb. When she finally walked out of the bedroom, Joe looked up and said, "Wow, babe, you look beautiful!"

Maria blushed and said, "Thanks, honey. It's the best I could do with what I've got."

"You've got it all!" Joe replied. He gave her a big hug and a kiss and ran his fingers through her hair. "You know, I love your hair this way. That was one of the things that attracted me to you in the first place."

After dinner, they drove down Main Street and through Joe's old neighborhood. He drove by Gary's house, and they looked across the street and saw Mrs. Wicker standing out on her front porch, watching the snow fall. Joe pulled up to the curb, and they got out and walked up to her house. Maria wanted to thank her for the gift, but she wasn't sure what to say.

When Mrs. Wicker saw them walk up, she smiled her sweet smile and just said, "It's a lovely night for giving thanks, isn't it?" She slowly and carefully walked down the steps to the sidewalk. Then she held out her arms and gave Maria a great big hug. "Happy Thanksgiving, my dear. I'm so happy you stopped by. Won't you both come in for a spell? It's quite cold out here, and I would like to have some time to talk with you two a while."

They all walked up on the porch, Joe holding both women's arms to help them on the slippery steps. When they got inside, Mrs. Wicker invited them to have a seat on her new sofa as she sat down in the matching easy chair.

"Mrs. Wicker, thank you so much for the gift you gave us. We could sure use it. But you didn't have to. You hardly even know me," Maria stated.

"My dear child, it's not how much we know someone that counts, it's how much the Lord wants us to give that is most important. I've known Joseph for quite some time, and I remember the first time I saw you with him, I knew that you two were meant for each other. And when Joseph told me you are going to have a precious child, well, I knew that the Lord wanted me to help you both out. I'm just sorry it wasn't more. But I'm on fixed income, you know, and there is only so much to spare. I hope you didn't mind."

"Mind? Of course not. We were overjoyed. I have to tell you, this Thanksgiving wasn't turning out very well this year. As a matter of fact, I wasn't even looking forward to celebrating at all. But because of you, Joe took me out to a wonderful Thanksgiving dinner today, and we had a fantastic time."

"I know you did, my dear. I can see it in your eyes. It was certainly my pleasure. By the way, when are you due? You look like you're almost ready to deliver now," she said with a smile.

"I'm not due till the end of January. I wish it were sooner. Sometimes I just feel like a big blob wobbling around."

"Just look at my manners," Mrs. Wicker apologized. "Would you two like something to drink? I have a pot of hot spiced cider in the kitchen, just waiting for someone to enjoy. May I get you two a cup?"

"That sounds great," Joe said.

"Can I help?" Maria inquired.

"Oh, no. You two just sit there and make yourselves comfortable. It won't take a minute."

Mrs. Wicker came back into the living room a few minutes later with a sliver tray holding three beautiful china cups and saucers of steaming spiced cider. As she set the tray on the coffee table, she said, "I have been collecting cups and saucers just about all my adult life. When my husband was alive, he used to comment on how many cups and saucers were enough. But I know deep down he knew how much they all mean to me, and he was always ready to put up another shelf to hold them. He was a precious man, and I do miss him so." She stopped talking for a few seconds and seemed to be reflecting on her marriage. "Oh, but enough about me. Here, you two, let's just enjoy our cider."

They talked and sipped cider for several more minutes, but then Joe commented that it was getting late and they should be getting home before the snow got too deep. Mrs. Wicker thanked them for stopping by, and Maria and Joe thanked her again for the money. After the hugs, they made their way out to the car and back home.

After they had changed into their pj's and crawled under the covers, Joe wrapped Maria in his arms and gave her a warm kiss. "I hope you enjoyed the day, babe."

"Oh, honey, it was perfect. And Mrs. Wicker is such a dear, sweet lady. We need to go visit her more often."

Joe looked at Maria in a way that made her wonder what he was thinking. "What?" she said.

"Babe, I know your mom doesn't like me very much. And your dad isn't much better. And you know how much it bothers me when we are around them and your mom is always putting me down."

"She doesn't always put you down," Maria said. But she knew in her heart he was right.

"Whatever! Anyway, I've been thinking, I know you miss them, so what would you think if we went up to Bend for Christmas?"

Maria was almost in shock. *Thank You, Lord,* she prayed. "Oh, Joe, you would do that?"

"Well, I got to thinking, with the money we have left over from Mrs. Wicker, we would have more than enough for gas money up and back. And since Christmas is on Monday, we could go up on Sunday and come back Monday afternoon. I know it wouldn't be a lot of time, but at least you would have a chance to be with them on Christmas. That's only if they want us to come. And if our old beater can make it that far!"

Maria didn't want to tell Joe her mom had asked just that morning if they could come up. "I'm sure they would want us. I'll call Mom tomorrow and tell her our plans. Oh, thank you, Joe."

Joe held Maria in his arms for several minutes, and they just lay there quietly. Joe was wondering about what he was going to do after the first of the year when his health insurance was canceled. How was he going to pay for the new baby? How were they going to manage if he didn't find a better-paying job?

Maria was thinking about the baby inside her. Was she up to the challenge of being a mom? Could she love her baby unconditionally like God wanted her to? Could she love her husband unconditionally like God wanted her to? She started crying quietly. She didn't want Joe to know of her distress. Then she heard the soft snore that notified her that Joe had gone to sleep. She prayed to God for His guidance as she, too, fell asleep.

Chapter 24

Leah
November 23

Leah woke up early, just like most every other morning. Her mind had been racing ever since she had made up her mind to commit suicide at the inn. She had spent several days going through old photos and mementos, sending most of them through the shredder. Her life with Philip was over, and she wanted nothing to do with memories that someone else might look at.

This morning, she came across a baby album that she had long forgotten about. It was of Jessie. Leah didn't even remember that she still had it, and it must have been mixed in with other stuff she had moved to Oakland. Anger grew inside her as she looked at the pictures. She was in some of them, but always off to the side or in the background. Memories of those times brought tears to her eyes, and she wept openly as she took each picture and ripped it to small pieces. By the time she was finished destroying the album, she had cried so hard she made herself sick. She hurried into the bathroom and threw up.

Leah walked to the bathroom sink to wash her face and looked at herself in the mirror. She could hardly believe whom she was looking at. She hadn't taken care of herself in several days, and the mirror magnified every flaw. Gray hair streaking through dirty blond. Dark circles under her eyes. Crow's-feet spreading to each side. A double chin that hadn't been there when she was younger. The smile that Philip had admired when they first met was long gone. In its place were downturned corners of her mouth with vertical lines dancing above and below. Pale skin from too little sun and too much sorrow. As she looked at herself, she suddenly saw her mother, the mother she remembered.

Leah's mother was a sad woman in her later years. Oh, how she had tried to keep the family together and happy. After Leah was born, everything seemed so right. A loving husband, an adorable daughter, and a comfortable life. For six years she had been happy and satisfied. Then, when Jessie came along, life became a struggle. A complicated pregnancy followed by a premature baby. Jessie required so much more than she felt she could give. And along with Jessie's health problems, there was the jealously coming from Leah. These were things Leah remembered from watching her mom and talking with her later in life. Leah said her mom had told her that one day, shortly after Jessie came home from the hospital, Leah had asked her if they could take Jessie back and get a better one.

Leah kept looking in the mirror and thinking how her mother continued to grow more and more unhappy as the years passed. Her mom and dad argued constantly, and the girls just went to their room and covered their heads with a pillow to block out some of the noise. How they managed to stay together, Leah could never understand. But they did. It wasn't until after Leah and Philip were married and moved to San Francisco that Leah received word that her mom had died from complications of pneumonia. At least that was the way it was written in the official death certificate. But Leah knew her mom had died of a broken heart.

And now Leah was headed in the same direction.

But at least I have a plan, she thought. *I won't wait for fate or chance or karma or whatever anyone wants to call it. I have planned my demise. I am in control of my life, and death!*

That thought gave her a new purpose. She must do something today to celebrate, she thought. "Oh, my," she said aloud, "this is Thanksgiving Day, isn't it? I shall fix myself up and go out for a fine meal. I shall celebrate the fact that I am in total control of myself."

After a long, hot shower, Leah fixed her hair, put on some makeup, and put on one of her favorite dresses. She had had it for several years, but it still was in style, and she liked the way men had looked at her when she wore it. She put on a sweater to protect her from the chill of the day and made her way to a small local restaurant around the corner from her apartment.

The restaurant was packed with couples and families celebrating Thanksgiving, but there was a small table in the corner that was perfect for Leah. As she ate her meal in silence, she couldn't help but wonder what her former friends would think when they read her obituary. Would they wonder if they could have done anything to help prevent it? The thought made Leah smile as she took a bite of cranberry sauce. She thought how revenge seemed so fitting right then. *Let them all suffer,* she thought. *The same way they made me suffer for so long.*

She finished her meal and slowly strolled back to her apartment to prepare for another restless night.

Chapter 25

December 1

I was walking back to the inn after inspecting the bridge across the Little Jordan. I talked with the owners the week before and told them that it seemed to be on its last leg. I said I hoped it would last through the winter. It shouldn't be a problem, I figured, if there wasn't too much of a spring snowmelt or at least if it didn't melt too fast. That was when the problems would occur. The Little Jordan was just a trickle most of the year. In fact, during the summer, sometimes it completely dried up. But if there was a heavy rain or rapid snowmelt, it could fill up fast. I figured I'd just have to pray it would last until Scott could round up someone to replace it.

It had been snowing a lot up higher in the mountains, but around the inn, there was only a few inches left on the ground after the Thanksgiving weekend storm. That made it easier for me to take care of things outside.

I walked back to the pump house to check and make sure I had a full tank of gasoline for the emergency generator. We usually had to use it at least once every winter when a storm would knock out the power. We could survive without it, but it would be a little primitive, with only the gasoline and propane to provide light and heat. Guests could get a little testy when things got that bad. I chuckled at that thought. Better safe than sorry, even if we weren't having too many guests this winter.

I knew I should get back to work on the renovation project, but my heart just wasn't in it today. I had finished the two rooms for Doc and Leah, but nothing else had been done. I heard a noise around the corner and walked around to see Elisabeth and Sarah playing in the backyard. They were all bundled up against the cold, and they looked so cute running around the outside firepit, chasing each other.

I wondered if living up here at the inn, isolated from other children their age, was a good thing for the girls. They always seemed so happy here, and their mother was such a caring mom. Their education didn't seem to be a problem at all. Lydia was an excellent teacher. She was patient and thorough. She could also be strict when she had to be. But there was something missing. Of course, I knew for certain one thing missing for these girls was a dad in their lives. I knew all about their father, Cade, and how it was a good thing he wasn't filling that position right now. Lydia had finally told me all about Cade, and I was always alert to the fact that he might try to find Lydia and the girls someday. That was one of the reasons Lydia and the girls spent very little time in town, or anywhere for that matter, beyond the inn.

I didn't consider myself a matchmaker, but I had often wondered about any eligible males in New Bethlehem who might be a good fit for Lydia and the girls. So far, I had drawn a blank there. But I had noticed how Lydia acted around Doc, and I wondered if there was anything there. I knew Lydia was too professional to jeopardize her position at the inn by flirting with guests, but I couldn't help but think that Doc needed someone in his life as much as Lydia and the girls needed someone in their lives. *Time will tell,* I thought, *time will tell.*

Martha was standing at the sink, looking out the window, as I walked by. I saw her standing there and gave her a smile and a wave. She waved back, with a dishrag in her hand and a smile on her face. *How can I be a matchmaker,* I thought, *if I can't even figure out my own life?* I started thinking about the years since my Hannah had passed away. It had only been five years, but it seemed like forever ago. Sometimes it seemed like every day just blended into the next for me. I had been so accustomed to having Hannah by my side. She was my confidant, my leaning post, my sounding board, my comfort, for so many years. That first year after she passed, I wasn't sure I was going to be able to continue. If it hadn't been for Martha and her insistence that I take care of things, the inn would probably have suffered. But she was there, with her woe-is-me attitude, worrying about every little thing. Deep inside I had figured I needed to take care of Martha more than myself.

But beyond all her worrying about things, she was very good at taking care of things at the inn. And over the years, we had become good friends. Sometimes I looked at Martha and wondered if she had any feelings for me like I had for her.

The only problem for me was, every time I had those feelings, visions of Hannah appeared. How could I do that to Hannah's memory? How could I ever love another woman the way I loved Hannah? "Oh, Lord," I prayed, "I need Your guidance now more than ever. How can I overcome this longing I have in my heart? Am I wrong to feel this way? You have given me such a wonderful life here, and sometimes I think I haven't been faithful to You in taking care of the gifts

You have given. Please help me, Lord, to know the way You want me to go."

Martha watched Gabe walk by the window and wondered what was going through the mind of that old fool. She had grown so fond of him over the last six years and couldn't think of how things would be without him in her life. Oh, she knew he probably could never be interested in her romantically. She could never take the place of Hannah. She had seen that firsthand that first year she worked here as Hannah struggled with the final months of her life. She saw how he worshipped her and took care of her. Even though there was a caretaker for her, Gabe did most of the work in taking care of his Hannah.

Martha also knew that neither she nor Gabe was spring chicken anymore. But as she thought about her future, she also knew that she still had longings. She still had feelings. She still had a desire to have a man in her life to love and be loved. And deep down inside, she knew beyond a doubt that she loved Gabe that way. But would he ever notice? she thought. Probably not.

Chapter 26

Doc
December 10

Doc had just returned home from church when his phone rang. Usually, when he received a call on his home phone on the weekend, it was an emergency and his answering service was trying to contact him. He reached for it, prepared to change clothes and head for the clinic. "Hello, this is Dr. Meriweather," he said.

"Lucas, this is Carolyn Miller. I tried to call you on your cell phone, but it went straight to voice mail."

"Hi, Carolyn, I haven't talked with you since Thanksgiving. How are you doing?" He looked at his cell phone and realized the battery was dead. "I'm sorry, my cell phone is dead. Forgot to charge it last night."

"I'm doing okay, I guess. Anyway, I called your office number, and they gave me your home number. Lucas, would it be all right if we could meet somewhere today and talk? I have been thinking about some things you said when you were here on Thanksgiving, and I would like to talk about it."

Doc was puzzled. Other than the fact that he dodged her romantic advances, the only other thing of importance they had talked about was his faith. From the way she reacted, he was pretty sure that wasn't it. Whatever it was, he felt compelled to meet her and find out more. "Sure. I just got home from church. I need to charge my phone up and change clothes. How about we meet somewhere for a late lunch? My treat. Say, McDougal's? I hear they have killer sandwiches. I could meet you there about two thirty. How does that sound?"

"That sounds perfect. I go there often, and I love their salads. They also have some booths that provide lots of privacy. What I want to talk with you about is personal. I just couldn't think of anyone else I could talk to about this. I trust you. I'll see you there at two thirty."

"Okay, see you then. Bye." When he hung up the phone, Doc's mind was racing. *What in heaven's name could be so important and so private? And she can only talk with me. I hope I'm not getting myself into something I shouldn't,* he thought.

Doc walked into McDougal's at twenty after. It was dark inside, and it took a few seconds for his eyes to adjust. He saw a hand wave and saw it was Carolyn sitting in a booth near the back of the dining room. The place wasn't very busy this time of day, and the booths around her were empty. Well, she wanted privacy, he thought. As he walked over to her, she stood up and gave him a very long, warm hug and a kiss on the cheek. He felt like the hug was more like a plea for help than anything of a romantic nature. "Good to see you again, Carolyn."

"It's really good to see you too, Lucas. I hope I'm not making a mistake asking you to meet me here. What I have to say is very personal and very upsetting. I just didn't know who else to talk to. But first, let's get a bite to eat. I'm starved."

As they sat down, the server came over and asked them if they would like anything to drink. They both ordered ice tea with lemon. While they looked at the menu, Doc noticed that Carolyn seemed on the brink of breaking down and crying. But she held herself together, and when the server returned, she ordered a Cobb salad. Doc ordered a Reuben with plank fried potatoes.

When they were alone again, Carolyn started talking first. "I want you to know how much I enjoyed our Thanksgiving dinner together. I'm sorry I came across so strong, and I admire how gentle you were in deflecting my advances. I could tell you are a real gentleman, and I haven't found a lot of them around lately."

"You don't need to apologize. If anyone should, perhaps it should be me. I'm kind of dense sometimes, and I'm not entirely aware of what's going on around me. 'Cause I had a really good time too. You have a nice apartment, and the meal was excellent. You are a wonderful cook. I'm kind of a klutz in the kitchen, so when I have the opportunity to eat someone else's cooking, I jump at the chance." Doc wanted to take the emphasis away from her intended plans for that day and keep the conversation on a more platonic level.

Carolyn started talking about her cooking skills and the fact that she had at one time wanted to be a chef. She even went to culinary school for a while, but then some things changed in her personal life, and she gave it up. She never said what those changes were, but it sounded like something major. Was that what she wanted to see him about? he wondered.

They chatted a few more minutes, and their food arrived. Conversation trickled to a minimum as they ate their lunch. Doc dived into his sandwich and fries like he hadn't eaten in days. Carolyn just nibbled around the edges of her salad and didn't seem too interested in it.

"Is something wrong with the salad?" Doc asked. "I could order you something else."

"No, the salad is great. I guess I'm just not as hungry as I thought."

Doc finished his sandwich and looked into Carolyn's eyes. He could see that there was a great deal of pain she was holding inside. He waited for her to speak. He wasn't sure what it was, but he didn't want to push her. He wanted her to feel comfortable talking to him.

"Lucas," she began. There was a crackle in her voice, and her hands were trembling. "Remember when I told you I like to have flings? I hope you don't think I'm too bold, but ever since my ex left me, I have been bouncing from one relationship to another. There have been too many one-night stands to count, and I'm not very proud of who I have become. I have never spent much time around religious people, and when you told me you would pray for me, I was kind of in shock. Why on earth would someone pray for me?"

Doc started to interrupt, but she stopped him and said, "Lucas, let me finish. I have to tell you something, and I need your help. I don't know if I can finish what I am about to tell you, but I'm going to try. But you have to just listen until I finish, okay?"

"All right," Doc said. "Go ahead."

"Last Wednesday night, I went out after work with a couple of women I work with. We went to a bar over on Curtis Street. As you probably know, Curtis Street is not in the best part of town. Anyway, they wanted to go, so I went. We had several drinks, and then this guy came over to talk to us. The other two are married, and they said they had to get going, and they left. There I was all by myself with this guy. It wasn't really strange territory for me, because I have been down that road way too many times.

"So he sat down and ordered us another round, and we started talking. He was coming on pretty strong, but I had enough drinks in me that it didn't bother me. We sat there for a while, and he asked me if I would like for him to take me home. He said he could see that I had had too much to drink to drive home and he would be glad to give me a lift. He was kind of cute, and I thought, What the heck? Let's see where this goes. Anyway, we left the bar, and the last thing I remember is getting into his car. I don't have any memory of the rest of the night.

"I woke up the next morning in a fleabag motel room down by the tracks."

Carolyn started to cry, and Doc reached for his handkerchief and handed it to her. She dabbed her eyes and continued to cry. Her voice got very soft, and he could hardly hear what she was saying.

"I had no clothes on, and I had several bruises on my body. My right eye was swollen, and I had a pounding headache. I know he raped me, but I have no way to prove it. I couldn't wait to get out of that dump. I grabbed my clothes, got dressed, and washed my face and called a cab. All I wanted to do was to get as far away from that place as possible. I know I should have called the cops, but I just couldn't. I was so humiliated and felt so violated, and I just couldn't imagine trying to tell this to a policeman.

"When I got home, I stripped down and threw my clothes in the trash. I stood in the shower until I used up all the hot water. I felt like I couldn't get all the filth off me."

Her voice crackled as she spoke the last statement, then she began to cry uncontrollably. Doc reached over and took her hand in his, and she squeezed it so hard he almost had to pull away. She was shaking all over, and the sobs continued. Doc caught a glimpse of the server out of the corner of his eye. She had started to walk over to ask them if they needed anything else. He caught her eye and motioned for her to stay away. She took one look at Carolyn, nodded, and turned around.

For several minutes, they sat there, Carolyn crying, Doc holding her hand. Finally, the crying subsided and she spoke again. "You must think I'm a horrible person."

"No, I don't. Carolyn, I see a woman in pain. You have gone through a terrible, traumatic experience. You have every right to feel the way you feel. I know in hindsight we could say you should have called the police. But no one knows but you how mixed up your emotions were at that time. He probably slipped you something in your last drink, and that's why you don't remember anything. You had no way of knowing that was what was going on.

"Carolyn, I want you to know I appreciate you having the confidence in me that you could tell me what happened. But now, what is it you want me to do to help you? I don't want to do anything that would make you angry or think I was trying to persuade you to do something you don't want to do. But if you do want to report this to the police, I will help you in any way I can."

"I'm not sure yet. I know if I report it, they will want to know who was at the bar with me, and I just couldn't face my friends if they knew. That's another reason I called you. When I woke up that morning and saw where I was and what had happened to me, I thought of what you said about praying for me. I know that sounds stupid that I would think of that, but I did. I thought, 'Lucas, you could sure pray for me now!'

"I thought, 'If there is a God, why did something like this have to happen to me? Is He punishing me for not believing?' I just didn't know, but I knew you would have the answer."

Doc felt a huge weight settle on his shoulders. *This woman came to me to lead her to the Lord. She is depending on me to show her the way.* "Carolyn, will you allow me to pray for you right now?"

Carolyn started crying again, but through her tears she nodded her yes.

"Father God, I lift up my sister, Your child, to You right now. Lord, You have seen the horror she has gone through. You have seen her broken spirit, her wounded body, her anguish, and her tears. Father, You alone can heal these wounds. You alone can make her whole again. You alone can give her the strength to move forward. Lord, I ask that Your Holy Spirit be here with her right now, at this time, to give her that peace only You can give. Give her wisdom, Lord, give her strength, give her comfort in Your gentle touch. And, Lord, I give thanks for Your mercy and grace. I pray, Lord, in the name of Your precious Son, Jesus Christ. Amen."

"Lucas, I do want to believe there is a real God. I do want to know Him. And I do believe Jesus died for my sin. I learned enough in my youth to know all about how He died. I know that when I was a little girl, my mom used to sing to me a song that went, 'Yes, Jesus loves me, the Bible tells me so.' I have been such a fool for so long, though, I don't know if I'm still good enough."

"Carolyn, none of us are 'good enough.' The Bible tells us, 'For all have sinned and fall short of the glory of God.' But the Bible also tells us, 'For God so loved the world that He gave His only begotten Son, that whoever believes in Him shall not perish, but have eternal life.' Do you believe that, Carolyn? Do you believe Jesus died for your sin? Do you believe He was raised from the dead and sits now at the right hand of God? Do you believe that by accepting all these things, you are a new child as of right now?"

"Yes, I do," she said through her tears.

"Then please repeat this prayer with me." As he spoke the sinner's prayer, Carolyn repeated each word. Doc could feel the Holy Spirit move in her as she spoke the words. Her body trembled as she spoke, and Doc could see the change taking place before his very eyes. He, too, began to cry. But they were tears of joy for this woman before him. He thought how he had failed in ministering to her from the first time he met her. How the Lord had forgiven him and given him another chance to introduce her to his Savior.

Carolyn slowly began to dry her tears. She smiled at Doc for the first time since they sat down. She thanked him for all he had done for her. She seemed to have a renewed resolve to move forward. "I know now what I have to do. I am going to the police. I will tell them everything. I will call my friends and tell them what happened. I will ask them if they can remember anything about the guy. I will hold my head up high and do whatever it takes to get this creep off the street. No offense, Lucas, but I don't need you there beside me. I know now I have an inner strength. I know God will be right there beside me all the way. Thank you so much, Lucas. Thanks for everything. Thanks for being the kind of friend I have needed for too long. I will never forget you. I hope we can continue to be friends."

Just then, Doc's cell phone went off. It was his answering service. He smiled and gave a silent prayer for the call not coming until now. He looked at Carolyn, and she smiled at him and said, "Go ahead. It must be important."

He punched the Answer button. "This is Dr. Meriweather."

Chapter 27

December 15

"Mr. Belknap, this is Joe Alexander." That was the way the phone conversation started. Joe was at the bottom. He had been looking all over town, and there wasn't any work to be found where he could get medical insurance for Maria and the baby. As much as he hated the thought of moving up to Bend and living under the thumb of his in-laws, he saw no other option.

"Hello, Joe. What a surprise! I never expected to hear from you. By the way, I understand you are bringing Maria home for Christmas. That's great. We are really looking forward to seeing her."

Joe had to bite his tongue to keep from saying something he would regret. It was time to swallow all his pride and cater to this man who disliked him so much.

"What can I do for you, Joe?"

"Mr. Belknap, I suppose you heard that after the first of the year, my hours are going to be cut and I'm going to lose my health insurance. I've been trying to find something else here, but there just isn't anything open right now. I know last summer you told me you could probably get me on at a business a friend of yours owns. I was wondering if that offer still stands?"

"Well, I don't know, Joe. A lot has changed since last summer. The economy is still in a slump, and I'm not sure he has any openings right now." Derek Belknap was enjoying this. He relished the thought of the power he had over this punk kid who robbed his baby girl of a better life. If it weren't for Maria being in the middle of all this, he would tell Joe where to go in no uncertain terms. But he knew that to try to drive a wedge between Maria and Joe would probably alienate her from himself and his wife. So he tempered his remarks and continued, "I'll tell you what? I'll do some checking around. I know a few people, and someone might have an opening someplace. I know you need health insurance, so I'll be sure to include that. The pay probably won't be much, but you two could probably move in with us for a while until your finances improve."

Joe knew that was coming, and he hated the thought of moving in with Maria's parents. But if that was the only way he could make things work, then that would have to do. "I really appreciate this, Mr. Belknap. I would appreciate it if you wouldn't say anything to Maria just yet. I wouldn't want her to get her hopes up if things don't work out."

"Okay, Joe. I'll keep things just between us. Looking forward to seeing both of you on Christmas Eve. Hope you have a safe trip." Then he hung up. No goodbye. He didn't even give Joe a chance to say anything else.

Figures, Joe thought.

When Derek Belknap hung up the phone, he turned to his wife, Wanda, who had been listening to his side of the conversation. "Would you believe Joe actually called to ask me to find him a job? I think I might have misjudged him a little. I never thought he would swallow his pride like that."

"So what are you going to do? You know I would love to have Maria and the baby stay with us. But I don't know how that would work out with Joseph here also. You know he hates us."

"Wanda, I'm beginning to think maybe we haven't given him enough credit. I mean, he has been doing his best down there, trying to take care of Maria. And all the reports we get from her makes me think she really is in love with him. Anyway, I'm going to talk to Larry Wilkins first thing tomorrow. His handmade-furniture business is going strong, and he may have an opening for a driver or something. I know he carries a good health insurance policy on his employees. We talked about that just a few months ago. He said it was the best thing he ever did. Keeps good employees around. He is a pretty shrewd businessman."

"Well, if you think it's the right thing to do, okay. But he's still going to have to prove himself to me." Wanda turned and headed for the guest room. When her back was to her husband, a smile spread across her face at the thought of Maria and the baby living with them. She had plans to make, a baby crib to buy, new curtains for the windows in the guest room. Nothing was too good for her baby girl.

Chapter 28

December 19

Leah Gardiner had made her plans for this dramatic, climactic ending of her life on earth. It was 6:00 p.m., and she was in a taxi on her way to the San Francisco International Airport. Her flight to Klamath Falls was scheduled for nine fifteen and arriving in Klamath Falls at around 11:00 p.m. She had made a reservation at a Best Western and had hired a driver to take her from Klamath Falls up to Shepherd's Inn. She had made absolutely no plans for a return trip. There was no need. There was no one to hide her plans from, no one who would even know she had made plans. And if after her death someone noticed that fact, it would just reinforce the fact that she had committed suicide and didn't accidentally overdose.

She wanted the whole world to know she was in command of her life.

The letter she had prepared was neatly tucked inside a small notebook inside her suitcase. The letter would be placed in a conspicuous location inside her room on Sunday evening.

Leah sat in the cab, thinking about all the preparations she had made for this trip. Of course, when she had first made the reservation, she had not planned to end her life. But now that all the plans were in place, she was certain that it wasn't just coincidence that she changed her usual travel period from the fall to the end of December. She didn't really believe in coincidence, anyway. She had always believed things happened for a purpose, even though she wasn't sure where or when that notion had manifested itself in her.

Leah leaned back in her seat and smiled as the cab made the exit from the 101 freeway at the airport exit. She should have plenty of time for a light dinner before boarding her flight.

Chapter 29

December 19

Martha and I had just returned from town with a load of groceries for the next week. Martha had planned the menu through the end of the month, and now we were unloading the truck. The inn was in tip-top shape as usual, and Martha had gone out of her way to make sure everything was perfect for Christmas. I had gone up behind the inn a few days before and cut down a large Christmas tree for the great room. It stood about ten feet tall, but with the open-beam ceiling, there was plenty of room for the tree on the opposite end of the room from the fireplace. Decorations had been completed, and presents were suddenly appearing under the tree.

Everyone at the inn seemed to be really excited about this particular Christmas. It seemed like they knew that something special was going to happen this year.

It had been unusually warm the last few days, and it had started raining around noon. I had stopped in at the sheriff's office while we were in town, and the weather report for the next week didn't look very promising. A pineapple express storm was moving across the pacific northwest, and rain was in the forecast up to at least six thousand feet. The elevation at the inn was about forty-five hundred feet, and there had been a lot of snow falling at the upper elevations for the last month. What little snow that had remained at the inn had already melted by the time we got back.

I checked the water level in the Little Jordan as we crossed the bridge, and so far, it was still way below bridge level. I just hoped it would stay that way.

December 19

Joe hadn't heard anything back from Maria's dad about a possible job in Bend, and he was becoming more and more concerned. He realized it had only been four days, but he was getting desperate. Maria was almost eight months along now, and in less than two weeks, they were going to be out of insurance. Joe had been independent all his life, and the thought of having to rely on welfare or handouts to take care of his family made him angry.

Joe had just come home from work, and as he walked through the front door, he could tell something was wrong. Maria was almost always there to greet him when he came through the door. Tonight, the house was very quiet. There was no light in the living room, and only the light over the stove in the kitchen was on. The door to the bedroom was closed, and there was no sound coming from anywhere. Joe walked over and slowly opened the bedroom door and saw Maria curled up in bed with the covers over her head. "Maria, are you okay?"

Maria turned over and pulled the covers from her head and looked at him with a feeble attempt at a smile. "I'll be okay. I just have a headache, and my back hurts. I thought if

I could just lie down for a while, it might get better. I didn't realize it was time for you to be home yet. What time is it?"

"It's almost six thirty."

"Oh my gosh," Maria said as she threw the covers back. "I must have fallen asleep! I'm sorry, Joe, I don't have dinner ready. I came in here at around four and was just going to lie down for a few minutes."

"Are you sure you're okay? That's not like you to zonk out like that. Do you want me to call the doctor?"

"Don't be silly. I just have a little headache. It's nothing. I'll get right into the kitchen and finish dinner. It just might be a little late. Guess I've just been overexcited about our trip to Mom and Dad's for Christmas."

"I'll help, okay?"

"Oh. Don't be silly. I'm fine. You've been working all day. Just go sit down and relax. I'll have something ready in about half an hour." Maria pushed her hair out of her face as she got out of bed and headed for the kitchen. She felt terrible, but she wasn't going to let Joe know. She was afraid he might try to get her to the doctor and they might tell her she shouldn't be traveling this close to delivery time. There was no way she was going to miss this trip to Bend. She loved her parents so much, and she really missed them. Her heart was longing to return to the place she had called home all her life.

Chapter 31

December 20

Leah awoke in her motel room and looked at the clock. "Oh, dear!" she exclaimed. "It's almost nine o'clock! I'm going to be late." She reached for her purse and the phone. She was supposed to be picked up by her driver at nine, and there was no way she was going to make it.

"Hello, this is Leah Gardiner. I am supposed to have a driver call for me at 9:00 a.m. I'm sorry, but I have overslept and won't be ready for at least an hour. Could you please notify him of my situation?"

The dispatcher on the other end of the line couldn't believe how some of these rich people could be so inconsiderate of others. What did she think, he was just sitting around, doing nothing, waiting to cater to her? But regardless of what she thought, she knew that customer service was what the boss wanted, and that was what he would get. She was going to be nice to this rich biddy, no matter how bad a taste she had in her mouth. "Oh, that's fine, Ms. Gardiner. Richard—that's your driver's name—is on his way there already. I'll just give him a call and tell him to wait. Let me give you his cell number, and you can call him when you're ready. That way, he can come to your room and take care of your luggage. Will that be all right?"

"Okay, I guess. Just let me find a pen to write with." Now she was upset. She had to get up and rummage around for a pen so she could copy down the number. Didn't this person know how inconvenient that was? she thought.

It was almost ten thirty before Leah called her driver. She had gotten up and prepared some coffee in the tiny little coffeepot in her room. After her shower and makeup, she got dressed and went down to the lobby for breakfast. It was nothing special, and nothing close to what she had been used to all those years she had been married to Philip. But it would have to do. It was nearly eleven o'clock by the time they were headed north on Highway 97.

The day had started out gloomy and didn't look like it was going to change anytime soon. A drizzling rain was falling, and the damp cold seemed to soak into a body. Leah had finally started to get warm in the plush leather seat of the Lexus sedan she was riding in. The driver had made an attempt at small talk when they started out, but she put a stop to that quickly. She was in no mood to carry on a conversation with this hired person. How on earth could he have anything interesting to talk about?

Normally, it should take only about an hour and a half to make the trip from Klamath Falls to New Bethlehem. Today was not going to be a normal day.

"What are those flashing lights up ahead?" Leah inquired. They were only about a half-hour out of town, driving along the shore of Klamath Lake. The highway snaked along in places between the railroad tracks on the lakeside of the highway and steep cliffs on the right. In several places, there were guardrails, retaining walls, and steel mesh screens to help keep falling rocks from reaching the highway.

"Looks like a rockslide, ma'am. They're stopping traffic. Not sure how long we'll have to wait."

"Now that's just terrific! Can anything else possibly go wrong today?" It was obvious Leah's insults were being directed at her driver.

"I'm really sorry, ma'am, but there's not much else I can do. I'll keep the motor running and the heater going. Is there anything you would like? I have some refreshments in the trunk. Would you like a soda or something?" He was trying hard to please his client. He wanted a big tip, and he knew this was probably going to make a big dent in the amount she would give him, if she gave him anything at all.

"No, thank you. I'm fine." Leah sat quietly after that, not interested in conversing with this person.

"Would you like to listen to some music, ma'am? I have several CDs of different types of music." He wanted to continue telling her what types of music he had, but she cut him off.

"I am not interested in listening to music. I just want to get on my way as soon as possible."

"Yes, ma'am. Is this place you're going to—Shepherd's Inn—is it for vacation or family or something?" He was really trying hard to make the wait as painless as possible, but it looked like he wasn't doing a very good job of it.

"Young man," Leah shot back, "the reason for my trip should not be of any concern to you. What I do with my time is my business. Is that clear?"

"Yes, ma'am, I'm really sorry. I was just trying to be friendly. I apologize. I guess my mind has been kinda messed up lately and I wasn't thinking. I've been worried about my daughter, and that makes me say stupid things sometimes."

"Why are you worried about your daughter?" she said. As soon as she said it, she regretted it. Now, she thought, she was probably going to have to listen to some long-winded sob story about who knew what with his daughter.

"Well, ma'am, my daughter is six years old, and she has been diagnosed with leukemia. The doctors have it in check right now, but they say she really needs a bone marrow transplant. My wife and I don't know how we're going to pay for it. Insurance covers some of it, but she has to go to Portland to have it done, and we just can't afford it. We keep praying that something will happen and we'll have the money somehow."

"I'm truly sorry to hear that...what did you say your name is?"

"It's Richard, ma'am. Richard Carter. My daughter's name is Bethany."

Just about that time, he could see that the traffic was starting to move again. "Looks like they got the road open again. That's great. Shouldn't take long now."

"Very well," Leah replied. "I am anxious to get out of this car and unwind in front of a roaring fireplace."

"Sounds pretty nice. I hope you enjoy your stay up there. Are you going to need me to come back up and pick you up when you're ready to go back home?"

Leah wasn't sure how to phrase her response. Before she thought, she almost said she wouldn't be going back home. But she caught herself just in time and said, "I'm not certain of my plans yet. I'll contact your company later."

"Okay," Richard replied. He didn't want to push her any further. All he wanted to do was get her unloaded at Shepherd's Inn and get his tip, if any, and head back home. He was glad there wasn't any ice or snow on the road, and he hoped it would stay that way until he got back to town.

Once traffic began moving again, there were no further incidents along the way, and they arrived at the inn at around two in the afternoon. After he got her luggage out of the trunk and deposited in the lobby of the inn, Leah handed him a twenty-dollar tip and thanked him for a comfortable trip.

"Thank you, ma'am. I hope you have a Merry Christmas."

Leah turned to the check-in counter without a word. Richard took the hint and headed for his car.

Chapter 32

"Good afternoon, Ms. Leah. Welcome back to Shepherd's Inn. I hope you had an enjoyable trip from California. We have your room ready for you. It's been a couple of weeks since Gabe finished the remodel, so all the paint smell should be gone." Lydia was being her usual perky self even though she knew it was useless with Leah.

"Well, I certainly hope so. I would like to get into it as soon as possible. I need to lie down and take a nap. I am exhausted from my travels. Will you please wake me in time for the evening meal?"

"Of course, Ms. Leah. I'll have Gabe take your suitcase to your room right now." Lydia turned toward the kitchen and hollered, "Gabe, Ms. Leah is here. Will you take her bags to her room?"

I walked in from the kitchen, where I had been helping Martha move some supplies from the pantry to the kitchen cupboards. "Good afternoon, Ms. Leah. Glad you could make it up this year. Got your room ready for you. I'll get this suitcase in there right now, and you let me know if you need anything else."

Leah couldn't help but like Gabe Sinclair. She knew she had very high standards for comfort and convenience, and Gabe had always tried awfully hard to accommodate her wishes, unlike many of the people she confronted in her travels. "Thank you, but I think I have all I need right now." She followed him down the hall to her room. As they were walking, Elisabeth and Sarah came bounding down the hall in the opposite direction. They were about ready to say hi to Gabe when they saw Leah following him. They both remembered their encounters with her from previous visits, and they knew she didn't like them. Their whole demeanor changed, and they slowed to a walk and gave a quick "Hi, Gramps! Hello, Ms. Leah." And then they didn't wait for a reply as they walked on past.

After I took Leah's bags to her room and made sure she had all she needed, I returned to the lobby, where Elisabeth and Sarah were waiting for me. Both girls were looking at me with concern on their faces. They loved this time of year, with all the decorations, singing, storytelling, and sweets of all kinds, but something was bothering them.

Sarah started in first. "Gramps, why did that lady have to come here at Christmastime? She is always so crabby, and she doesn't like us."

Then Elisabeth chimed in, "Yeah, and she always stares at us and tells us to leave her alone."

"Well, girls, I don't have an answer for you as to why she decided to come visit us at Christmastime. But I do know that things don't just happen by chance, and I have a good, strong feeling that we are going to make a very important difference in her life this year. I can't tell you what it is, or how I know this, but you two will just have to trust me.

"And I want both of you to act the way you have always acted around her, with politeness and manners. I know it is hard to do sometimes with people who are hard to get along with, but I know you girls can do just that. Am I right?"

The girls didn't say a word; they just smiled and nodded in unison. That was one thing about these two girls that I loved. How much they acted and reacted at the same time and the same way. I know twins often seem to communicate with each other without saying a word, and these two were living proof of that.

I thought back to three years ago, when they celebrated their first Christmas at the inn. It was the first time they had ever had a real Christmas tree for Christmas. Lydia had told me they weren't allowed to have a real Christmas tree when they lived with their father. He said it was silly and a waste of money. Lydia said she had a small artificial tree she used to set on the dresser in the girls' room. She would sit with them at nights before bed and tell them the story of Jesus's birth and the shepherds and wise men. She would sing them songs she remembered from her youth. She would also buy small gifts for both of them and hide them until Christmas morning. When she had shared this chapter of their lives with me, I couldn't help but feel sadness for these three souls who had endured such sorrow for so long. It filled my heart with joy that they now could enjoy all the excitement, wonder, and beauty that came with this time of year.

A short time later, as everyone was gathering around the table for dinner, Leah came walking into the room. She took one look at the huge tree standing in the great room and gave a distinct "Huh." Without another word, she took her place at the table.

One thing that was a nonnegotiable event at Shepherd's Inn was the holding of hands and saying of grace before every meal. All the residents knew it, and all the guests knew it the first time they sat down to a meal. Leah was caught off guard the first time she had dined at the inn and was holding hands before she realized what was going on. She had regarded the event as an encroachment on her privacy, and after the meal, she had told me she didn't intend to take part in our "ritual." I had looked at her with an intensity that caused even her to consider her choice of words.

"Ms. Leah," I said, with a combination of hospitality and tact, "one thing you are going to have to understand is, as a guest of Shepherd's Inn, we will do our very best to make this an enjoyable stay for you. If you need anything, all you have to do is ask and we will do whatever is necessary to accommodate your wishes. However, there is one 'ritual' we perform here at the inn that is at the very core of who we are at Shepherd's Inn. You might not be aware, but this place was named after the Good Shepherd, Jesus Christ. Now, you may not believe in Him like we do, but we will not sacrifice our belief and faith and actions for any mortal man, or woman. When we gather around the table to partake of food, we always thank Him who provided it. We know that everything we have is from the Lord, and we can't wait to thank Him for it.

"Now, you don't have to bow your head, you don't have to listen to what is being said, but when we gather and hold hands, we complete the circle of family with no beginning and no end, just like our life with our Lord. I hope you can understand our belief in this demonstration of faith. I respect your feelings, and I hope you respect ours. I make no apology for our actions."

When he had finished, Leah wasn't sure what to say. On the one hand, she was feeling outrage that this lowly innkeeper had the nerve to speak to her in such a way. On the other hand, she couldn't help but harbor a small amount of admiration for the resolve she saw in his statement. It occurred to her that Gabe Sinclair was obviously a man of conviction and a man who did not drift with the current of daily opinion, which was the case with most of the people she had dealt with over the years. But nevertheless, she was not about to allow him to see weakness in her as she replied, "Well, considering the fact that this is *your* inn, and I am 'just a guest,' I suppose I have no other option but to submit to your liturgical demonstration."

So even though Leah showed her disgust with the tree in the great room, as they all sat at the table, she held out her hands to Martha and Lydia, whom she was seated between.

And so began a visit to Shepherd's Inn for Leah Gardiner that no one at the table would ever forget.

Chapter 33

December 22

Doc was in the clinic early. He wanted to make sure everything was in order before he left for his trip to the inn. He planned on leaving Napa around noon and drive partway today. He wasn't sure how far he would get, and he was in no hurry. He wasn't scheduled to check in at Shepherd's Inn until Saturday, so he was just going to drive until he got tired and find a motel for the night. He knew it would be an easy two-day trip as long as the weather didn't get too bad.

"Good morning, Doctor," Michelle greeted him. Michelle Green had been Doc's assistant ever since his wife died. She loved animals (had three dogs and two cats of her own). She was a tremendous asset to the clinic, and he really appreciated her dedication. She had an on-again, off-again boyfriend who worked at a Napa Valley vineyard. They were currently *on again*, and whenever that happened, she was always in an excellent mood. Although even when they weren't, she was the best at keeping the clinic running smoothly. "Are you all ready for your trip?"

"Yep, just wanted to check and make sure everything was okay here before I leave."

"Now, don't your worry about a thing while you're gone. You know Dr. Gordon will take care of things, and I'll be able to help. I'm not going anywhere for Christmas, so I'll be as close as my phone. I have even switched all your calls over to my number so if there are any emergencies, I can handle them."

Doc knew she was right. Every time he had been away from the clinic, she had taken care of everything. That was why he had planned on giving her a raise at the first of the year. Business had been very good, and he could well afford it. He had prepared a letter informing her of the raise and placed it in a very fancy wrapped Christmas gift box. He had the box under the counter, and after her last comment, he reached down and picked it up. "I have a little something for you this Christmas. Now, don't open it until Christmas morning, okay?"

Doc had always given Michelle a bonus for Christmas, and she thought that might be what was in the box. "Okay," she said, "I promise. Now, don't worry about a thing. Just get in your car and get out of here!" She had the biggest smile she could muster when she said it.

He gave her a big hug and a thank-you and headed for the door. "Have a very Merry Christmas, Michelle."

"You too, Doctor. And have a safe trip. I'll be praying for you."

"Thank you. See you next week."

It was almost noon by the time Doc got back home. He was all packed and ready to go. All he had to do was put his bags in the car and he would be on his way. Just as he walked through the door, his cell phone went off. He looked at the caller ID and saw the call was coming from Carolyn Miller.

"Hello, Carolyn. How are you doing?"

"Hi, Lucas. I'm doing just fine. I just wanted to call and tell you something. If you haven't already made plans, could we meet for lunch someplace?"

"Wow," Doc replied, "you're fortunate you caught me. I was just loading up to head out of town. I'm going up to Oregon for Christmas. There is a rustic old inn up in the mountains, run by the greatest people you could know. I have spent Christmas there every year since my wife and son died."

"Oh, well, that's okay. What I wanted to talk to you about can wait." Carolyn started to continue, but Doc cut her off.

"But I don't have to leave right away. And I probably should have something to eat before I hit the road. So yes, let's meet for lunch. McDougal's again? How does that sound?"

"Sounds perfect. Shall we say twelve thirty?" Carolyn's voice sounded overly excited and upbeat.

Doc figured he would still have plenty of time for lunch before he headed out. He loaded the car, checked the house before leaving, and headed for his car. He had no idea what Carolyn wanted to talk about, but he was really looking forward to seeing her again. They hadn't had any contact since their lunch a week and a half ago.

Doc arrived at McDougal's about a quarter after noon. The place was packed with the usual business lunch crowd. He looked around and didn't see Carolyn anywhere. He told the hostess he was expecting someone about twelve thirty. She seated him in a booth near the rear of the dining room but in clear view of the front. Carolyn walked through the door about five minutes later.

Doc stood when she walked over and gave her a hug and a kiss on the cheek. Her return hug was warm and friendly, unlike the one she gave him on Thanksgiving Day.

He noticed she had a spring to her step and a cheerful attitude. He was anxious to find out what she wanted to talk to him about.

"I hope I haven't made a mess of your travel plans. I would have understood if you had told me you didn't have time to talk."

"No, it's no problem at all. I gave myself plenty of time to get to the inn where I'll be spending Christmas. So what is it you want to tell me?" He was obviously very curious after their last conversation.

"First of all, I want to tell you I went to church last Sunday!" The excitement in her voice told Doc much more than just the words. "There is a church just a couple of blocks from my apartment. I drive by it all the time and never even noticed it was there. Well, anyway, it's just a small church on the corner, and it looks like it came out of an old-time story. This middle-aged gentleman greeted me at the door and asked me if he could give me a hug. He said his name was Jim Craig and he was the unofficial greeter. He asked me my name and told me how happy he was to meet me. While we talked, a woman came and stood beside him. He introduced me to her, her name was Sharon, and we three talked for a couple of minutes. He said the church is nondenominational. I'm not sure what that means, but I intend to find out." Carolyn was talking very fast, like she just couldn't wait to tell him everything before she forgot and left something out.

"So Sharon invited me to sit next to her and Jim, and I really enjoyed the music and people coming up to me and shaking my hand and welcoming me. I felt like I was with a room full of old friends. The pastor came over to me during the greeting time and introduced himself to me also. His name is Arnie Louis. When he got up to talk, I thought he was talking straight to me. I could feel my face getting red and hoped no one else noticed. Lucas, he spoke about a woman who had had an affair. The church leaders wanted to stone her to death. But Jesus told them if they hadn't sinned, then they could stone her. But the most amazing part was when Jesus told the woman He didn't condemn her." She started to cry quietly and picked up her napkin and wiped her eyes. "Lucas, that woman was me. I know now that Jesus doesn't condemn me."

Doc was searching for words to reply. He couldn't believe what she had just told him. "Carolyn, I am so glad you understood that message. It is one of the most important scriptures in the Bible. But many people don't understand how we are not to judge. But you got it. That's great!"

"But there is a lot more I want to tell you. Why don't we order lunch first?"

When the server came back to the booth, they gave him their order and waited for him to bring their drinks. As soon as the ice tea was placed in front of them and the server left, Carolyn started in again with her story.

"After we talked on the tenth, I went home and turned off all the lights and got down on my knees and prayed. I wasn't even sure if I was doing it right, but when I was finished, I knew what I had to do. The next morning, I went to the police station and filed a report. I was a nervous wreck by the time I got there. I wasn't sure if they would believe me, and I knew they would want to know why I didn't report it when it happened. Well, I was taken into a back conference room, and this woman detective came in. She said her name was Lisa, and I couldn't believe how nice she was. She asked me to tell her everything that happened, who else was there, everything. We talked for over two hours. She even asked me to look at some pictures of guys who had been arrested for the same thing.

"While I was looking at the pictures, one face jumped off the page. I caught my breath when I saw that face. I will never forget what he looked like. I showed the picture to Lisa, and you'll never guess what she told me. She said he had been arrested Saturday night for the same thing. It was almost the same scenario as mine. Seems the woman he picked up had been with friends also, and when he took her out to his car, one of her friends was still outside the bar, smoking a cigarette. She saw how her friend looked like she had passed out and he was stuffing her into his car. The friend was parked just two cars down from him, so she followed him. While she was following, she called 911 and told them what was going on. Anyway, long story short, the friend told the cops the name of the motel, and they were there when he was taking her into the room. Would you believe it was the same motel where he took me?

"Lucas, you can't imagine how relieved I am that that creep is off the street. Lisa told me my testimony will be extremely helpful when he goes to trial. At first, I thought I didn't want to have to testify, but I prayed about it and God told me it would be all right.

"I want you to know how grateful I am to have a friend like you. If it hadn't been for you last week, I don't know what would have happened. I had even considered just taking some pills and ending it all. You literally saved my life."

"Carolyn, I'm happy I could be there for you. And I'm really glad things turned out the way they did. But I didn't save your life. God did."

"I guess you're right. It's just that I'm so new at this it's hard for me to get my arms around it all." Carolyn reached over and took Doc's hand in hers. "I can hardly believe how everything turned out. I am so lucky to have you as a friend."

"Carolyn, I don't believe 'luck' had anything to do with it. As far as I'm concerned, luck only works for gamblers. With Christ there is no gamble. He knew what you needed, and He placed me in your life to assist Him in taking care of that need. I was supposed to be there for you. Can you grasp that?"

"I'm beginning to think so," Carolyn replied. "I know I still have a lot to learn, but I'm really looking forward to it. I even got a call from that pastor on Wednesday night. He said he just wanted to let me know how happy they were that I visited last Sunday and invited me back. He told me they have several small church groups that meet in people's homes. He was sure there was one that I would like. I can't believe I'm going to get involved with a real church. If you had told me that a couple of weeks ago, I would have told you off in words I won't even repeat now."

Lunch arrived, and they turned their attention to their meal. While they were eating, Carolyn asked Doc about his trip to the inn for Christmas. He told her all about the inn and the wonderful people who run it. After a while, he realized it was getting late and he needed to be on the road. They walked outside, and Doc walked Carolyn to her car. Before she stepped inside, she turned and gave Doc a big hug and a kiss on the cheek.

"You are the best friend I have ever had. I want you to know that," she said. Before he could even answer, she turned around, got in the car, and shut the door. She started the car, fastened her seat belt, and turned and gave him a wave. Then she drove away with a smile on her face.

"Wow!" was all Doc could say. He walked to his car and sat inside for a few minutes, trying to digest what had just taken place. He closed his eyes and said, "Thank You, Lord, for Your grace and mercy for Carolyn. Thank You for putting me in her life at the time she needed You." He started his car and headed toward Shepherd's Inn.

Chapter 34

The trip for Doc had been uneventful so far. It had rained during the entire trip, but other than that, traffic was relatively light. He arrived in Weed, California, a little before 7:00 p.m. and hoped there would be at least one vacancy in town. As it was, even though there were lots of travelers this time of year, he found a very small motel in the center of town that still had their vacancy sign on. He walked up to the counter and rang the bell for service. A voice from the back hollered, "Hold your horses, I'll be there in a minute!"

Wow, what kind of place is this? he wondered.

Just then, a short wide elderly woman appeared from a room in the back. She had gray hair that looked like it had been trimmed with sheep shears. Her attire was a plain housedress that looked like it had been stuffed under her pillow for several days before she put it on. It looked like she didn't have a tooth in her mouth, and she walked in with the aid of a cane. "Hello, sonny, lookin' fer a room, are you? Well, you're in luck. I got one room left. Lots of folks travelin' fer Christmas, you know. Is it just yourself, or you got a wife and young'uns out in the car?"

"No one but me. I just need a place to lay my head for the night." Doc wasn't sure whether to just leave and try to find something else or just take what he knew was a sure thing. From the looks of this person in front of him, he could only imagine what the room would look like. *What the heck!* he thought. *It's just for one night, how bad could it be?*

"Just fill this out. I'll get you a key. Is it just for one night? Most folks don't stay here more than one night unless they plan to do lots of skiing on Mt. Shasta. 'Course, that ain't likely now 'cause of all the rain and warm weather. I hear the slopes are closed 'cause it's rainin' way up on the mountain. That ain't good, you know, 'cause if too much snow melts, we could have some pretty bad floodin'."

Doc finished filling out the registration form and turned it around. The lady looked at it and said, "You're from Napa, huh? Hear that's a pretty place up in the hills with all them wineries. You make wine?"

"No, ma'am, I'm a veterinarian."

"You take care of our precious little critters, huh? I like that. It's good to know there's folks who learn how to take care of animals. Guess that's why the good Lord put all kinds of people on this good earth to take care of all His stuff. You a believer, young man?"

Doc was mildly surprised at how straightforward this woman was. They had just met, and here she was, asking him about his faith. "Yes, ma'am, I am. I gather you are too, is that right?"

"Yes, indeed, sonny. I got washed in the baptismal waters when I was only eleven years old. Guess how long ago that was?" She looked at him with great expectation that he would volunteer an answer.

"Oh, I'm sorry. I'm not particularly good at guessing someone's age." He wasn't about to step into that trap. Because no matter what he said, he knew he would regret it.

"Well, I'll tell you, sonny. That was well before World War II. I'll be eighty-seven my next birthday!" she exclaimed with what seemed like a genuine pride. Her smile was as wide as she was, and he confirmed there was not a tooth in her mouth. "Well, I reckon you don't want to be standing here gabbin' with me all night. You probably want to get a good night's sleep. Here's your key. That'll be $39.47, that's $35 for the room plus tax. Room's number 4. You can park anywhere you want. You need a wake-up call in the mornin'?"

"No, ma'am. I'll be fine. Is there someplace close where I can get a bite to eat?"

"As a matter of fact, there's a place right next door. Spanky's. My son runs it. Nothin' gourmet, but it'll fill you up." She gave him no other options, so he figured he had better get himself over to Spanky's as soon as he got settled.

When he opened the door to his room, he couldn't believe his eyes. He was expecting a run-down, unclean, poorly decorated, third-rate motel room. What he saw was a complete surprise. Not only was the room neat and clean, there was also a small lamp on the nightstand offering a warm glow to the room. The furniture looked brand-new, and the comforter on the bed looked like something from the Martha Stewart Collection. The bed was turned down, and there was a Hershey's Kiss sitting on the pillow. A Gideon Bible was not in the drawer of the nightstand but lying on the bed next to the Hershey's Kiss. There was a flat-screen TV on the dresser and a small table and chair in a corner of the room. *Okay,* he thought, *this is clearly not what I expected, but thank You, Lord, for all of it.*

After he spent a couple of minutes in the bathroom, which was also in perfect condition, he made his way over to Spanky's. The place was packed, but he saw one small table for two off to one side. The sign at the door said, "Seat yourself," so he made his way over to it.

Everything on the menu looked like it was prepared with lots of butter, bacon grease, and love. Comfort food with a capital *C. What the heck,* Doc thought, *I'm on vacation. Calories don't count now, do they?* He smiled at the thought and ordered the chicken fried steak with mashed potatoes and green beans. He didn't regret the choice he made. The food was excellent, and the tiny little waitress who served him rivaled waiters in some of the finest restaurants in Napa. *She deserves every penny she gets in this place,* he thought as he left her a nine-dollar tip on an eleven-dollar meal. He left the place with a full stomach and a smile on his face. He wouldn't soon forget the hospitality shown him in the little mountain town of Weed, California.

As he placed his head on the pillow, preparing for a good night's sleep, he thought about all that had happened in the last couple of weeks. He thanked God for giving him the opportunity to serve Him in ministering to Carolyn, working with his assistant, Michelle, and meeting some interesting people along the way. He also asked for peace in the coming days at Shepherd's Inn as he would be surrounded with people he loved like his own family. *Tomorrow is another day,* he thought. *Wonder what the Lord has in store for me.* Then he turned out the light.

Chapter 35

December 22

The weather had been extremely unusual the last few days. By this time, there was usually at least a foot of snow on the ground at the inn. Now there was only rain. It had been raining lightly for the last three days, but the forecast was for heavy rain starting on the twenty-third and continuing through Christmas morning. A cold front was moving in from the west, and by Monday the rain was expected to turn to snow, finally!

I had been keeping a watchful eye on the bridge over the Little Jordan as the creek level kept rising. It was still a few feet below the bridge level, but with more rain and warmer temperatures, there was a strong possibility the creek might overflow its banks. If that happened, I wasn't sure the bridge would hold out. *Well, nothing to do now but pray,* I thought. "Lord, it's all in Your hands," I said.

Back inside, the girls were quietly playing in the corner of the great room. They were getting excited about Christmas, and their mother had had to scold them about making too much noise. She reminded them that there was a guest at the inn and they must respect her privacy. Of course, both girls knew what could happen if they caused Ms. Leah to become upset. They had suffered through her comments on more than one occasion over the years and didn't want to suffer through them again.

Leah had kept herself confined to her room most of the day. She did come out for breakfast but asked Martha if she would bring her lunch to her room. Martha politely replied she would be happy to do that for her and then went into the kitchen and had a very animated conversation with the pantry.

Chapter 36

Doc woke early to the sound of rain outside his room. The sky was just starting to turn from dawn to light, but the clouds hung heavily over the mountains, and there wasn't much light to be had. He wondered if he would have any problems heading north since he had to go over a mountain pass between Weed and Klamath Falls. Whatever the case might be, he thought he had better get up and get going. He still had a few hours' driving ahead of him, and he wanted to give himself plenty of time in case of trouble.

Spanky's was open for business by the time he had shaved, had showered, had dressed, and was ready to go. A hearty breakfast of eggs, sausage, hash browns, and biscuits were the special of the day, so he took advantage of it. *I'm going to have to remember this place next year,* he thought after finishing his meal. Both last night's and this morning's meals were about the best he had had in a long time. "Who'd have thought," he said as he walked to his car. "Especially from the looks of the place from the outside! Oh, well, you sure can't judge a book by its cover."

Heading north from Weed, he put in a CD of Casting Crowns and continued his journey to his favorite place, Shepherd's Inn. "No cruise control on this trip," he said to himself. "Not with all this rain. I sure hope there will be snow by the time I get there." Little did he know what was in store for him once he arrived.

Chapter 37

December 23

Maria called her mom on Saturday morning to tell her they weren't going to be able to get away until Sunday. Joe had to work for a few hours in the morning to get some last-minute deliveries made before Christmas since the store would be closed until Wednesday. "But we will be able to stay over until Tuesday before we have to come back, 'cause Joe has Monday and Tuesday off. He has to take the car over to a friend's house after work today. He said something wasn't working right and he wanted to get it fixed before we leave. So we'll get up first thing in the morning and head out. I checked, and it looks like just rain tomorrow, so we shouldn't have any trouble getting there by noon."

"Well, all right," Wanda replied with a hint of disappointment in her voice. "I had prepared for you to arrive today and made plans. But if it's not to be, then I guess there's nothing I can do about it. How are you feeling, by the way? After all, you are eight months along. You need to be taking better care of yourself."

"Mom, I'm fine. And I am taking care of myself. We have been going to Lamaze classes, and Joe has been really good about doing what he needs to do in the delivery room.

I have been a little tired lately, but the doctor said I should expect that. Don't worry, Mom. Everything is going to be fine. We'll see you tomorrow, okay?"

"All right." Wanda snipped the reply. "You just be careful, and you tell Joseph to drive very carefully tomorrow. He will be transporting a very precious cargo!"

"Okay, Mom, we'll be careful. See you tomorrow. We love you! Bye."

When Maria hung up the phone, she felt a shiver all over. She wasn't sure what it meant, but she had a feeling that something was going to happen, and she didn't know if it was for good or for bad. She walked into the kitchen to grab a snack, and as she reached for the door of the fridge, she felt a small pain in her back. Nothing very severe, but enough for her to notice. *Wonder what that's all about,* she thought.

Her cell phone rang before she opened the door. Heading back into the living room, she noticed the pain was still there, but it didn't seem like something she should be worried about. *Just prego aches and pains,* she thought. She looked at the phone, and it was Joe.

"Hi, honey," she said with a smile in her voice. "Are you still at work?"

"No, we got done early. A couple of the orders were for people who are out of town, and we didn't know it until we got here this morning. Anyway, I'm heading over to Jeff's house now. He said he'll run the car into his shop and check it out. It's just running rough, and I don't want to take any chances tomorrow. Did you talk to your mom?"

"Oh, yes. I just got off the phone with her. Of course, she was not happy we aren't coming up today. She let me know she had made plans. But she perked up a little when I told her we could stay till Tuesday. I also checked the weather, and it's supposed to be just rain tomorrow all the way, so we shouldn't have any trouble."

"I wasn't worried about that," he replied. "I've got studs on the car, and I grew up in the snow, remember? I could drive up there in a blizzard!"

"I know, Joe, but I'm glad we don't have to. That's all I'm saying."

"How are you feeling this morning? It sounded like you didn't have a very good night last night. Are you doing okay?"

"Honey, I'm fine. Just a little tired is all. You try sleeping with an extra thirty pounds around your middle and see how you like it." She snapped. She was not in a great mood already, and she didn't need Joe making it worse. "I'm fine. Just get the car fixed and come home, okay? I'll feel better when you get here."

"Okay. I'll call and let you know about how long it will take. Love you! Bye." He hung up before she could even reply.

"I love you too," she replied into a dead phone. *I hope you still love me!* she thought as she looked at herself in the mirror hanging in the hall. Then she started to cry.

Chapter 38

Leah had stayed in her room Friday after she had gone to breakfast. Martha had brought her meals to her room and inquired if she was feeling all right.

"I'm just fine," Leah snapped back, "as if that is any of your business. I would appreciate it if you would just leave me alone. I have a great deal of reading to do, and I would appreciate peace and quiet. Is that too much to ask?"

Martha was almost at the breaking point. She had tried to be nice to Leah, but there was only so much she could put up with before she snapped. "If that's what you want, then that's what you'll get. I'm sorry if I have offended you." It was all Martha could do to get the last statement out without exploding. Before Leah could reply, Martha walked out the door and closed it not too softly.

Back in the great room, I was sitting in one of the easy chairs, listening to the radio. It was tuned to a news station, and I was listening to the latest weather forecast. It wasn't good, and Martha could see the concern on my face. I could also see the concern on Martha's face, so I asked her what was wrong.

"I don't know how much more of that woman I can take. She is the most selfish, self-centered, hateful woman I think I have ever known. If it were up to me, I would kick her out on her ear and let her figure out how she was going to get back to California."

"Now, Martha, she is only going to be here for a few more days. I'm sure we can put up with her for that long. I know she can be a little hard to get along with."

"Hard to get along with!" she cut in, raising her voice a couple of notches. "That's an understatement. If she was like that around her husband, it's no wonder he went looking for greener pastures."

"Martha, regardless, she is still a guest, and we will all treat her like one. We'll just have to bite our tongue and smile."

"I know." Martha calmed a little. "And I will do just that. Guess I just had to vent a little before the next episode."

Lydia had been working on the books in the little cubbyhole office around the corner from the front desk. Since the end of the year was just a little over a week away, she wanted to be sure everything was up-to-date. She took great pride in her bookkeeping skills, and last year the Brewers gave her an end-of-the-year bonus for her excellent work. She was hoping she would get another bonus this year. The girls were outgrowing their bicycles, and she wanted to get them new ones.

She had been working for quite a while, so she was taking a break and doing a little web surfing. Even though the service was slow dial-up, she could still go to some of her favorite sites. Now she was catching up on news by reading the *Portland Oregonian* online.

In the middle of the regional news section, an item about an arrest in the Salem area caught her eye. As she was reading the particulars of the case, she suddenly froze. A shiver ran down her spine, and she was having difficulty breathing. She had read that two men had been arrested in Salem for attempted robbery the day before.

> *Salem police arrested two Olympia men in connection with a failed attempt to burglarize the home of a Salem couple in an upscale neighborhood in southwest Salem. Lester Stubblefield and Cade Summers were arrested after a brief run through the neighborhood with police in foot pursuit. Not only were the two men unfamiliar with the home they were attempting to enter (which was equipped with a security system), they also were not familiar with the neighborhood as they ran down a cul-de-sac with high security walls and gates on each driveway. After discovering their error, they surrendered to the pursuing officers without further incident.*
>
> *Stubblefield and Summers both have arrest records in their home state, but according to a statement from Salem PD, they just recently moved from Olympia to Salem, and their ID still listed an apartment in Olympia as their residence. After further investigation, police found a rent receipt in Summers's name for a hotel downtown that rents rooms on a weekly basis.*

Cade is in Oregon, she thought. *Did he find out where we live? Was he trying to work his way over here?* She couldn't move. She hadn't experienced fear like this since the last time she saw him. *What am I going to do? Should I tell Gabe?*

Will he make us leave? Breathe, Lydia! Get control of yourself. Everything is going to be all right. She thought it, but did she really believe it?

She started thinking about what she could do to find out more about where Cade was then. She was afraid to do any investigating on her own. *What if Cade found out and told the police what I did to him in Olympia? What if he had made a report and the police arrested me?*

Lydia had so many things going through her head that she had forgotten what she should do first. "Father God," she began, "please forgive me for not seeking Your wisdom first. Lord, please tell me what You want me to do. You have sheltered me and protected me these last three years, and I… we are so grateful. You have provided for us in so many ways and so much more than we could have imagined. I turn to You now, Lord, to guide me and give me strength."

I have to talk to Gabe, she thought. *He's got like a hotline to God or something. He'll know what we should do.*

Lydia walked into the great room, and Martha and I were both sitting, listening to the radio. The weather report had just finished, and I had turned toward Martha, about to say something, when my eye caught Lydia coming toward us. I wouldn't have given it a second thought, but the look on her face was one I had never seen before. She looked to me like she had just seen a ghost. And I was pretty sure there were no ghosts at Shepherd's Inn other than the Holy One.

"Lydia, what's wrong, child?" I said. "What happened?"

Martha and I both knew of Lydia's past, so she felt comfortable talking to both of us about what she had just read. "Gabe, I just read an article in the *Oregonian* that said Cade had been arrested in Salem for attempted burglary. He was arrested with his drinking buddy, Lester. Gabe, it scared me to death! What is he doing in Oregon? Do you think he found out where we are and was headed this way?"

Martha's excitability has a hair trigger, and it went off. "Oh, my Lord! What are we going to do, Gabe?"

"Now, you two just settle down a bit. I know this sounds pretty serious, but let's just take a couple of minutes and think about it." I think I have a way with calming a serious situation, and this was one of those times when I worked my best. "First off, are you sure it was Cade they arrested?"

"Of course, I'm sure. It said so right in the article. Cade Summers and Lester Stubblefield were mentioned by name. It even said they were from Olympia and had just moved to a place in downtown Salem."

"Okay, so we know he's in Salem, but we also know he is in jail, right? Didn't it say they were arrested?"

"Yeah, but maybe he got out on bail or something. You know they have overcrowded jails everywhere and maybe they didn't have room for them, so they let them out on bail!" Lydia's voice was full of excitement, and she was starting to hyperventilate.

"Calm down, darlin'. It ain't going to do us any good if you go and pass out on us. I don't think they would let them out that quickly. But besides that, what makes you so sure he found out where you are? Maybe he and his buddy were just on the move. It's a free country, and maybe they got into some trouble in Washington and decided they should change their environment.

"I'll tell you what? First part of the week, I'll go into town and talk with Belinda Claybaugh. Maybe she can do a little internal investigating and find out just what's going on. I won't tell her anything about you and Cade. I'll just say Lester is maybe somebody I used to know. I don't think that would be an outright lie. At least I hope not. Well, on second thought, it would be a lie, so I'll think of something. But the first thing we need to do is some serious prayin'."

Lydia was already starting to feel a little better. She knew I would do everything I could to protect her and the girls. But she still couldn't shake the thought that Cade had somehow found out where she was living and he wanted to settle a score. That was what she was thinking as she sat down with Martha and me and the three of us began to pray.

Chapter 39

Just as I was saying "Amen," we all heard the sound of a car pulling into the parking lot. Lydia's heart jumped into her throat as she immediately forgot about Cade and remembered that Lucas Meriweather, DVM, was arriving today. She almost started to hyperventilate again, but she kept her breathing under control and hurried to the front door to see if it was really him.

Doc was just getting out of his Jeep Cherokee. He was immediately getting soaked from the heavy rain, and he made a mad dash for the front porch. He almost fell when he jumped up the steps, but he caught himself just in time. He saw Lydia standing in the doorway and thought, *That would be just great. Mr. Graceful falling flat on his rear end in front of the most beautiful woman at Shepherd's Inn. Boy, I had better not let Martha hear that!*

Doc was surprised at the look on Lydia's face when he finally caught his balance and walked up to her. She had a look like he was her knight in shining armor or something. Little did he know how important his appearance was for her right at this moment.

As hard as it was to keep her composure, Lydia resisted the urge to rush out and give him a big hug. Instead, she just said, "Welcome, Doc. How was your trip? Not too bad, I hope, with this rain and all. Come on in. We have your room all ready for you. Would you like me to get you a towel? Do you want me to bring in your luggage for you?" *Shut up, Lydia, you're sounding like a schoolgirl.*

Doc was not as careful with his composure as he walked up and gave Lydia a big hug. He wasn't sure why, but he knew they both needed that hug. He felt much better for doing it.

As for Lydia, she almost melted in his arms. He had never hugged her like that before. She wondered what it meant. Whatever it meant, she was glad he did it.

After hugging Lydia, Doc gave Martha and me a hug too and said, "Boy, it's good to be here. I have been looking forward to seeing all of you, and it seemed like the time was moving very slowly for me the last few weeks. But now I'm here, and I feel great. Where are the twins? I can't wait to see them."

About that time from down the hall they all could hear the thundering footsteps of Sarah and Elisabeth, and they rounded the corner and raced up to Doc. "Uncle Doc, Uncle Doc," they chimed in unison, "you're finally here!"

Doc knelt as the girls both ran into his arms. He grabbed the girls, one in each arm, and gently held them as he stood back up. Lydia couldn't help but notice how easily he picked them up with his muscular arms. She was ready to melt again.

All thoughts and fears of Cade had vanished in just a few moments. Lydia was in love with Lucas Meriweather, and she had no idea what she was going to do about it. But she knew one thing: she was going to try to do something.

Chapter 40

Joe got home a little after four and found Maria lying on the sofa in the living room. A gust of wind caught the door as he came in, and it slammed with a crash. Maria, frightened by the noise, tried to jump up but could only raise her head. "What was that noise?" she said.

"I'm sorry, babe. The wind just ripped the door out of my hand. I hope I didn't scare you."

Even though Maria was still coming out of a hard sleep and all her senses weren't working, she could still tell that Joe had been drinking. Ever since that day he found out his work hours would be cut after the first of the year and he came home drunk, he had been drinking more and more. Not enough to get drunk every night, but she could still tell when he had had a couple of beers after work.

This time she was really upset, for several reasons. First, she felt horrible. She had a headache, a backache, and she felt like throwing up. And Joe and Jeff were probably drinking beer while Jeff was supposed to be working on their car, so how good of a job could he do while drinking?

Don't start anything now, Maria, she thought. "Oh, that's okay," she said. "I needed to get up anyway. Did you get the car fixed?"

Joe walked over and gave her a hug and a kiss. "I think so. There was something in the fuel line. Jeff really knows his stuff. He said it should work fine now. It ran okay on the way home. Boy, is it raining out there! I haven't seen it rain like this around here in, like, forever! I sure hope it lets up a little tomorrow. What's for dinner?"

"Leftovers. I'm trying to empty out the fridge before we go. Hope you don't mind." Maria wasn't thinking about left-overs or whether Joe minded or not. What she was thinking was that the only thing Jeff knew was how to screw things up. He was a klutz. He hadn't been able to keep a job as a mechanic. He had been fired from three different shops, and now no one would hire him. So now he was a pizza delivery guy. How he could con his friends into letting him work on their cars, she couldn't understand. She thought it might have something to do with the stories he liked to tell his buddies about the women he met when he was delivering pizza. Joe had let slip that he told them about women coming to the door without much on. She knew his stories were more than likely mostly a figment of his wild imagination, but Jeff had always been a teller of tales and he could make up stories that made him look like some superhero. She couldn't stand the guy, but he was a friend of Joe's, so she put up with him.

"Leftovers are fine. I'm not very hungry anyway. I had some pizza at Jeff's. I'm going to go put some stuff together for the trip. I haven't packed anything yet. Give me a holler when dinner's ready, okay?"

"Okay," she said to his back as he was already heading for the bedroom. *Joseph Alexander, sometimes you can make me so mad! Maybe I should just stay in Bend! It would serve you right!*

Dinner was an uncomfortable occasion for Maria and Joe. Joe was just picking at his food. He hated leftovers, and he wasn't hungry anyway. Jeff had brought a pizza from work, and he had eaten about half of it while Jeff worked on his car. The pizza, along with a couple of beers, had been more than enough for the rest of the night.

Maria, on the other hand, was starving. She had eaten hardly anything all day because she felt so bad. She still had a headache and backache, and Joe wasn't making either one of them any better. They both tried a little small talk, but there was so much friction in the room that even talking about the little things was useless. They both knew that tonight was not going to end on a good note.

By the time they had finished dinner, their talking had come to an end. Joe started clearing the table, and Maria was glad of that. He usually would just walk into the living room and start watching TV. Tonight, however, she was going to let him do it all. "I'm going to bed," she said. "My back is killing me, and I have a gigantic headache. Please don't just leave the dirty dishes in the sink. Will you please wash and dry them and put them away?" Joe looked at her as if he wanted to say something, but she cut him off. "Can you at least do that for me?"

"Sure, babe" was all he said. He could sense that any other answer would be suicide.

Maria ran a tubful of hot water and bubble bath, hoping that would help with her aches. As she was lying in the tub, trying to read from her daily devotional, she couldn't help but wonder what their future would bring. What were they going to do next month when there was no more insurance? Was she going to become another welfare case, having to depend on the government to take care of her because she couldn't take care of herself? "O God, please help me. I have really made a mess of things. I don't know what to do. I love Joe so much, but sometimes he makes me so angry I can't stand to be around him. I don't think he loves me the same way. I sometimes feel like he doesn't like me anymore because I'm not the same 'sexy thang' he called me when we were going together. God, I'm a mess. I'm fat, I'm getting pimples again, I hurt all over, and I just wish this baby would hurry up and get here. I don't know how much more I can take. And, God, I don't know how much I'm going to be able to stand once we get up to my parents' house. I know they are going to try to get me to stay there and Joe is going to get all upset and they are all going to get into it and I'm going to be in the middle. Some Christmas, huh? Please, God, tell me what to do."

As Maria stepped from her bath and was toweling off, she could hear the TV going in the living room. She slipped on her nightgown and walked into the hall. She glanced into the living room and saw the back of Joe's head in the recliner as he was watching a rerun of *Cops*. She quietly walked into the bedroom and climbed into bed. As she lay there, looking at the faint glow of the streetlight through the blinds, she once again turned to her heavenly Father as she prayed and cried herself to sleep. She wasn't aware when Joe quietly walked into the room a couple of hours later and climbed into bed beside her.

Her back was to him as he lay down, and he gently placed his arm around her and whispered, "I love you, babe."

Chapter 41

December 24

Sunday morning broke with continued rain. When I woke up, I could hear the rain pounding on the roof and running down the gutters. It was still dark outside, and there was a chill in the room that I couldn't explain. I turned toward the clock on the night table, and there was no light coming from it. *Power's out!* I knew immediately.

I jumped out of bed, threw on my jeans and shirt, hurried into my boots, and went straight out to the pump house. The rain was still coming down in sheets, and in the ten feet I had to cover from the main house to the pump house, I was soaked.

I threw open the door and pulled the chain on the battery-operated work light inside the door. After double-checking that everything was ready, I pulled the starter rope on the generator. Nothing! I pulled again. Nothing! "Lord, I could sure use a little help here." On the third pull, the motor caught, and the generator purred like a contented kitten. I then went to the breaker panel, threw the switch, and we had electrical power again at the inn. "Thank You, Lord." I double-checked to make sure the gas tank was full and then went back into the main house.

Martha was walking into the kitchen when I came through the back door. I didn't think she was expecting to see me, and she let out a little scream when she saw my drenched figure come in the door.

"Lord Almighty!" she exclaimed. "Gabe, you look like a drowned rat! Have you been standing out in the rain all morning?"

I explained to her that my appearance was the result of just a few seconds between the main house and the pump house.

"I have never seen it rain like this since I've been here," she said. "I take it the power lines are down, right? I could tell by the way the lights aren't as bright as they usually are."

"Yep," I said. "When I woke up, I noticed the clock wasn't working. We should be okay now. The generator is working fine, and we have lots of gas to last a few days. We'll just have to conserve as much as we can. Anyone else up yet?"

"Not that I'm aware of. I just got up myself. I couldn't sleep with all the rain. That downspout outside my window sounded like the Little Jordan was running right through it."

The Little Jordan, I thought. "I had better go see how the bridge is doing. I'm guessing, with so much rain last night, the creek should be just about out of its banks."

I went to the back room and got my heavy raincoat and rain boots, grabbed a flashlight, and headed out the front door for the creek. Since it was still dark and the rain was coming down so hard, I could hardly see just a few feet in front of me. As I got closer to the bridge, I could hear the roar of the Little Jordan in the distance.

I couldn't believe what I was looking at when I got to the bridge. It was still standing, but the water was rushing under like I had never seen. There were only a few inches between the water level and the bottom of the bridge. If the rain kept up much longer, I was sure the water level would be over the bridge in a few hours. The bridge itself seemed to be holding up okay, but the banks of the creek were starting to erode in places, and I couldn't be sure they would hold up under the bridge. At least we weren't expecting any guests up here for a few days, but in the back of my mind, I knew that expectations and reality can often run in opposite directions. "Well, Lord, we just place all our trust and faith in You. If it be Your will, place Your protecting hand on this bridge and this place. Lord, we are at Your mercy, but we know that is more than enough. Thank You, Lord, for Your protection, mercy, and grace. We also pray for this holy night to celebrate Your most precious gift to us all. In His name I pray. Amen."

I turned and walked back to the main house. *Better get a big fire going in the fireplace,* I thought. *No telling how long we're going to have to hunker down.*

Chapter 42

Maria was up early. She had slept very little during the night, and her backache seemed to be getting worse. Since Joe would be doing all the driving today, she figured she should let him sleep a little longer. She wanted to get an early start on their trip. The rain was still coming down hard, and she just hoped it didn't turn to snow before they got to Bend. She was never very good at driving in snow, and just to be in the car while someone else was driving made her nervous. She knew she should get over it if she was going to live in this snow country the rest of her life. Oh, how she wished they could move somewhere warm and sunny all the time. But fat chance that was ever going to happen. She knew it would always be only a dream.

Back to reality, she thought as she started the coffee going. It smelled so good, and even though she knew she shouldn't be drinking it now, she really wanted a cup. "Maybe just one cup won't hurt."

"Mornin', babe!" Joe had quietly walked up behind her as she was standing at the counter. "How's your backache and headache this morning?"

"Good morning, honey. Oh, my head feels okay, but my back is still killing me. I'm glad I have a doctor's appointment on Wednesday. Maybe she can give me something for it. I didn't get much sleep last night. I hope I can sleep some on the drive today. Otherwise, I'll be a wreck when we get to my folks' house.

"By the way, thanks, honey, for cleaning up the kitchen last night. It looks great. I just didn't feel like doing anything. You understand, don't you?"

"Oh, no sweat, babe. Remember, I used to live by myself for a while before we met. I got fairly good at cleaning up after myself. Guess I have gotten a little out of practice since we got married. You spoil me, you know?"

"Anytime you want to start cleaning up after yourself again, I won't get in your way!" Maria shot back. She was in no mood for a fight or humor, and she wasn't sure where he was going with his comments.

"What time did you want to get started?" Joe shot back. He wanted to change the subject as quickly as possible.

"The sooner, the better, as far as I'm concerned. I don't like to drive in all this rain. And it's Christmas Eve day, and lots of crazies are going to be on the road today."

Joe looked at Maria with a look of "you worry too much" and said, "I guess we can get started anytime. Are your folks going to church this morning? If we leave too early, they would still be in church when we get there."

"Mom told me to text her when we leave and she would make sure they were home by the time we get there. I think they were having an early service this morning because of the extra crowd of CE Christians showing up today. I know I shouldn't say that. Even though some people just show up at church for Christmas and Easter, at least they are there. We can plant seeds whenever we have the chance. And their church is also having a Christmas Eve service at seven, so we can all go then."

"Okay, if you want, we can just get ready and leave and stop up the road and get some breakfast. I'm not hungry yet. I'll go jump into the shower if you'll bring me a cup of coffee when it's ready." As Joe started to turn toward the bathroom, he stopped, turned back to Maria, and said, "I really love you, babe!" And then he was gone.

Where did that come from? she wondered. *I'm not sure, but I really liked it.* Maria started humming a Christmas carol as she reached for a cup from the cup rack on the counter. She stopped in mid-tune and said, "Father, forgive me for being so crabby lately. I know Joe is the one for me and we are going to be fine. Please give me the strength and wisdom to handle the day-to-day stuff that can so easily get in the way of a great marriage. And please give me the strength to get through the pregnancy. We are so looking forward to starting our family with our little baby boy. You have blessed us, Lord, in so many ways, and I am so very thankful. I know You have plans for us, and I have faith that Joe's job hunt and the insurance problem will be solved. We just place it all in Your hands, Father. Please be with us today as we travel. You know, Lord, how scared I get, so I ask You to take that fear from me and give me courage. Thank You, Lord, for our many blessings. Thank You for Your Son. In His name I pray. Amen." She poured a cup of coffee, hesitated, and reached for another cup. As she walked toward the bathroom with two cups of coffee in her hand, she started humming that Christmas carol again. *This is going to be a Christmas we will remember always,* she thought.

It was just getting light when they loaded their bags in the car and headed out. Maria's back was still hurting, but not as much as it had during the night. She let her seat back about halfway and hoped she could get at least a little sleep. Joe had the radio on, and he had it tuned to a station that was playing just Christmas music. He started to change the station, but Maria asked him if he could just leave it there for a while. "Okay, I guess. If it makes you happy," he said with a heavy dose of sarcasm.

"Now, what's that all about?" she snapped. "You make it sound like it's such a chore for you to listen to Christmas music. Well, don't let me, 'cause you to have to *endure* a little discomfort! Change it to whatever you want. Don't worry about what I want!" She knew as soon as she spoke that she shouldn't have. But it was too late to get the words back. "I'm sorry I snapped at you."

"No problem," he said. "Just try to get some sleep, okay?"

Twenty-five miles north of town, there was a little restaurant that served the best biscuits and gravy for miles around. They stopped and ate breakfast, made a rest stop, and got back in the car without getting too wet. As Joe turned the key in the ignition, the starter turned over for a long time before the engine finally fired. The car was running rough to start with, and he pressed the accelerator a couple of times and it finally started running smoother. Joe looked at Maria, and she was looking back with a look that said, "So much for Jeff fixing the car." "Don't start in with me," he said. "Everything is fine. It's probably just the rain that's making the car hard to start. We'll get there just fine." He didn't wait for a reply; he just put the car in reverse and backed out of the parking space.

Back on the road, he was noticeably quiet, and Maria decided she didn't want to make waves. *It's Christmas, think merry thoughts,* she thought to herself.

About an hour after they left the restaurant, as they were just about to reach the top of a small rise in the highway, suddenly, the car started to shake as the engine cut out. It didn't quit completely, but it was running so rough Joe was worried that something really bad was wrong. Joe was ashamed he didn't know more about cars. Most of his friends knew how to work on them, and one friend, Matt, rebuilt old Junkers.

"What's going on, Joe?" Maria said as she woke up in panic from a shallow sleep.

"I don't know," he said. "Everything was going fine, and all of a sudden, this happened. I don't know what to do."

Just then, they passed the sign that signaled the turnoff for New Bethlehem, one-half mile. "I'll turn off there. Maybe there is a gas station or garage that can look at it." As he said it, he knew there was no chance there would be a place open in a little backwater town out in the middle of nowhere on Sunday. Especially since it was Christmas Eve. He just didn't have any better ideas at that moment, and he was worried.

From the time they turned off Highway 97, the road to New Bethlehem was mostly downhill, so Joe took his foot off the gas pedal and coasted down the road. The car slowed to about thirty miles an hour, but there was no one else in sight, so he wasn't worried. After about a mile, the road leveled out some, so he had to give the car a little gas. It was still running rough, but at least it was still running. Panic was starting to settle in on him as he thought about what would happen if the car quit before they got to town. It was still pouring down rain, and he couldn't imagine having to get out and walk in it. *And what about Maria?* he thought. That was when he did something he very seldom did. He prayed.

It was about half past ten on Sunday morning, Christmas Eve day, pouring down rain, when Joe and Maria arrived in New Bethlehem. Although they had lived within a couple of hours of the town all their lives, neither one of them had ever been here. What Joe saw was despair. All the business seemed to be on one main street in town, and it wasn't a long street. All the shops looked closed, and there wasn't another soul in sight. Even though it was midmorning, the heavy rain gave the town an almost-ghostly appearance. He had traveled almost half the distance down the main street, and his thoughts were about the prayer he had just said. *So much for prayer, God! Look what good it did me.*

Driving past a small Ace Hardware store and local restaurant named Rob's Diner (both closed), he noticed a lighted sign almost at the edge of town. As he got closer, his heart took a leap. The lighted sign said "Chevron." *Could it be?* he thought. *Could I be so lucky to find a gas station open in this Podunk town? But there probably isn't a mechanic on duty."*

Maria saw it at about the same time, and she said, "Oh, Joe, look. Pull in there. It looks open. Maybe they can fix the car."

"Don't get too excited, Maria. Most gas stations now just have a flunky pumping your gas and taking your money." (For those who don't know, Oregon has a law that you can't pump your own gas. Don't ask me why; just trust me!)

The sign on the front of the station said, "Noah's Chevron." Underneath there was a list of services provided, including engine repair.

As the car rolled across the line that notified the attendant that a car had arrived, a black man, who appeared to be in his mid-fifties, rose from a chair in the office, laid the book down that he had been reading, and walked out to greet his first customer of the day.

Joe was getting out of the car as Noah came around the front. "Mornin', folks. Kind of a nasty day to be out drivin', isn't it? Need some gas today, huh?"

"Something's wrong with my car, and I don't know what it is. It just started running rough up on the highway just before we got to the turnoff. I sure hope you can help us.

My wife is eight months pregnant, and we were on our way to Bend to her parents' house for Christmas."

"Now, don't you worry none. I'll see what I can do. Why don't you two just go on inside and have a seat? There's a pot of coffee on the counter, and I even got a box of doughnuts if you're hungry. They might not be very fresh, but they'll at least chase the hunger away."

"I can't believe you are open today. It doesn't look like there is anybody else in town."

"Now, son," Noah replied, "this here is New Bethlehem. We don't always do what you would think normal folks do. I was supposed to be open today 'cause you folks were coming by. You see, the Lord works His best on folks who believe in Him."

Chapter 43

Noah Bismarck was born Noah Elijah Vincent in Mississippi in the late fifties on a small farm outside Hattiesburg. His great-great-grandfather was born a slave in 1841, and he had been given the last name of his owner. Noah's family had little in the way of creature comforts, and life was hard for all of them. When Noah was fifteen years old, he ran away from home and thumbed his way, along with riding the rails, all the way from Mississippi to Harlem. For several years, he lived on the streets, taking odd jobs wherever he could and taking handouts when he couldn't find work.

When he was in his early twenties, he knew he had to find a way to better himself, so he hopped on a freight train and started moving west. It took him almost a year to finally wind up in Bismarck, North Dakota. He arrived there in the early summer and found a job at a farm outside of town. At first, he just did odd jobs because he really had no marketable skills. But he was a hard worker, and when he said he would do something, it got done.

The foreman took a liking to Noah and began to give him more and more responsibility around the farm. Noah seemed to have a natural talent for working on farm equipment, so he started working on tractors and combines and anything else that had an engine.

After he had worked on the farm for about two years, the foreman came to him one day and asked him if he would like to go to school to learn more about being a mechanic. Noah couldn't believe what he was hearing. Here he was, a poor black man from the South who didn't even finish high school, and these folks wanted to send him to college.

Up to this point, Noah had never been much for going to church or even believing in God. When he was a child, his parents always took him to church in Mississippi, but after he ran away from home, he also ran away from God. But when he was given the chance to go to school to become a real mechanic because his boss believed in him, something changed.

At the end of that day, after talking to the foreman about all the particulars of him going to school and continuing to work on the farm, Noah lay down in his bed that night and opened up an old Bible that he had carried with him for years, even though he never opened it until now.

During the winter in Bismarck, North Dakota, there is more to do than many people think. The most important thing is keeping the livestock fed and taken care of. The bitter cold can wipe out farm animals if they are not taken care of. There's also much to do to get all the equipment ready for the next spring. That far north, the days are short in the winter, and it was during those long nights that Noah did most of his study. By the end of the second year, he could take an engine apart and put it back together in record time. He could analyze what a problem was just by listening. The foreman said he had never been around anyone so skilled at engine repair. So Noah quit farming and became a full-time mechanic. He worked primarily on the farm where he started, but he also helped other farmers in the area whenever needed. His needs were few, so he saved as much money as he could for the next four years.

After all those years in Bismarck, Noah finally got tired of dealing with the bitter, cold winters and decided to seek a more agreeable climate. He packed up all his belongings, which were few, loaded them into his old Ford pickup, which he had running like a brand-new vehicle, and headed west. He wasn't sure how far west he would go; he just figured he would know when he got there.

After a few days of driving west on I-94 and I-90, he found himself in Ellensburg, Washington. He was tired of the freeway, so he decided to head south on Highway 97 down into Oregon. While sitting down to a meal in Bend, Oregon, he was reading the local newspaper and saw a help-wanted ad for a mechanic in New Bethlehem. He had no idea where New Bethlehem was, so he asked the waitress. She told him it was just about an hour and a half south of Bend. With nothing to lose and everything to gain, he paid for his meal, said a little prayer, and pointed his truck in the direction of New Bethlehem.

When Noah got into town, he went to a pay phone and called the number listed in the ad. The voice on the other end of the line sounded old and feeble. When Noah asked if the job was still available, the old man said yes and told him he owned a Chevron station on the edge of town and told him to come on over.

That was the day Noah met F. G. Crownover.

F. G.—no one ever knew what the F. G. stood for—was a crusty old fellow well into his eighties who had owned the station from back when you could buy a gallon of gas for fifteen cents. F. G. still pumped the gas most of the time, but the mechanic who worked for him had gotten married and he and his wife moved to Pendleton. Since the station was one of the few places in town with a mechanic on duty, especially on weekends, F. G. needed to get someone hired fast.

"What's your name, young fellow?" F. G. asked.

Before he could reply, Noah thought how he hated the last name of Vincent. He was always reminded of how that name came about from his great-great-grandfather being a slave. "Name's Bismarck, Noah Elijah *Bismarck*," he replied. *My, that sounds good!* he thought.

"Where you from, and what brings you to a little backwater town like New Bethlehem?"

"Well, sir, I come from all over. I've worked my way from Mississippi to New York to North Dakota to here. I've chopped cotton, lived on the street, sold newspapers on the street corner, worked on farms, and learned how to be a darned good engine mechanic. I can take a car engine apart and put it back together blindfolded. I love what I do, and I just want a chance to settle down in a town like this and do what I do best.

"I ain't married, I don't have no kids, and I don't need a lot to make me happy. If you've a mind to give me a job, I'd be happy to show you what I can do before you pay me a red cent."

"See that old four-hole Buick sittin' there in the bay?"

"Yes, sir," Noah said, "and a mighty fine-looking car, if I may say so."

"That's mine. Bought it new back in 1954. The last guy I had workin' for me couldn't seem to figure out why it wants to overheat whenever I drive over forty miles an hour. You fix my Buick and you've got a job. How does that sound?"

That night, after the station closed, Noah took F. G. for a drive in the '54 Buick. They went out to Highway 97 and opened it up. The heat gauge settled in just around the two hundred mark the whole time, even when Noah got it up to eighty miles an hour. When they got back to the station, F. G. said, "Let's get you a timecard so you can start work tomorrow mornin'. That is, if it's okay with you?"

"Mr. Crownover, that sounds just fine to me. I don't suppose you could tell me where I might be able to rent me a room around here? I been sleepin' in my pickup for the last several days, and I could sure use a nice bed and a hot bath someplace."

"Tell you what? I have a little house out back where my last mechanic lived. It ain't much, but I don't charge a lot of rent either. If you want to go check it out, I'll go get the key." F. G. went into the office and took a ring of keys off a hook behind the counter. "This one right here is for the house. The rest of the keys on here are for everything else around here. If you'll be staying here, I reckon you probably should be the one to open up things in the morning.

"Oh, and before you start, you have to know one thing. Folks around here, even the kids, call me F. G. If you talked to anyone in town about a Mr. Crownover, they probably wouldn't even know whom you were talking about." F. G. laughed when he said that.

Two years later, F. G. Crownover went home to the Lord. He had no living relatives, and his station was put up for auction by the state. Noah Elijah Bismarck was the only bidder.

Chapter 44

Joe opened the door for Maria, and they both went into the station. It was warm and dry and smelled of doughnuts, coffee, and gasoline. Joe found the coffeepot and some cups hanging on a peg board rack behind it. On the counter beside the coffeepot was a box of Winchell's doughnuts. He poured each of them a cup of coffee and held the box down for Maria to choose.

"Yuck, get those out of my sight. I think I'm gonna throw up!" Maria looked pale and tired, and Joe could see pain in her eyes.

"I'm sorry, babe. Do you want the coffee? Maybe something warm in your tummy might help." He was bending over backward trying to please her. He knew he was in the doghouse because of the car problem.

"No! I don't want anything except to get out of this town and get to my parents'. My back hurts, my head hurts, the baby keeps kicking like he is doing gymnastics, and riding in that car is like riding in a covered wagon!" Maria had held it in as long as she could. She started to cry and reached for a tissue from her purse.

Joe felt helpless. He didn't know when or even if the car could be fixed. He figured there was no place in town even open today where they could go and be more comfortable.

He was at the end of his rope. He thought about what he could say to make Maria feel better, but nothing came. He figured his best bet was to go out into the garage and see if the mechanic had found out anything yet.

"I'm gonna go check and see if he found out anything. I'll be right back. Okay, babe?" He didn't wait for an answer.

Noah had the hood up on the car, and the engine was running, just barely. He had it hooked up to the diagnostics and was checking some gauges.

"I had a friend of mine work on it yesterday," Joe offered. "He said there was a clogged fuel line and he got it running fairly good. It was doing fine when we left Klamath Falls. But just before we got to the turnoff up on 97, then it just started running really rough like it wasn't getting any gas."

"Well, son, looks to me like that friend of yours needs to find himself a new profession. There ain't nothin' wrong with your fuel line. It's your fuel pump that's gone belly-up. You're downright fortunate you made it as far as you did."

"Can you fix it? Does it need a new one?"

"Well," Noah started with a slow, easygoing pace to his conversation, "normally I'd say I could have it fixed in a couple of hours or so. You see, in this car the fuel pump is in the gas tank. I have to drain and drop the tank and replace the pump. This here bein' Sunday and Christmas Eve, the parts store is closed up tighter than a drum. I know the owner is out of town, visitin' with family, so I can't call him up to see if he could give us a hand."

Before Noah could continue, Joe cut in, "So what can we do? Can you fix the one that's in there? How are we going to get to Bend today?" He was rambling, and he knew it. He just didn't know what to do.

"Now, son, before you get yourself so worked up, just listen to me for a minute. First of all, what in tarnation were you thinkin' taking your wife out for a three-hour drive on a day like this, especially in her condition? I swear, from the looks of her in there, I think she could drop that foal just about any minute. And what are you doin' hangin' around fellers who think they can work on cars but just make things worse? I ain't your pa, and I may be speakin' out of turn, but I think it's time you got your head on a little straighter and calmed yourself down.

"You seem like a pretty levelheaded young man to me. You just got yourself in over your head today. So settle down, think about how you are going to take care of that pretty wife and baby in there, and let me do what I do best, and that's fixin' cars. You suppose you can do that?"

Joe wasn't sure what to say. He had never had anyone talk to him like that. Especially a total stranger. Anger swelled up in him at first, and he had to hold back the urge to take a swing at the old man for talking to him that way. But on the other hand, he realized what the old man had to say was probably pretty close to right on. He knew for sure Jeff had worked on his car for the last time.

"Okay," he finally said, "but can you fix it today?"

"Tell you what?" Noah said in the same slow, easygoing manner. "I can't fix your fuel pump. And I can't go buy you a new one. But I do have an ace in the hole. You see, there's a car out back that happens to be exactly like yours. It seems the young feller who owns it was doin' what most of you young folks do these days. He was using his dad-gummed phone to 'text' his sweetheart while he was supposed to be driving. Well, he drove, all right, right up a lodgepole pine tree alongside the road. Good thing for him he had his seat belt on at least. But it wasn't no good for the car. Smashed to whole front end up. But I'm guessin' his little tree-climbing experiment didn't do one bit of harm to the fuel pump on that car.

"So let me give him a call and see if he won't mind if we 'borrow' his fuel pump so we can get you on the road. How does that sound?"

Joe couldn't believe his luck. What a coincidence that the same make of car would be where they could get another fuel pump. "That sounds great. Can you call him now?"

"Sure enough. Just let me wash my hands and I'll go in and call him. Now, you get back in there and tell that pretty little wife of yours that everything is going to be just fine. Old Noah has everything under control."

"Will do. Thank you, Noah."

When Joe walked back into the office, he could see that Maria had stopped crying, but her eyes were still red and puffy.

"Good news, babe! It's just a bad fuel pump, and Noah—that's the guy's name—said there is a wrecked car out back just like ours and he's going to call the kid who owns it and see if we can use his fuel pump. Let me tell you, I have a good feeling about this. That old man, Noah, there's something different about him. I'm not sure what it is, but it's like he has some special powers or something. It's not so much what he said to me, it's how he said it. At first, I just thought it was luck that things were working out this way, but I just have this feeling that it's a whole lot more than that."

Maria looked at Joe and saw something in his eyes and his face that she had never seen before. Joe had never been one for believing much in faith in God. He did go to church with her sometimes, but she could tell he was not a strong believer. But now she saw the Spirit of God moving in him like she had never seen before. This was a Joe she would like to see more of.

"That's great, honey. Did he say how long it will take? I don't know how much longer I can go without lying down somewhere."

Before Joe could answer, the door from the garage opened and Noah walked in. "Well, how are you doing, ma'am? I'm sorry I don't have a more comfortable place for you to sit."

"That's okay. I'll be all right. Do you know how long it will take to fix the car? I really need to lie down, and I was hoping we could make it to Bend soon."

Noah could see the strain in her face and hear it in her voice. "I'm afraid it's going to take a few hours to get you folks ready to travel. But tell you what? I live in a little house out back, and if you want, you can go back there and lie down on the couch. It ain't much, but it's a darned sight better than these old chairs."

"Oh, that would be great." Maria said it with excitement in her voice, but in her mind, she was thinking, *Oh, great. This old guy lives alone probably, and his place probably looks like a dump. But anything would be better than this chair.* "Just let me call my mom and tell her what's going on. Maybe they could even come and get us. What do you think of that, Joe?"

She caught Joe completely off guard. Just what he needed. Having his in-laws come to bail him out. But it was more important to get Maria comfortable, so he just said, "Sounds good to me."

Maria took out her cell phone and punched in her mom's number. Her mom's phone went directly to the message prompt, so she knew it was probably off. She left a message and asked her mom to call as soon as she could. Then she noticed it wasn't quite noon and they were probably still in church. He mom was always good about turning her phone off when she was in church.

Noah pulled a beat-up old umbrella from behind the door and motioned to Maria to follow him to his house. "You just stay right her, young man. I'll be right back. No sense for both of us gettin' wet." The rain was still coming down in sheets, and the wind was bringing it in almost sideways. But Noah held the umbrella in a way that Maria could stay reasonably dry, while Noah was soaked by the time they got to the door. He opened it, and Maria stepped into something she would have never guessed. First, the place was immaculate. It was a small house, looked like only one bedroom and a bathroom off a living room / kitchen combination. The kitchen was spotless, the floors were mopped and waxed, and the furniture, though older and worn, looked clean and comfortable. Noah guided her to the sofa and helped her sit down.

"By the way, I don't think we have even been properly introduced. My name is Noah Elijah Bismarck. And you are?"

"Nice to meet you, Noah. I'm Maria Alexander, my husband is Joe, and this"—she motioned to her belly—"is little Dexter. Thank you so much for all that you are doing for us. I can't tell you how much we appreciate this. I don't know how we can pay you for all this, but maybe I can get my dad to send you a check when we get to Bend."

"Now, don't you go worrying yourself about stuff like that. The Lord has blessed me in so many ways, and one of them is financial. If I can do something like this for a couple like you two, especially at a time like this, well, that's about all this old man needs. You just think about lying down here and getting some rest. If you need to use the facilities, they are right over there." He pointed toward the bathroom, although it wasn't hard to miss. "And there's some sweet ice tea in the fridge if you want any. Just make yourself at home, and we'll come get you when the car is ready to go. And I'm going to write down the phone number in the station, so if you need something, just pull out that cell phone of yours and call me. No sense in you getting out in this rain any more than you have to."

Noah wrote the number on a pad and placed it on the coffee table. Maria noticed the pad next to a ceramic figurine of the lion and the lamb. She imagined herself as the lamb right now and couldn't help but picture Noah as the lion.

Noah went into the bedroom and came out with a colorful, handmade quilt. Maria had just taken off her shoes and was stretching out on the sofa as Noah placed the quilt on her and said, "You get some rest now. Okay?"

"Noah, I don't know how to thank you for all you are doing."

Noah just smiled, and without saying a word, he quietly slipped out the door and ran back to the shop.

Joe was pacing back and forth in the office. He felt good about Noah being able to fix the car, but he was now getting worried about how long it would take. He really wanted to get to Bend before dark, but it was starting to look like that wasn't going to happen. He really didn't want Maria's dad to come down and pick them up. That would just be another reason for them to not like him. And besides, since her dad had never gotten back to him about a possible job in Bend, Joe figured he had already written Joe off as a loser. He just wasn't in the mood for more humiliation.

"Okay, son, let me get ahold of that young feller and see if I can 'persuade' him to let us use his fuel pump."

Joe listened to Noah's side of the phone conversation and couldn't believe the gift Noah had for getting things done. In no time at all, he had convinced the guy on the other end of the line that it was his God-given duty to help these folks out in their time of despair.

When he hung up, Noah rubbed his hands together, looked at Joe, and said, "Okay, let's get this show on the road!"

Noah worked with skill and patience as he went out back and worked on the wrecked car. He had put on a set of rain clothes and rubber boots and had a big rain hat on his head and tied under his chin. The fact that the rain was cold and the wind was blowing hard didn't seem to bother him in the least. It took a while, but he finally had the gas tank off and had it hauled into the shop.

Joe asked if he could help, and together, they worked for over three hours replacing the fuel pump and getting the gas tank installed.

All the time they worked, Noah kept up a steady stream of chatter. He told Joe about his life in Mississippi, the story of his great-great-grandpa and life as a slave. He regaled him with stories of life on the streets in Harlem. His coming to the Lord because he could see the power God had in his life. By the time they were about to wrap up the job, he had almost given Joe his complete life history. And all the while working with skill to get the car repaired.

As Joe sat and listened to all Noah had to say, he couldn't help but marvel at Noah's past. But he couldn't help but wonder why, with all that he had learned, all that he had saved, he was still in a dump like this, working on Christmas Eve.

"Noah, how come you never got married?"

"Well, son, guess I just never found the right woman. Besides, I think the Lord had plans for me to do His bidding without having to worry about a woman by my side. I don't mind, though. I've got the pleasure of all these townsfolk being my family. Why, women are always bringing me little dishes they've made for me. Guess they think an old codger like me don't know how to cook." He smiled and continued, "Boy, do I have them fooled. I know they like to do it, though, and I don't want to hurt their feelings. And some of their fixin's is pretty darned good."

"But why do you stay in a nowhere town like this? You could move to a big city like Portland and probably make a ton of money. You are really good at what you do."

Noah stopped what he was doing and looked up at Joe with a gentle look of a teacher about to give his student a particularly important lesson to take through life. "Son, I know most of you young folks think you've got to go out and make a ton of money. Too many of you want to have it all and have it right now! Why, I watch TV now and then, and I see these young couples who are still wet behind the ears and demanding a fancy house, a brand-new car, and all the toys they think will make them happy.

"Well, let me tell you, all that *stuff* don't never make no one happy. And I mean *really* happy. 'Cause bein' really happy comes from bein' satisfied in your soul. And nobody can be happy in his soul unless he has the Lord in there with him. Do you understand what I'm talkin' about?"

Joe almost didn't hear Noah's last sentence. He was trying to grasp the thing about the soul. "Uh, yeah, I think I do."

"Son, I reckon you've probably heard this before, but I'm gonna tell you again. Find a job you really love, and you'll never have to work another day of your life. Well, that's what I have right now. I ain't got a lot of needs. I've got my little house out back that's big enough for me. I have this station that fills the needs of the folks in town, and I've got my Lord watchin' my back every step of the way.

"There ain't nothin' I would rather do than work on cars. And as far as bein' stuck here on Christmas Eve, well, let me tell you, I ain't stuck. I am doin' the Lord's work.

"Why, what do you suppose would have happened to you two if I hadn't been open today? See what I mean? Doin' the Lord's work."

"Yeah, I guess so. But you're going to be all alone on Christmas Eve. Doesn't that bother you?"

"Son, I have never been alone in my entire life. Even back in those early days when I was roamin' around the country, trying to figure out who I was, I know the Lord was with me every step of the way. Who do you think gave me the gift of workin' on cars if it weren't the Lord? And who do you think gave me the gift of helpin' strangers if it weren't the Lord?

"And besides all that, as far as bein' alone tonight, well, that ain't gonna happen. There's a Christmas Eve service over at the church tonight, and I plan on bein' in the front row. Sittin' there with all my family."

It was almost 4:00 p.m. by the time Noah finished installing the fuel pump. It was already starting to get dark, and with the dark clouds and rain, it was even darker. Joe was anxious to get Maria and get on the road. He figured they could still make it to her folks' house before it got too late. He asked Noah how much he owed him, and Noah replied, "Son, these last few hours have been the highlight of my day so far. Let's just consider it my Christmas gift to you two. No, you go and get that wife of yours and get her up to her mama's place."

"Wow, I don't know what to say! Thanks, Noah. Thanks a lot. I really appreciate it. I guess I owe you one."

"Son, you don't owe me nothin'. A gift is a gift. That's all there is to it."

"Okay, thanks. Bye the way, what's the best way to get back to the highway?"

Noah gave Joe directions. "Turn right out of the lot, then right at the next corner." But Joe was thinking about getting Maria and getting on the road, and he didn't pay much attention to what Noah said. He hurried out back to the little house and quietly opened the door.

Maria was sleeping on the sofa, and as he looked at her lying there so peacefully, he reflected on what Noah had told him about happy in his soul. He knew they still had some problems to solve, but he was more certain now that things would work out.

"Babe, it's time to wake up. The car's fixed, and Noah didn't charge us a dime. Can you believe it?"

Maria opened her eyes and smiled up at Joe. But he could see in her eyes that she was still in pain. She pulled the quilt back and started to sit up. But as she placed her hand under herself to push up, she felt a sharp pain in her back.

"Oh!" she cried. "That hurts so much. Please help me, Joe."

Joe hurried over and took her hands and helped her to her feet. As she stood, he could see that it wasn't an easy thing to do.

"Are you going to be okay to drive the rest of the way to Bend?" he asked.

"Oh, sure," she said with little conviction. "I must have twisted wrong when I tried to get up. I think I'll be fine."

Joe picked up the umbrella, and they headed for the door. Maria walked slowly along the walkway to the back of the station. Once they got inside, Noah helped her over to a chair.

"Now, you gonna be all right, little lady?" he said.

"Oh, would you two quit worrying so much about me? I'll be fine. I'm pregnant, I have pains, I'll deal with it. Lets' just get going.

"Oh, by the way, Noah, Joe told me you aren't charging us for the repairs. Thank you so much. You are a dear, sweet man. We won't forget what you did for us. I hope you have a very merry Christmas."

"And a merry Christmas to you both. Now, get yourselves out there in that car and get up to your mama's place."

Joe opened the door for Maria, and she slowly and carefully eased into the front seat. He then hurried around to the driver's side and climbed in. As he was backing out of the garage, Noah was watching and waving goodbye.

Just about that time, the phone in the office started to ring, and Noah headed in to answer it. He didn't look back to see Joe take a left out of the lot.

Chapter 45

I was sitting in the great room, reading my Bible, when Elisabeth came strolling in, followed by Sarah. Those two girls seemed to be joined at the hip. I hardly ever saw them far from each other. And unlike most siblings, the girls hardly ever argued with each other. But they could sure stick up for each other if someone else got on their case.

I always got a smile on my face when they were around. *I sure do love those little girls. I'm sure the Lord knows that, because He hears me talking about them all the time in my prayers.*

"Gramps, why are the lights acting so funny?" Sarah asked.

"Well, little darlin', the electricity to the inn isn't working, so I had to fire up the emergency generator. I suppose we'll have to put up with dim lights for a while till the power comes back on. I'm going to call the power company today and see if they can check on it. I just hope it won't take too long."

Elisabeth looked at me with a worried look on her face and said, "I'm scared, Gramps. I could hear the rain all night, and I couldn't sleep. Are we going to have a flood like they did in the Bible?"

"No, little one, we're not going to have a flood. If you remember, after the flood in the Bible, God sent a rainbow and said He would never again destroy the people of the earth with a flood.

"But things could get a little messy around here. Seems like the Little Jordan is filling up pretty fast, and I'm not too sure that decrepit old bridge is going to hold up much longer. But don't you girls worry none. We're all going to be just fine right here.

"Why don't we go into the kitchen and see what Martha is rustling up for breakfast?"

That perked the girls up, and they jumped up and headed for the kitchen. I was following them in when Doc came strolling down the hall.

"Hey, Gabe, is everything okay with all the rain last night? I didn't think it ever rained that much around here. And by the way, where is all that snow you promised me when I called you last month? You know we always have snow. That's one of the reasons I like coming up here." He gave me a big smile when he said it.

I smiled back and said, "Don't know what to tell you, Doc. I reckon you'll have to take that up with the good Lord. Seems He's in charge of all that's goin' on around here. Anyhow, the last weather report I had said the rain might turn to snow by tomorrow."

"Okay," he said, "guess I can live with that. How's the bridge holding up? Have you been down to look at it this morning?"

"I was down there first thing this morning. Water is up almost to the bottom of the bridge, but so far it looks fairly good. Although, if all this rain has melted the snowpack up on top, then we could have the Little Jordan out of its banks by nightfall. Guess we'll just have to pray that that doesn't happen." I turned toward the kitchen, and Doc followed me to where the wonderful aroma of bacon, ham, and sausage was erupting.

"Gramps," Elisabeth said as she saw me come into the kitchen, "Aunt Martha said we are having pancakes this morning. But I told her you call them flapjacks. And she told me you're just a silly old man."

Martha's face turned about three shades of red as she looked at me and then quickly turned back to the stove. I tried my best to suppress a laugh, but Doc started to giggle, the girls started laughing, and I couldn't keep it in. Martha turned back toward me with a smile as wide as I had ever seen, and then she started laughing. Our funny bones had all been tickled, and we were all laughing out loud when Lydia came walking in.

"My goodness, what is so funny this morning?" she asked. "I could hear all of you way down the hall. You'd better be quieter. You might wake Ms. Leah, and then you know what would happen."

Suddenly, everyone stopped laughing, gave Lydia a "spoil sport" look, and then we all started laughing again. There was joy in our home, and no one was going to stop it today.

Ms. Leah came walking into the kitchen about that time, and it was clear she did not share in the mirth. "It's a good thing I was already awake when you all started your ruckus. The sound was enough to wake the dead." When she said it, she remembered what her plans were for tonight, and she had a great fear move through her.

"Is everything okay, Mr. Sinclair? I could hear the rain all night. Are we going to be secure here today?"

"Things are going to be fine," I replied, "but the power went out during the night. Maybe a tree fell on the lines or something. I started the emergency generator, so we have electricity. It's not quite as good, but it should work okay until we can get power restored. I'll call the power company today and see if they can get an emergency crew out.

"As you can see, the kitchen is working fine, and we should have a wonderful breakfast of bacon, ham, sausage, and 'flapjacks' in no time."

With that remark, the twins started laughing again, and we all joined in, all except Ms. Leah.

After breakfast, we all helped Martha clear the table and clean up the kitchen. Then we all worked our way into the great room—all except Ms. Leah—and sat around the fireplace. Lydia pulled out several copies of Christmas songs, and we all started singing and watching the flames of the fire dance to our music.

As we continued, I looked to each one and gave thanks for our little family gathered here. I was reminded of how we all came to be and the small miracles the Lord provided for us to make it all possible.

Suddenly, I felt a presence, a stirring of my spirit that I couldn't explain. I had this mixed feeling that something was going to happen tonight that was going to be out of our hands. I had no idea what it was, but I was as certain as I could be that whatever it was, it would be revealed to us in due time.

The singing continued for a while, and then everyone went about taking care of last-minute details for Christmas.

I continued to be worried about the bridge. I thought about calling the sheriff's office and asking them to put a "Road Closed" sign at the bottom of the hill just in case the bridge washed out. Instead, I called the power company's emergency number and got ahold of the dispatcher. He told me he was working with a skeleton crew because of Christmas and they were all already out on calls all over the county. He said he would get someone out to check our lines as soon as he could, but he couldn't promise anything before tomorrow.

I busied myself all day with bringing in wood for the fireplace, checking and filling the gas tank on the generator, and walking down to the bridge to see if it was still standing. The rain was not letting up, and the water level was brushing the bottom of the bridge by early afternoon.

Martha made a light lunch for all of us since we had such a big breakfast and we were planning a special meal this evening. We had all decided that because of all the rain and mud on the road, we would forego heading into town for the evening service. I just didn't feel like getting out, and someone would have to stay behind anyway to be here for Ms. Leah. So we all whiled away the hours of the day waiting for Christmas Eve.

Chapter 46

Joe was happy to have the car working again and was in fact anxious and somewhat excited about getting up to Bend. He was still very worried about Maria. Her backache seemed to be getting worse, and she was starting to breathe a little differently. He could tell she was in some distress, but she was trying to put up a good front.

As he pulled away from the station, he didn't even realize he was headed back the same way he came in. Noah had told him to go right, but he hadn't been paying attention. Besides, it was already dark, and he didn't recognize his mistake. But he did remember Noah had told him to take the first right after leaving the station. Just a block away, he came to an intersection. He didn't see any signs directing him to the highway, but he didn't give it a second thought. *Take the first right and it'll take you right back to the highway.* That was what his memory told him, and that was what he did.

Maria looked around after they turned and said, "Are you sure this is the way we're supposed to go?"

"I think so. Noah told me to take a right at the first corner, and that's what I did. Don't worry, we'll get there."

The road didn't look like it was well traveled, and Joe started questioning himself about his decision. About that time, Maria let out a little yelp of pain and reached over and grabbed Joe's arm.

"Honey, I really don't feel good. I don't know if I can make it all the way to Bend. Maybe we should go back and see if there is a motel in the town. I could call Mom again and let her know we will be there first thing in the morning."

Just as she was saying that, Joe saw a faded sign indicating, "Shepherd's Inn, one-half mile ahead."

"Look, maybe this place has a room. I'm already heading in that direction, and it doesn't look like there is any place to turn around. Let's go check it out."

"Okay," Maria said, "just find me a place to lie down."

The road got even narrower the farther they went, and it changed from blacktop to gravel. The rain was still coming down in sheets, and he was having trouble seeing where he was going. Then he saw what looked like a small bridge ahead, and beyond that he could see lights coming from a large building. *Thank goodness,* he thought.,

The bridge was just one lane, but it looked okay, so Joe slowly drove across and headed toward the lights. As he got across the bridge, he heard a loud noise, but with the rain coming down so hard, he couldn't be sure what it was, and it was so dark he couldn't see behind him. He didn't think it had anything to do with the car, so he kept driving.

When he pulled up in the parking area of Shepherd's Inn, Joe parked as close to the front door as he could. There were only a couple of other cars in the lot, so that was not a problem. The lights looked so warm and inviting coming from inside the inn, and Joe hurried out of the car and around to open Maria's door. He helped her out as she was still in lots of pain, and just getting out of the car was a major undertaking for her. The fact that the rain was getting them soaked at the same time didn't help her or her disposition.

After finally getting her out of the car, he helped her as best as he could to get her up the stairs and under cover of the front porch. The sign on the front door proclaimed, "Welcome to Shepherd's Inn."

Chapter 47

I had called the sheriff's office a little after three and asked Sheriff Claybaugh if she could put a "Road Closed" sign at the turnoff for the inn. I had been watching the Little Jordan slowly rise all afternoon, and now the water was starting to wash over the bridge. I didn't have a lot of confidence that the bridge would hold up if someone tried to cross. Of course, we weren't expecting any guests tonight, but I didn't want to take any chances that someone would drive up. The sheriff wasn't in the office, and the dispatcher said there had been a bad accident out on the highway at the New Bethlehem turnoff and the sheriff and a deputy were busy right now. She said she would pass along the message and they would get a sign up as soon as they could.

When Sheriff Belinda Claybaugh finally got back to the office and retrieved the message, she went in the back room and got a "Road Closed" sign and a sandbag to hold it down. As she was putting the sign in the trunk of her car, Joe and Maria were turning right onto Shepherd's Inn road.

I had gone down to the creek about four thirty to check the water level again and walked downstream a way to check and make sure a tree or something else wasn't blocking the water flow. As it was, everything was clear, and this was just the highest level I had ever seen the Little Jordan in all my years at the inn. Guess you could call it the storm of the century. I was about a hundred yards downstream when I saw the lights of a car coming up the road toward the bridge. My heart leaped into my throat. "Oh, Lord," I prayed, "please keep those folks safe if they try to cross the bridge." I started hurrying back upstream, but the ground was littered with branches and rocks and I had trouble running without falling down.

I helplessly watched as the car slowly crossed the bridge, pushing water that was covering it. I realized I was holding my breath as the car slowly made its way across. As soon as all four tires were back on solid ground, I started to breathe a sigh of relief when, all of a sudden, the entire bridge just folded itself together and collapsed into the creek. The driver of the car didn't appear to notice as he headed on up to the inn. I slowed a little and walked on up to where the bridge had been. All that was left were the concrete supports on either side.

"Lord, thank You for protecting those folks. I have no idea who they are, but You know, Lord, and You kept them safe." I then started walking back up to the main house.

The phone rang inside the inn, and Lydia hurried in to pick it up. She couldn't imagine who could be calling on a night like this, but she was always prompt in picking up the phone. She considered it part of her duties to not keep anyone waiting. "Hello, Shepherd's Inn, Merry Christmas, this is Lydia. Oh, hi, Sheriff, how are things down in New Bethlehem? Isn't this rain something else? The roads up here are getting really muddy. Hope nobody else tries to come up here tonight. We don't have any reservations anyway. What's that? You're going to put up a 'Road Closed' sign at the bottom of the hill? Gabe thinks the bridge might wash out? Oh, I hope not. That rickety old bridge might not be the best, but it's the only way we have of getting out of here." Just then, there was a bright flash and a loud clap of thunder. "Hello, Sheriff, are you still there? Hello, hello? That lightning strike must have knocked out the phone. Oh, well, I'm sure they'll get it fixed as soon as this rain lets up." That was Lydia. Always upbeat, even when things weren't going well.

Just as Lydia was hanging up the phone, the door opened and in walked Joe and Maria, looking like a couple of drowned rats. Lydia looked at them with a surprised look on her face. "Hi, there! Where on earth did you two come from? You shouldn't be out on a night like this."

Joe started to speak. "We made a wrong turn and got lost—"

Maria quickly cut him off. "It's a lot more than that! We were on our way to my parents' house for Christmas, and we had car trouble down in New Bethlehem. We finally got the car working okay, thanks to that nice old man at the gas station, and then Mr. I-Know-Where-I'm-Going got us lost." She gave Joe a glaring look as she spoke. "We saw the sign at the bottom of the hill pointing to Shepherd's Inn, so we thought you might have a room for the night. I'm not feeling well, and my back is hurting really bad. Do you have any vacancies?"

Lydia gave them that look, knowing she was going to have to give them some really bad news. "Oh, my, we don't have any rooms right now. We closed most of them off and hauled away all the beds 'cause we're going to remodel for next summer. Maybe you could just drive on back down to the bottom of the hill, take a right, and you'll be back in town in no time. I'm sure there would be a couple of vacancies there."

I was walking in the door just as Lydia was making that last statement. "You two ain't goin' nowhere tonight. I was just down by the creek, checking on the water level, when I saw your car come across the bridge. Why, you two no more than got your rear tires off that bridge when the whole dang thing just washed away. Figured you didn't even hear the commotion 'cause it was rainin' so hard." I gave them both a once-over look and noticed that the woman looked like she was about due any moment. "What in tarnation are you two doin' out on a night like this? And you, young lady, in your condition." I then looked at him in a fatherly way and continued, "And you, young man, you ought to be ashamed of yourself for bringin' her out on a night like this, it bein' Christmas Eve and all. What in heaven's name were you thinkin'?"

Lydia finally cut me off and tried to smooth things over a little. "Now, Gabe, don't be so hard on this lovely couple. They just got a little lost and wound up here. Isn't it a blessing that they made it across the bridge? The Lord was looking out for them, that's for sure. But what are we going to do about getting them a place to stay tonight?" She paused a moment and then turned to Joe and Maria. "By the way, I'm Lydia, and this is Gabe. And what are your names?"

"We're Joe and Maria Alexander," Joe said, then rubbed Maria's belly and continued, "and this is our little Dexter."

I jumped right back into the conversation. "Well, it's a real pleasure meeting you two. I guess I should say *three*. Now let's see about getting you a place to stay tonight." I turned to Lydia, "There's that cabin out back that we've been using for storage. There's a bed in there, and we could get Martha to put some clean sheets on it and get the bathroom cleaned up for them. That shouldn't take long."

I then looked back at Joe and Maria. Maria looked like she was about to pass out. "Why don't you two come on over here and sit down? Little miss, you look like you need to give that young'un you're carrying a little rest."

Joe and Maria headed toward the sofa, and Maria said, "Oh, thank you so much. I really am tired. And I need to call my mom and tell her where we are. I'm sure she is really worried." Maria reached in her purse and pulled out a cell phone.

"That cell phone ain't gonna do you a bit of good up here. We don't get any cell service at all. That's why some folks who come here to stay like it so much. They aren't bothered by the dang things," I said. "You're welcome to use our phone if you want."

Lydia then jumped back into the conversation. "Sorry, hon, but our phone line's out. Must have gone down with the bridge. I was just on the phone with the sheriff when the line went dead. Oh, by the way, Gabe, Belinda said she's going to put up a 'Road Closed' sign at the bottom of the hill. Hopefully, no one else will try to come up tonight."

By this time, poor little Maria was fit to be tied. I could see she was about three shakes from having a nervous breakdown. And clueless Joe was just sitting there, looking like a lost puppy.

"What are we going to do?" Maria exclaimed. She was looking at Joe like she expected him to fix things and fix them *now*!

Mild-mannered Lydia was still busy trying to calm everyone down, including herself. "Now, don't you worry about a thing. We'll get that room fixed up real soon, and then you two can just get a good night's sleep. We'll let tomorrow worry about itself. Gabe, will you go ask Martha to get the cabin ready?"

"Oh, sure," I said. "You want me to be the one gettin' my head bit off. I swear that woman can worry herself half to death thinking she is the only one doing any work around here."

I was just starting to head for the kitchen when Martha walked in the room, speaking to no one in particular, and not paying any attention to anyone in the room.

"Well, I finally got all that mess cleaned up in the laundry room, so I better get in the kitchen and finish up getting supper ready to go." She finally looked up and saw Joe and Maria. "What are you two doing here?" Then she turned to Lydia and continued, "I didn't know we were having more guests tonight. Where are they going to stay?"

Lydia took the burden away from me and said, "It's okay, Martha, they will be staying in the storage cabin. All you need to do is put clean sheets on the bed and clean the bathroom. Shouldn't take any time at all."

Martha was now starting to get wound up. "Easy for you to say! All you do is stand here at the counter, acting all sweet when people come in. Look at all the stuff I have to do to get things ready for them. And what are we going to do about feeding them? I didn't plan on having two more mouths to feed tonight. And supper's going to be late now 'cause I have to get that room cleaned up." Then she started walking away toward to storage room and speaking to no one in particular again. "But that's okay. You folks just sit there and take it easy while good old Martha takes care of everything. Oh, yes, we can always depend on good old Martha!" And she was gone.

Lydia just stood there for a moment, looking at the blank space that had moments before been Martha. She gave serious thought to busting out with a good cry, but she thought of everyone else in the room and decided to just suck it up. But deep down inside the wound would not heal quickly. As much as she loved Martha, she couldn't understand sometimes why she could say such hurtful things. *But enough of that,* she thought. *Time to get on with the business at hand.*

Lydia turned back to Joe and Maria. "Sorry about that. Martha really does have a good heart. I think sometimes she just tries too hard to make sure everything is exactly right. I'm sure she'll be fine by suppertime. And don't you worry about that either. I know there'll be plenty of food to go around. There always is."

Chapter 48

While all this was going on in the great room, Leah had been lying in bed in her room, reading through some literature she had brought with her from Oakland. She was reading an article about one of her ex-husband's many companies, of which he was the board chairman. Her thoughts wandered back to a time not that many years ago when she lived right in the middle of that life. *Funny,* she thought, *how so important I felt being married to such an influential person as Philip Gardiner. What kind of a person must I have been to believe I was enjoying myself? And knowing he was fooling around all that time, especially with my sister! Oh, how I hate them both for what they have done. Oh, how I hate how my life has turned out.*

As she was running all those thoughts through her mind, she became distracted by the flickering of the table lamp next to her bed. She was thinking how, before, she would never have even considered staying in such a remote, run-down dump like this. She supposed the term *rustic charm* would be the description a real estate person would put on the inn. But *run-down dump* was more to her liking.

Finally, she got out of bed and headed down the hall to inquire as to what could be done about the poor lighting conditions. This was just not acceptable.

Leah walked into the great room and observed Lydia, Joe and Maria, and me. Then she zeroed in on me.

"Could you please explain to me why the lights in my room keep going up and down? I'm trying to read, and it's just impossible to concentrate with all that flickering."

"Sorry, Ms. Leah," I said, "but remember, I told you we are using the generator now 'cause all the power lines are down. We'll just have to make do with what we have."

I don't think that was the answer she was looking for. "Well, I didn't come all the way up here to have to live like a Neanderthal! I expect you to do something very soon. In the meantime, I will be taking my evening meal in my room. And I would appreciate it if *you people* could keep the noise down out here. I can't concentrate with all this commotion going on." And then she went back to her room.

As she entered the hallway, Doc was just arriving from his room. Leah almost ran into him as they passed, and she mumbled something about rude people.

Doc walked into the room, looking straight at me, and said, "Who put a burr under her saddle?" Then he noticed Joe and a very pregnant Maria standing next to Lydia and continued, "Well, hello, folks. What brings you up to Shepherd's Inn on Christmas Eve?"

Joe started to open his mouth to reply when Maria cut him off. "We took a wrong turn in town and wound up here thanks to my geographically challenged husband! Now, because the bridge washed out, we can't get back down the hill."

"The bridge washed out?" Doc said very excitedly. "How long will it take to fix it? I need to get back home by the end of the week."

"Can't be too sure," I said. "Just depends on how long this confound rain keeps up. But the last weather report I got earlier today said the rain might turn to snow sometime tonight or tomorrow. You may get that white Christmas, after all."

Doc said, "Okay, guess I'll have to live with that." Then he turned to Joe and Maria. "So why were you two out on Christmas Eve, anyway?"

Maria started talking first. "We *were* going to my parents' house for Christmas."

Joe jumped in with a short burst. "We *always* go to her parents' house for Christmas." (Even though this would be their first.)

Back to Maria. "As I was saying, we were going to my parents' house when we had car trouble. Mr. Wonderful here had a loser friend of his work on our car in Klamath Falls yesterday, and he just messed it up. Lucky for us that nice man at the Chevron station in New Bethlehem was able to get it fixed, but it took several hours. By the time he got finished, it was dark, and the rain was pouring down, and Mr. Navigator here took a wrong turn. We were afraid to turn around 'cause the road was really narrow and there was no place to do it without getting off the road. It looked way too muddy to do that. Then we saw the sign to this place and thought you might have a vacancy."

"So when did the bridge wash out?" Doc asked.

I jumped in then. "Not two seconds after them two got across. Seemed like the Lord was just holdin' it up long enough for them to make it across, and then He said, 'Let 'er rip!'"

"Well, praise God you got here safe. Don't you worry now. These folks will take really good care of you."

As Joe was taking all this in, he finally realized we had been saying Doc. He turned to Doc and said, "Did I hear them call you Doc? Are you a regular doctor?"

"Oh, heck no. Allow me to introduce myself. I am Lucas Meriweather, doctor of veterinary medicine. Why do you ask?"

"Maria's been having a lot of back pain, and I thought you might be able to give her something for it."

"Sorry to disappoint you," Doc replied. Then he turned to Maria, "But I know you probably shouldn't be taking much of any kind of medication with that baby coming and all. How far along are you?"

"Eight months," she replied as she rubbed her hand across her belly and then on her back. "I think I'm just tired from riding in the car so long. I'll get a good night's sleep and should be fine in the morning. Joe just worries too much."

Joe started talking to Maria as if there were no one else in the room. "Maria, you know that's not true. You've had that backache for the last several days. And you took a long nap while Noah was working on the car, and we had just been driving for a few minutes when we got here. There is something wrong, and I know it. I wish we had just stayed at home and taken you to the doctor."

Lydia had been over at the check-in desk, getting a registration form ready, and realized that things seemed to be getting out of control very quickly. Lydia hated confrontation and arguments about as much as anyone, so she thought this would be a good time to jump in and defuse the situation. "Okay, all I need for you to do now is fill out this registration, and by that time, Martha should have your room ready."

Maria just glared at Joe as he walked over and started working on the paperwork.

Martha came back into the room just about the time Joe finished with the paperwork. She looked like she was still carrying the weight of the world on her shoulders. "Well, I got that room ready, such as it is. I started a fire in the fireplace to take a little of the chill off. If you need anything else, you'll just have to wait. I have to go get supper ready."

She was heading for the kitchen when Lydia said, "By the way, Martha, Ms. Leah came in a while ago and said she would be taking her evening meal in her room."

I do believe I could see steam rising from Martha's head. She stopped, turned to Lydia, and said, "Well, isn't that just a fine 'How do you do?' Who does she think she is, queen of the Nile?"

"Now, Martha, watch your temper. You know how your blood pressure goes up when you get all excited," Lydia replied.

Martha just glared at her and said, "Whatever!" as she headed for the kitchen.

Lydia was back in control. Since Joe had finished filling out the registration form, Lydia quickly looked it over and said, "Okay, that should do it. Let's get you two into that room."

Maria was still sitting on the sofa, and before she got up, she said, "Joe, will you go out and get the suitcase out of the car? I need it before I go to bed."

"Don't you worry about that," I said. "I'll go get it for you. No sense in you getting all wet again. You could catch your death. Just give me your keys and I'll be right back."

"Thanks a lot," Joe said as he handed me the car keys. "I'll help Maria get to the room."

Joe, Lydia, and Maria headed for the room, and I grabbed my raincoat and headed out front. Doc headed for one of the easy chairs by the fireplace, and I said, "I'll be right back."

When I got outside, the rain was still coming down in buckets. I could hear the water roaring down the creek and wondered just how long we would be stranded up here before we could get out. I thought about how we had relied so much on that bridge to get us in and out of here and never even considered having an alternate route out in case of emergency. I stood there on the porch for a few seconds before going to the car. "Lord, we have a lot on our plate now with all that's going on here. Please, Lord, take care of that young lady in there, along with her little baby. And, Lord, we could sure use some help figuring a way out of here soon. And, Lord, forgive me for not doing enough to keep everyone safe up here."

After I got the suitcase deposited in our new guests' room, I came back in and sat down in a chair beside Doc. We hadn't had much of a chance to talk since he got here, and now seemed like a good time. But before I could say anything, Doc put down the copy of Field & Stream he had been reading and looked me right in the eye.

Chapter 49

"Gabe, you know how much I like coming up here for Christmas. But after all these years, Christmas is still hard for me. When my wife and son were killed by that drunk driver on Christmas Eve, well, it just ripped a big hole in my heart. For the longest time, I carried a lot of hate for that guy. I couldn't understand how God could take my family from me and let that thief live. Yeah, I call him a thief 'cause look what he stole from me.

"Even though I questioned God, I know that if I hadn't known Him back then, I probably wouldn't have made it. That entire first year, I was walking around like I was in a fog. I couldn't concentrate on my work, and I almost lost my clinic. My customers were noticing how I wasn't taking care of things like I should have. My employees were about ready to quit, and I didn't even really care. If it hadn't been for my friends getting me to come up here, I can't even imagine what would have happened.

"I remember that first time I came here, how you took me under your wing. It seemed like you knew what I was going through even though I hadn't even told you about it. And then to find out that you had lost your wife a few months earlier to cancer, I couldn't figure out how you could be so understanding after all you had gone through.

"I sure wish I had had a chance to meet Hannah. From what I have been told, she was an absolute saint. I know you probably still miss her."

"Yep," I said. I was surprised and happy that Doc was opening up like this to me. For the first couple of years he was coming up here, he was pretty closed up about his family. I could tell he was carrying around a load that was way too heavy for just one man. As a matter of fact, it seemed like his attitude got a little better about the time he came up here after Lydia started working here. I don't know. Just a thought.

"I do miss Hannah a whole bunch. But you know, we had such a good life up here for so long. Do you realize I've been caretaker here for over thirty-two years? And Hannah working right beside me as housekeeper right up until the time she took sick. I tell you, it was downright honorable how the owners, Scott and Cory, hired someone to take care of Hannah right up until the day she died. It's been five years last August. Yep, I miss her too. That's for sure."

"What's the story on Ms. Leah?" Doc said. "She seems to think she is so much better than the rest of us."

"Now, don't be too hard on that woman," I said. "Story is, she's been carryin' a heavy burden for quite a while now. Seems she has a younger sister who is quite the looker. Ms. Leah's husband kinda strayed from his marriage vows, and he and Ms. Leah's sister are now gallivanting around Europe someplace. He has lots of money, so while she was still married to him, Ms. Leah lived high on the hog. She got some of his money when he left her, but not enough to live the way she used to."

Doc was showing some real, Spirit-filled concern for Leah. "That's too bad. I sure hope she can find peace someday soon. I know we can all use some of that."

"Yeah," I answered. "I think since she has been coming here, even though she acts like she doesn't want to have anything to do with any of us, she is starting to get a little better at joining in. But this year I don't know what happened. She hasn't been herself. Stays in her room most all the time and even wants her food brought in to her. I tell you, something is going on with that woman, and I just can't put my finger on it yet."

About that time, Lydia came walking back in from getting Joe and Maria settled. I said, "Did you get them taken care of? Is the room going to be okay for them? I know it wasn't in the best of condition the last time I looked."

"Oh, they're going to be fine. Gabe, you wouldn't believe what Martha did. You know how grumpy she was when she went to get the room ready? Well, she not only put clean sheets on the bed, she also moved a lot of stored stuff over into the corner and put some blankets on it, so it was hidden. Then she swept and mopped the floor and cleaned up the bathroom really well. She got a good fire going in the stove and brought in some extra wood. She also turned on a little lamp by the bed, turned back the covers, and put some Hershey's Kisses on the pillows. Now, wasn't that just the sweetest thing?"

"She has a heart of gold," I said. "She just doesn't always let it shine. I wouldn't take a thing for her. She is one of the best things that's happened here since Hannah went to be with the Lord."

"I'm going to the kitchen and see how Martha's doing with supper," Lydia said. "I know she could use some help, but I bet she won't let me. What do you think?"

I couldn't help but laugh at that when I said, "You got that right!"

Just about that time, Elisabeth and Sarah came into the room and walked over to Doc and me. Elisabeth started in, "Gramps, why is Ms. Leah so mean?"

"Now, hon, Ms. Leah isn't really mean. She just gets a little cranky at times. Did something happen?"

"Well, we just passed her in the hall, and we wished her a Merry Christmas, and she told me there was no such thing as Christmas. She said we were stupid to believe in Jesus." Both girls started tearing up a little, and Elisabeth continued, "I know she's wrong, Gramps, but why did she have to say that to us? We were just trying to be friendly like Mom told us Jesus wants us to be."

My heart was breaking for these little girls. They were the sweetest things around Shepherd's Inn, and I was getting pretty upset myself with Leah's antics. "Oh, Elisabeth, Sarah, I'm sorry she made you feel so bad. But like I said, she just gets cranky at times. She's had some stuff happen in her life, and sometimes it gets to be a little too much for her. Remember, God wants us to forgive people when they do things that hurt us. That's what the Bible says, right?"

Sarah answered that one. "Uh-huh. We learned that in Sunday school. But she was still wrong, wasn't she?"

I said, "Yes, darlin', she was wrong. So maybe we should say a little prayer for her tonight before we go to bed. What do you say?"

"Okay, Gramps." And suddenly, both girls were their usual selves. They gave me and Doc a great big hug, and in unison they shouted, "Merry Christmas."

Martha walked in from the kitchen, caught the twins as they were about to run down the hall, and said, "You two go wash up for supper." Then she turned to Doc and me and said, "That goes for you two also. This might not be the best

Christmas Eve dinner I have ever prepared, but I have a feeling it is going to be one we won't soon forget.

"Gabe, will you go and tell that young couple they can come have supper with us? That is, if she is feeling up to it. If she wants, I can fix her up a plate and her husband can take it in to her."

"Sure thing, Martha. I'll get right to it. Is Ms. Leah all taken care of?"

"Oh, yes, such as it is. When I took her food to her, she said she wasn't hungry after all and asked me if she could just have a glass of ice tea. I swear, Gabe, that woman is either working for the Lord and testing us or she's working for the devil to push us over the edge."

"Martha, sometimes we just have to do everything on faith and let everything sort itself out. I have a hunch you're right, though, about tonight's meal being one we won't soon forget."

Doc then said, "I'll go check on the couple, Gabe. Maybe I can tell how she is feeling by talking to her. I usually don't get a reply when I talk with my patients. This will be a little different. But I have a feeling she may be a little farther along than she thinks. Or perhaps that child she is carrying is a little more anxious to come into this world than she thinks. I just hope he waits long enough to get the bridge fixed."

"Yeah," I said. "There's a lot riding on getting the bridge fixed so we can get them out of here and up to her folks. I imagine they are probably getting pretty worried about now. I sure wish we had some way of getting in touch with them."

A few minutes later, we were all starting to gather around the table. Martha had fixed a little plate for Maria. She had said she wasn't very hungry. Joe took it to her and then came back in to join us at the table.

When we were all seated, we joined hands, and Doc asked if he could say grace tonight. I could tell he was carrying a big load on his heart tonight, and the Lord was working overtime to give him all the help he needed to deal with his personal problems as well as everyone at the inn.

I sat at my usual place to the right of Martha, who always sat at the head of the table. I might be the caretaker here, but Martha was the head of the cooking department and wanted to be able to see everyone at the table while we ate. She said she could tell by looking at all the faces if her meal was a hit or a strikeout. She actually used that term because she was such a baseball fan. Well, I guess, to state it correctly, she was a Yankees fan. She said she had been as long as she could remember. Her daddy was a fan, and so was her late husband, Cal.

While Doc asked a blessing over the food and the night, as I held Martha's hand, I could feel a warmth and tenderness I had never noticed before. I could feel God's presence in the room, and a quiet, relaxed feeling came over me and, I believe, everyone at the table.

With the "Amen" completed, we all started to dig in. Conversation resumed, and the talk was all about Christmas. The twins were excited about opening gifts in the morning as well as the one gift we all get to open on Christmas Eve. Joe seemed to adjust to all of us quickly and talked some about him and Maria and starting a family. He was obviously still concerned about her health, but he seemed to loosen up a little, and we all became good friends almost immediately.

When we were finished with supper, everyone pitched in and carried their dishes into the kitchen, except for Joe, who wanted to get back to see how Maria was doing. We could tell he was really worried about her and the baby.

Doc asked Martha, "Would you like me to help you with the dishes tonight?"

"Oh, land's sakes, no. I have a system, and it won't take long at all for me to finish. But thank you for asking. Now you go on and get yourself back out there and visit with Gabe. I know you two still have a lot of catching up to do."

"Okay," he said, "if you say so. I really do appreciate all you do around here." With that, Doc went back out and sat next to me on the sofa.

Lydia was busy wrapping a couple of small gifts she always kept in reserve for occasions like this when unexpected company arrived on Christmas Eve. The twins wanted to help, but she told them, "You girls go on in and brush your teeth and get your pj's on. When you get ready, then you can come on out, we can open our Christmas Eve gifts, and then we can sing some carols. How does that sound?"

"Okay, Mommy," Sarah said. And off they went, bouncing away like a couple of little fawns running through the woods.

Since Joe and Maria were in their cabin and it was just the three of us in the room, everything seemed to get eerily quiet. The fireplace was crackling just a little, and the sound of the rain on the roof was down to just a hush of noise. We hadn't heard a sound out of Leah, and we were all just sitting there at peace, enjoying the moment. Little did we know how short that peace would last.

I was just starting to reach for my Bible when Joe came rushing into the room like he was scared out of his mind.

"Doc, Doc, you've gotta come quick. Something's really wrong with Maria. Her back pain got a lot worse, and now she tells me she thinks she is going into labor. That can't be right, 'cause her doctor told her last week she would go full term. Doc, you gotta do something!"

Doc stood there for a second like he had been punched in the stomach. "Hey, I told you, I'm a vet. I deliver dogs and cats, not people!"

Joe wasn't giving up. "But, Doc, you gotta do something. She's hurting real bad, and I'm scared for her and the baby!"

I said, "Now, just you settle down a little, son. Doc and I will come on back and see what's going on, and I'm sure we can figure out something."

Joe's panic wasn't getting consoled. "Well, hurry. You have to do something!"

Martha came in from the kitchen and said, "What's going on in here? Sounds like somebody's getting beat up or something."

I knew this news would put Martha completely over the edge, but I couldn't see any way to avoid it. "We think our little mama-to-be out there is about to make a Christmas delivery." And then I didn't have to wait long to watch as the chaos began.

"Oh, my Lord! Oh, my Lord! Gabe, you have to do something! Doc, you have to do something! What are we going to do?"

I actually thought for a moment that Martha was going to add one more casualty for the evening as she wobbled, weaved, and leaned against a chair. Finally, she regained some composure and got a little color back into her face as Doc and I started heading for the "delivery room," following a screaming lunatic also known as Joe Alexander.

"Hurry, Doc! I think she's going to die! Should somebody boil some water? Can we call in a chopper to take her to the hospital?"

If things had not been so serious, I would have been laughing my head off at this poor young man in front of us who didn't have a clue what to do for his wife. As for me, I had all the confidence in the world with Doc's ability to handle the situation.

As Joe, Doc, and I were heading out the back, the twins came running in like they were being chased by a bear. "Mama, Mama, what's happening?" Sarah and Elisabeth chimed in unison. "Why is everybody yelling?" Elisabeth added.

"It's okay, girls. Everything is fine. It's just that Mr. Alexander's wife might be having her baby tonight. But don't worry, girls. Your uncle Doc is going to take care of everything." As soon as she said it, Lydia realized how confident she felt that Luke was in charge. *Luke,* she thought to herself. *I thought of him as Luke, not Doc.* With everything that was going on and everything she should be doing to help, all she could think about was Luke. Suddenly, she became angry with herself for being so selfish. But she still couldn't shake the strong feelings she was having for Luke Meriweather.

Chapter 51

Ms. Leah had been lying on her bed, reading over her suicide note, wondering if she should make any additional comments. She had wanted it to be perfect, so there could be no misunderstanding of her intentions. Her bottle of pills was sitting on her night table, along with a glass of water to wash them down. As soon as she was finished with the note, she was going to take the pills and slowly drift away to oblivion. All her second thoughts had been carefully and meticulously sorted out, and her mind was made up. Nothing could stop her now.

Suddenly, she was shaken from her composure by the sound of shouting coming down the hall. *What on earth?* she thought as she got up and put on her silk robe, tied a perfect bow slightly off-center, and slipped her feet into the pink terry house slippers she kept by the side of her bed.

As she opened the door to her room, she could hear the voices much louder now, and it was obvious to her that something serious was going on in the main room of the inn. Hurriedly she walked down the hall toward the sounds, not because she wanted to find out what the commotion was about, but to voice her displeasure at being disturbed. She thought, briefly, about how selfish that might seem but quickly justified her thoughts because she was Leah

Gardiner. And that was all that mattered. "Would someone please explain to me why everyone is making so much noise and disturbing my rest?"

Martha was first to comment on Leah's remark, since she had regained her composure and was now looking at the fact that she was in charge of the inn since Gabe was predisposed in the "delivery room." "It looks like we may be having a special delivery for Christmas, Leah. Our newest houseguest is going into labor."

"Oh, for goodness' sake," Leah responded. "What a very inopportune time for this to occur."

Martha had finally reached her limit with the arrogant, self-serving attitude of Leah Gardiner. "It is not inopportune! It is a perfect time for a baby to be born. And now we have to take charge and make sure everything is taken care of. Leah, I want you to take care of the twins. You are to take them to their room, get them into bed, and read stories to them until they fall asleep.

"Lydia, I want you to get out there and see what Doc and Gabe need and give Doc a hand with any help you can provide. You've been through this before, so you would know more of what Maria is going through.

"Girls, I want you to go with Ms. Leah and don't give her any static. Do what she says and no sass, do you hear me?"

"Yes, ma'am, Aunt Martha. We will," Sarah replied. She looked at her sister as if to say, "We better do what she says, because we've never seen her like this before."

Leah was still standing there with her mouth half-open, as if she was preparing to say something, when Martha looked her way again and said, "Well, don't just stand there. Get going and do what I told you to do!"

Leah could not recall the last time she was treated with such little respect. She was about to come back with an appropriate response, but something inside her said, "Keep your mouth shut and do what she said." "Come on, girls. You heard what she said. Let's go get you ready for bed." And off this unlikely trio went, marching down the hall, twins hand in hand and Leah following behind, not having a clue what to do with these little creatures.

Chapter 52

The fire in the stove had burned down, and there was a slight chill in the room. But Maria was perspiring heavily, and her breaths were coming in short gasps. It was obvious to Doc and me that she was for sure going to give birth tonight, no matter how far along she was or what her husband thought.

Joe had gone straight to her side and was holding her left hand in both of his. "Babe, I got Doc to come help, okay? Everything is going to be fine now. Where do you hurt? Can I get you something?"

About that time, another contraction gripped Maria's body, and she let out a loud wail and gripped Joe's hand so hard he almost yelped in pain.

Doc quickly assessed the situation and determined this was not going to be a normal delivery. But with no medical instruments and no experience with child delivery, he knew he was going to have to rely on the Great Physician to see him through. He quickly said a small, quiet prayer and started talking with Maria.

Lydia had come into the room and was assessing what she could do to help. Part of her mind was on her two little girls in the hands of Leah, and another part of her was selfishly hoping she didn't do anything to embarrass herself in front of Doc. *Get your mind on the situation at hand,* she thought. *This girl needs your help.*

Doc started talking with Maria and asked her and Joe how far apart the contractions were. He was certain it was only a matter of minutes before this baby was going to arrive, regardless of what he or anyone else did. Maria was in too much distress to even answer, but Joe said he thought they were only a minute or so apart, which confirmed Doc's assessment of the situation. *Think!* he thought to himself. *What do I need to look for first?* He quickly ran his hands over Maria's belly, and fear crept up his spine and caused him to start sweating. "Breech!" he said out loud. "This baby is breech. Maria, I'm going to try something that might be more painful, but I want you to trust me. I'm going to try to turn this little guy around before he arrives. He will be so much happier to come out headfirst, and so will you."

I could see the fear in Maria's and Joe's eyes, but they both nodded, and Joe held Maria's hand a little tighter. He then did something that really surprised me. He bent closer to Maria and started to whisper in her ear. I couldn't hear what he was saying, but I could tell that whatever he was saying, it was making a profound difference in Maria. She appeared to be calmer, and the fear in her eyes, which I had seen only a couple of minutes before, was almost gone.

Joe continued to whisper to Maria and stroke her forehead as Doc continued to try to manipulate the baby to a head-down position. After several minutes of this effort, it was clear to Doc that it wasn't working.

Maria's contractions were now almost on top of one another. Lydia had brought over a bowl of water and a washcloth, and Joe was gently wiping Maria's brow. Doc was still trying his best to turn that little guy before he made his debut,

but everything he had tried was unsuccessful. If he had had more time, perhaps he would have been successful, but this baby was on his way, and there was nothing to do but pray.

Chapter 53

Leah ushered the twins into their room and stood by their door as they got themselves ready for bed. She had no idea what she was going to do, but she could still hear the sound of Martha's voice barking at her like a drill sergeant.

Sarah and Elisabeth were incredibly quiet as they got ready for bed. They had, on too many occasions, suffered the wrath of Ms. Leah for no reason except for being little girls. Finally, after they were all ready, Elisabeth finally reached over and picked up a book of children's poems and asked Leah if she could read it to them.

Leah slowly moved from her position by the door to a chair beside their bunk beds. As she took the book, she looked at the girls and, for a moment, envied Lydia. Having never had children, Leah often wondered what it would be like to have a child of her own. Of course, her career, her position, and her schedule would not have allowed for her to take time out from being the good wife for Philip to take care of a child. Regardless, for just a moment she wondered what it would have been like.

She opened the book, and the first poem she came to was titled "Little Gray Donkey." As she started reading, it amazed her how simple it was and yet the girls seemed to enjoy it, and they were even reciting along with her reading.

The little gray donkey Joseph led was tired as he could be.
But Mary was riding on his back, so he walked most carefully.
At last they came to Bethlehem, but the inn would spare no bed.
Their only shelter from the cold was lowly cattle shed.
The little gray donkey wearily lay down beside the sheep.
Stretched out on his four small aching legs and soon was fast asleep.
That night he dreamed that angel songs had echoed down the air,
And he woke to see the baby Christ and shepherds kneeling there.
Reverently, he went to look, and great was his reward.
For carrying Mary safe, he shared the birthday of our Lord!

As she continued reading, Leah grew a little impatient. Her plans for the evening had been rudely interrupted, but she took comfort in the thought that these two little pests would soon be asleep and she could continue with her plan. Regardless of what happened in the cabin out back, she would continue with her plan.

After several more poems and many irritating questions from the girls, they had finally exhausted themselves and fallen asleep. As she left their room and headed for hers, she heard the faint cry of pain coming from the room out back. Curious as to how things were going, she decided to go see for herself.

When she reached the door, she could hear the painful moans of Maria and the sounds of conversation from everyone else in the room.

I'll just slip inside and tell their mother that the girls are asleep. Then head back to my room. I'm sure they don't need me in there. I wouldn't know what to do, she thought.

Just as she opened the door, Maria let out a loud and painful scream, and as she looked down, she could see two very tiny feet in Doc's hands. As she diverted her eyes from the actual delivery, she looked up toward the ceiling and saw a shadow that sent fear through her entire body.

Quickly she turned and left the room without saying a word to anyone. Hurriedly she made her way back to the main house and into the safety of her room. Her thoughts were running wild. *What was that I saw in the room?* she wondered. *Was it an angel? But I don't believe in angels. It must have been shadows dancing across the room from the poor lighting. Yes, that must have been what I saw.*

Back in the delivery room, Doc had tried hard to turn the baby around without success. The delivery was starting, and little Dexter was entering this world feetfirst. Of course, Doc knew the hazards of breech delivery, and a C-section would have been the better alternative, but not under these conditions, so he turned to prayer instead.

One of the greatest fears of a breech birth is the umbilical cord getting wrapped around the baby and cutting off the flow of oxygen. Doc knew he would have to work quickly if that was the case.

"Lydia, will you please come help me?" he asked. "This baby is coming out feetfirst, and we need to work quickly to get him out and make sure he is breathing on his own as soon as possible."

As Lydia was moving toward him, he heard the door open, but he didn't take time to see who was entering the room. After just a few seconds, he heard the door close again, and he didn't give it another thought. He was too busy trying to save a couple of lives to worry about anyone else at the inn. And knowing who was now in the room, it didn't take much of a guess that it had to have been Leah, and he couldn't care less what she thought or wanted.

All this time, Joe continued to talk quietly to Maria, and even though she was in great pain, she seemed to be at peace as she looked into Joe's eyes.

With two tiny feet and legs already exposed, Doc told Maria to push, and she responded with a hard push and a loud scream. "Once again," he said, and she pushed again.

Suddenly, as if by some sort of miracle, the remainder of the baby emerged with little resistance. Lydia was standing beside Doc, and together they almost had to catch him as the delivery was complete. Much to Doc's delight, the umbilical cord seemed to be free of the baby, and he looked all right.

Doc turned him over in his hands and gave him a gentle slap on the back, which was answered by the sweetest sound we had heard all night. The cry of a newborn baby boy.

Doc handed the baby to Lydia and prepared to tie off the cord. As soon as he was finished, Lydia gently placed the baby on Maria's chest so she could see her little miracle.

There was not a dry eye in the room, me included.

Martha had come into the room shortly after everyone else. She was standing beside me, and as we watched the proceeding, she gently took ahold of my hand and held it through most of the delivery. While we were all watching Joe and Maria with the baby and crying our eyes out, suddenly Martha looked up at me, stood on her tiptoes, and gave me a great big kiss on the lips. It was a big surprise for me, but I didn't hesitate; I just kissed her back. Then I put my arm around her, and we continued to watch the new family.

Doc looked up at me as he was making sure Maria was all right and said, "I have never delivered a human before, and I was hoping everything would work out all right. But I never expected what happened tonight. I don't know if any-one else in the room noticed, but that baby should not have delivered so quickly. I have read some about breech birth and have even assisted a couple of dogs, but it was as if there was something or someone giving an extra push right at the end. God sure must have wanted to give me a hand."

"Doc," I said, "remember, this is Shepherd's Inn. Things happen here all the time that can't be explained. This place has been special like that as long as I have lived here. You're just going to have to get used to it." I smiled.

Chapter 55

Leah closed the door to her room and walked over to the side of the bed where she had placed her pills in the night table drawer. Even though she had been in a hurry earlier to find out what the commotion was, she had taken the time to put the pills in the drawer, out of sight, in case someone came in and saw them. It was just a natural action for her to keep her affairs private.

When she opened the drawer to retrieve the pills, she noticed they were sitting on top of the Bible that had been left in the room for guests. The Bible was on the night table when she had first arrived; however, she had quickly placed it in the drawer, out of sight. If it had been up to her alone, she would have just placed it in the trash. However, she knew that would probably be met with a tongue-lashing by Gabe.

As she reached for the pill bottle, a sudden fear raced through her entire being. She froze. Her heart began racing, and she began to perspire. Her hands started shaking, and she immediately realized she was afraid to die. Instead of picking up the pill bottle, she reached for the Bible instead. Her mind was racing, and she could still see the image of two tiny feet in the hands of the veterinarian. A new life coming into this world backward. A struggle to survive against all odds. She knew the problems that could arise from that type of birth.

She also knew that Doc was probably unprepared for such an event. Then she saw again the shadow in the room. *Was it really an angel? Do angels even really exist?* Her thoughts were running wild.

She picked up the Bible and opened it in the middle. Her eyes fell on the heading for Psalm 91, "Abiding in the presence of God." She began to read. When she read verse 11, she began to cry. "For He shall give His angels charge over you, to keep you in all your ways."

She reached for the pills, opened the bottle, and poured all the pills into her hand. Then she walked into the bathroom and dropped them all into the toilet. Walking back toward her bed, she took a moment to pull back the curtain and look out into the dark, rainy night. The rain had turned to snow, and the light of the moon penetrating the clouds cast just enough light to cause each snowflake to glisten as it cascaded to the ground.

"Forgive me, God, for being so blind for so long. I want You to take over because I can't do it by myself."

She climbed into bed, closed her eyes, and cried herself to sleep.

Chapter 56

Things in the delivery room were starting to settle down. Lydia and Martha got the baby cleaned up and back into the mama's arms. Martha had taken a small quilt throw and wrapped the baby. Maria said she was feeling fine, and Joe just stood there with a smile on his face. When we got everything taken care of, built up the fire in the stove, and asked again if they were going to be okay, we all left the new family to themselves and headed back to the main house.

As we walked outside, we were pleasantly surprised that the rain had turned to snow.

Chapter 57

It was early morning before we all were able to settle down and get to bed. I don't think any of us was really prepared to sleep, but we did go to our respective rooms to at least try. I had gone out and filled the tank for the generator, built up the fire in the fireplace, and made sure things were going to be safe and warm for the rest of the night. We didn't talk much. I think we were all still in a little shock and perhaps some awe at what had just happened. Not the way we had planned to spend Christmas Eve.

I woke up after a couple of hours of restless sleep and got up to start another day. The snow had been falling steadily, and there was already almost a foot on the ground as the first hint of morning light settled on the inn. I went outside and cleaned the snow off Joe's and Maria's car. I knew they didn't bring much in with them when they first got here, and I knew they probably would need some of the things they had left in the car. I even shoveled a path to the car so they wouldn't have any trouble. Just my nature, I guess!

Lydia came walking in right after I got back inside, and she was grinning from ear to ear.

"Have you had a chance to see how our new mama and baby are doing this morning?" I asked.

"Oh, they are doing simply fine. I was so proud of Doc last night. Did you notice how, when things got really serious, he just jumped in and handled that delivery like he had been delivering babies all his life? And I mean people babies, not dogs and cats!" We both laughed at that. "And how about Martha? I don't think I have ever seen anyone showing that much love and compassion for someone else as Martha did toward Maria."

I thought about the kiss Martha gave me when I answered, "Yep, she sure showed love!"

About that time, Leah walked into the room. She was in her robe and slippers, and she was holding a lace-trimmed, monogramed hankie that looked like it had been well used. Her eyes were all red and looked like she had been crying.

Lydia noticed also and was the first to speak. "Ms. Leah, is something wrong? Is there a problem in your room?"

"Oh, no," she said and started crying. "Quite the contrary, everything is perfect. But first, I want to apologize to all of you for the way I have been acting the last couple of days. I treated you so badly, and I want you to know that it will never happen again. I must explain something to you. Last night, while everyone else was busy helping one another, I was being very selfish. I resented being told what to do, and I was very much displeased with having to read stories to your girls. But after they fell asleep, instead of going directly back to my room, I went out back to see what was going on with Maria and the baby. When I opened the door, I don't think any of you even saw me. But let me tell you what I saw.

"First of all, I saw that little baby being born. I saw two little feet coming out. I knew that was not good news, and I had a fear for mother and child. But then I saw something I couldn't explain at first. I saw what appeared to be a shadow in the room over the bed. I was frightened like never before. I quickly closed the door and hurried back to my room.

"I won't go into detail as to what happened next, but after a few minutes, I opened the Bible in my room. That was the first time I had picked up a Bible in far too many years to count.

"And for the first time in my life, I spoke to God. I didn't even know how to pray, but somehow the words just flowed out of my heart. I heard the voice of God tell me, 'Don't be alarmed. I'll take care of everything.' A peace came over me like I have never known. I asked Him to forgive me of all my sin and thanked Him for sending His Son to die on the cross and take my sin away. I also prayed for Joe and Maria and their little baby and for everything I witnessed last night. I knew that the shadow I saw was an angel of God protecting that baby. And now I know there was more than one birth here at Shepherd's Inn this Christmas."

By this time, we were all three crying like little babies.

After a few minutes, we were all regaining our composure when Martha came breezing into the room with the biggest smile on her face I had ever seen. "Good morning, everyone!" She beamed. "I trust you all had as wonderful a night as I had. Isn't it a glorious morning? I can't wait to get into the kitchen and get breakfast started. I know everyone will be mighty hungry this morning."

Lydia and I looked at each other as if to say, "Who was that woman, and what has she done with Martha?"

Before we could let that soak in, the twins came scurrying into the room with eyes as big as spoons in anticipation of Christmas-morning surprises. But as they looked around the room, their eyes settled on Leah, and they both froze, unsure of what she might do next. After last night and their forced incarceration with Leah in their room, they weren't at all expecting the type of greeting they were going to receive.

"Merry Christmas, girls! Elisabeth, please come over here. I have something for you. First, I want to tell you I'm sorry for the way I talked to you last night. I was wrong. I should never have said those things. I hope you can forgive me."

I could see that Elisabeth was completely caught off guard, but bless her little heart, she recovered quickly and replied, "I forgive you, Ms. Leah, 'cause the Bible tells me to, and because I want to." Then she gave Leah a big hug.

"Elisabeth, I want to give you a Christmas present." Leah pulled a scarf out of the pocket of her robe and draped it around Elisabeth's neck. "This scarf belonged to my grandfather. It's made of pure silk, and his wife gave it to him on the day they were married. It's incredibly special to me, and that's why I want to give it to you. You are also incredibly special to me. You helped me last night to find out who God wants me to be."

With no hesitation, Elisabeth gave Leah another big hug and abruptly said, "I love you, Ms. Leah. And thank you for the scarf. I promise I will keep it safe for you. Merry Christmas!"

Leah then turned to Sarah. "And, Sarah, I have something for you too." She reached into the other pocket and pulled out a small worn teddy bear. "I was given this teddy bear when I was a little girl like you. I always kept it close to me, and when I got to feeling bad, I knew I could always count on my teddy to be my friend, no matter what. But now I know it's time to pass him down to you. I believe he will be your friend too, no matter what happens."

Sarah took the teddy bear and held it close to her. "Oh, thank you so much, Ms. Leah. He will be my friend, I just know it." Both girls then headed straight for the Christmas tree.

Doc, Maria with the baby, and Joe came walking in before we had a chance to absorb what had just transpired between Leah and the twins. I think we were all in a little shock.

I said, "Good morning, mother and child. Oh, and you too, proud dad!"

Lydia walked over to Maria and the baby, "Oh, let me see. How is he doing this morning? Oh, he is so cute! Look at all that hair. Oh, he is just adorable!"

Leah moved over with Lydia and started talking to the baby. "Well, how are you doing this morning, little one? You know, you had us all a little scared for a while last night. As soon as you're big enough, you need to give Doc a big hug for all he did."

Then everything just sort of went wild. Everyone was trying to talk at once, we all wanted a peek at the baby, and we could hear Martha in the kitchen singing Christmas songs at the top of her lungs.

Suddenly, Leah spoke in a very loud voice that put everyone on notice that she had something particularly important to say. "I can't wait to tell all of you, I asked Jesus into my life last night. I know now that I am a new person, just the same as this little baby here. I have a peace now that I guess all of you have known for quite a while. I'm just sorry it took me so long."

That led to more hugs all around. And during all that time, our newest little guest slept through the whole thing.

Doc said, "Last night sure was something, wasn't it? And, Joe, I was so proud of you and how you took charge of everything."

Maria looked at Joe with a look that reminded me of a high school crush. "Not as proud as I am. I love you, honey!" Joe put his arm around her and gave her a hug. A man of few words.

Chapter 58

We were all starting to gather around the Christmas tree. Martha had brought in some coffee and hot cider, along with some homemade cinnamon rolls. Just as we were starting to dig in, we heard a bullhorn announcing the arrival of the sheriff. It sounded like she had stopped on the other side of the Little Jordan.

I jumped up first and headed out to see what she had to say. I walked down to our side of the creek, and she said, "Mornin', Gabe. Merry Christmas. I got a call last night from a woman, said her daughter and son-in-law called her from New Bethlehem, saying they had car trouble. Called again this morning and said they hadn't got to her house yet and she thought they might be stranded around here someplace. Looks like I might have found them. She told me what kind of car they were driving, and we were out checking some of the back roads just in case they got stuck somewhere out there. Happened to see their car when I got to the creek. Good thing someone cleared the snow off it, or I wouldn't have been able to see it. Guess the Lord must have had His hand in that."

I said, "Amen to that!"

"Anyway, is everything okay here? Looks like that old bridge finally gave up the ghost."

"Yep, that young couple came driving up last night, and I was down the creek a way, checking water level. I watched them drive across the bridge, and as soon as they got their rear tires across, the dang thing just folded up and washed away. Another miracle at Shepherd's Inn!

"Then, last night, that little gal went into labor, and Doc got to deliver a healthy baby boy about the same time as the rain turned to snow.

"Everybody's doing fine this morning. Martha's fixin' a big breakfast, the girls are in seventh heaven, and we're in good shape. Lost the electricity a couple of days ago but still have plenty of gas for the generator. 'Course, you know the phone line went down last night while you were talking to Lydia. But other than that, we're blessed.

"I would like to ask if you could get in touch with Scott Brewster and let him know we need a new bridge pretty darned quick. We can't hold out forever."

"Don't worry about a thing, Gabe. I'll check with public works and see if they can give me a lead on a temp bridge at least. Shouldn't take much for now. I'll also give those kids' folks a call and let them know they are safe. I don't think I'll say anything about the new addition. I'll let them do that as soon as we can get you out of here."

By that time, everyone inside had walked out on the porch. Belinda gave a big wave and said, "You folks all have a very Merry Christmas!"

We talked for a couple more minutes, and when the sheriff left, I walked on back up to the inn. Everyone was inside now and back around the tree. I told them what Belinda was going to do, and everybody seemed content with waiting out a new bridge.

Chapter 59

Just as we started passing out gifts, the phone started to ring. Well, you can guess we were all surprised, because no one would be out on Christmas Day to fix a phone line.

Lydia jumped up and answered with her usual perky "Merry Christmas, Shepherd's Inn, how may I help you?" She listened for a moment and turned and held the phone out toward Maria. "It's your mom."

Maria looked at Lydia, then looked at Joe, then at the baby in her arms, and back to Joe, as if to say, "What am I supposed to do?" She finally walked over and took the phone from Lydia.

With a shaking hand, she held the receiver to her ear and spoke. "Hi, Mom." After a short pause, she continued, "Oh, yes, we are just fine. Mom, you and Dad have your first grandson. Yes, he was born last night just a few minutes after midnight. Oh, he's fine, Mom. We had an expert here to help." She gave a big smile to Doc. "By the way, Mom, old great-uncle Dexter is going to have to have someone else carry on his name. We decided on another name for an incredibly special reason. Your grandson's name is Christian Shepherd Alexander. Yes, Mom, I'll explain everything to you when we get home. Oh, and we have to wait for the bridge to be repaired so we won't be home for a few days. But don't worry, we are in excellent hands. Merry Christmas, Mom. We love you too. Oh, okay." She held out the phone to Joe. "My dad wants to talk to you."

Joe got a knot in his stomach, and all the joy he had been experiencing all morning suddenly vanished. He knew it had to be bad news. Everything had been going too well, and he knew it couldn't last. He hesitated for a moment and then went over to Maria and took the phone from her. "Hello, sir."

Joe listened for quite a while. There were a few "Yes, sirs" and "No, sirs," but for the most part, Maria's dad did all the talking. When he was finished, Joe said, "Merry Christmas to you too, Mr. Belknap, and thank you very much."

He hung up the phone and looked at Maria and Christian. "Your dad got me a job in Bend with a friend of his. I start work next week."

Maria looked stunned. Her arms started shaking, and Lydia hurried over and took the baby from her.

"I don't understand. I thought you didn't want to move to Bend?"

"Maria, a while back, after I found out my hours would be cut in January, I called your dad and asked him if he could help me find a job in Bend. I told him what happened with my job and that I needed something with insurance for you and the baby."

Maria knew how hard it must have been for Joe to ask her dad for something. Joe was such a proud man, and he didn't want her dad to know he needed help. "Oh, honey, that was so sweet of you."

Joe continued, "Anyway, there's this guy he knows who has a company that makes rustic wood furniture. Your dad told him about me and that I worked in delivery and set up at a furniture store in Klamath Falls. He said he told his friend that I was a real hard worker and would be an asset if he gave me a job. I couldn't believe the things your dad said about me. He made me sound like some superman in furniture delivery.

"Then he tells me he has faith in me and knows I will make him proud as the daddy to his new grandson. He even said we can stay with them until we can get enough saved up for a deposit on a house of our own. Can you believe that?"

In all my years working here at Shepherd's Inn, I had never seen so many tears of joy flow as these last two days. And at this point, there was no exception. Maria threw her arms around Joe and gave him a big kiss. I think he could taste the salt of her tears as he kissed her back. Everyone else was just standing there in awe. They knew they had just witnessed another miracle at Shepherd's Inn.

Leah broke the silence. "Everyone, I want to tell you something else. Last night, while I was getting accustomed to my new faith, I was reminded of a song I used to sing as a little girl at Christmas. It was 'Silent Night.' I realize it is now morning, but will you please sing it with me now?"

Epilogue

The volunteer fire department in New Bethlehem was always looking for a project to help the people of the county. They built a huge pavilion in the town park a few years back. They also took on the task of remodeling the house of a widow lady who lived on the outskirts of town. Her house had really gotten run-down after her husband died, and they spent weeks working on remodeling the kitchen, installing new thermal pane windows, painting the entire house, inside and out, and even doing some landscaping. When they heard that our bridge over the Little Jordan had washed out and we were stranded at the inn, they again sprang into action.

A crew showed up first thing Tuesday morning, taking measurements, checking the stability of the footings, which were still in place, and drawing up plans for at least a temporary bridge. After that, they headed for a big stand of lodgepole pines on the east side of town and proceeded to cut enough trees to make a base for the bridge.

Lodgepole pines grow straight, with very few limbs on the lower part of the trunk. Their diameter is fairly consistent, so one tree is almost the same size on each end.

By Wednesday at sundown, we had a new bridge and a link to the outside world, not that any of us were anxious to leave. Line crews had restored our electricity, and the phone line was still working fine.

The four days we had been together were the best four days I think I had ever had the privilege to be a part of. We played games, sang songs, watched the twins play with their new toys, and of course, we all took turns holding little Christian.

Maria was doing very well following the delivery, and Joe watched over her like a mother hen. It was downright comical sometimes watching them.

Leah was definitely not the same person she had been before her transformation. She talked about her life, her disastrous marriage, her fall from the lofty position she had held in society, and how much happier she was now. She even wanted to help Martha in the kitchen.

But when the bridge was completed, Leah decided it was time for her to get back to Oakland. She said she had a lot of fences to mend.

Maria and Joe were also anxious to get to Bend and show off their new little bundle of joy and prepare for their new life. Joe said they would stay in Bend and he would go back to Klamath Falls and take care of clearing out their house. Most of the stuff they had was almost secondhand rejects, he said, so it wouldn't take much to give it away or haul it off. He had called his old boss at the furniture store and told him he wouldn't be coming back. Guess that didn't go very well with the boss, but he said he did understand when Joe told him about the baby and the new job.

The weather had cleared on Christmas Day, and it got a little colder. The blanket of new snow on all the trees and bushes made for a beautiful scene every morning.

Leah called me on Friday and told me about a newspaper article in the morning paper. She told me that her ex-husband, Philip Gardiner, had been killed in an airplane accident in the Ozarks. Seemed he was headed for Florida to join up with Leah's sister, Jessie, for a New Year's bash at a fancy resort in Miami. Details were still a little sketchy about what happened, but along with Philip, there were three other people on the plane, including the pilot, and Philip was the only one who died. The others were injured but were all expected to recover. She told me she didn't feel much remorse and asked if that was the way a Christian should feel. We had a long talk, and I think she felt a lot better afterward.

Tuesday, January 2, a hearing was scheduled in Marion County Circuit Court in the matter of the *State of Oregon v. Cade Summers and Lester Stubblefield.* The subject of the hearing was to determine bail, since the two men had been in jail since their arrest a week and a half ago. Bail was set, and Cade put up his car as collateral. The two were released on bail the following morning.

While they had been incarcerated, Cade was looking at a picture he kept with him of Lydia, Elisabeth, and Sarah. A fellow inmate, walking by, happened to notice the picture and took a second look. "Hey, man!" he said to Cade. "I seen that chick before."

"You have?" said Cade. "Where?"

"I was livin' over near Bend a while back, and I worked for a time in a little town called New Bethlehem. I was boxin' groceries, and she always came in with them girls to buy groceries. I think she worked at some lodge or somethin' up in the mountains. I always thought she was really hot, you know, like I'd like to get to know her a little better."

The fist flew so fast the inmate didn't have a chance to dodge as Cade's right cross struck the guy on the side of his jaw. "Don't you ever talk like that about my woman, you hear me?" Cade growled.

As he was rubbing his chin and trying to shake the stars from his eyes, the inmate quickly replied, "Hey, man, I didn't mean nothin' by it. It's not like I did anything. I was just imaginin'."

"Well, don't even imagine," Cade replied as he scooped up the picture and walked over to the other side of the recreation area. *New Bethlehem. I have to get out of here and find out where this place is,* he thought. *I have some unfinished business to attend to!*

CPSIA information can be obtained
at www.ICGtesting.com
Printed in the USA
FSHW020900301020
75302FS